Forget Me

Books by Lisa Sherman

The Forget Me Not series
Forget Me

Coming Soon!
The Forget Me Not series
You Belong to Me

Forget Me

Lisa Sherman

SPEAKING VOLUMES, LLC
NAPLES, FLORIDA
2022

Forget Me

ISBN 978-1-64540-736-2

To my husband and children,
the best part of every day.

Acknowledgments

This book would not have been possible without the dedication and devotion of so many wonderful people to whom I owe an endless debt of gratitude.

To my parents, Elaine and Dennis, thank you for encouraging me to follow my dreams and put myself out there. For your love, support, and belief that I could do this. Mom, thank you for sharing the writing bug with me and for reminding me that other people have written books, so why not me. Dad, thank you for always letting me know how proud you are of me.

And thank you to my brother, sister-in-law, and my entire extended family for your enthusiasm and support.

To my wonderful agent, Nancy Rosenfeld, who saw something special in me and my writing. Thank you for giving me this treasured opportunity. I am forever grateful.

Thank you to my publisher for opening the doors of the publishing world to this debut author. To Kurt, Erica, and all the folks at Speaking Volumes who helped turn this book into a reality, working with you has been a dream come true.

Thank you to my fellow students and teachers in the Writing Popular Fiction program at Seton Hill University. Spending time and learning from and alongside you was the experience of a lifetime and one I will always cherish. Thank you to my terrific mentors: Barbara and Rebecca. Your guidance, advice, and generous conversations about story helped shape this book. This novel would not be what it is without the support of you both. A big thank you also to Vicki for our coffee meetups and for making me feel welcome. Special thanks to the Write Club and all my outstanding critique partners. Your feedback, encouragement, and above all, your friendship, is valued beyond measure.

Thank you to those who helped me as I started out on my writing journey. To my NIAY instructors, Emily and Abby, and my classmates, for sharing your stories and making me feel part of a writing community. Also, to Michele for being one of my first ever editors and helping me see myself as a writer.

Special thanks to Camille for your gentle guidance on this journey. Your words of encouragement continue to help light my way.

To the best friends a girl could ask for. You know who you are. Thank you for cheering me on and dreaming my dream alongside me. Your friendship means the world to me.

Last but certainly not least, my deepest thanks to my wonderful husband. Thank you for being my biggest supporter, my best friend, and the love of my life. Thank you for believing in me. For always believing in me. And to my children, thank you for being the amazing humans you are and for putting up with a few extra take-out dinners so your mother could write this book. I love you more.

Prologue

A swatch of yellow catches the sunlight glinting off the water. The elderly woman notices it first and shakes her head. *Damn litter. Wish folks would stop mucking up the river with their garbage.* She straightens her worn rubber boots and brushes loose strands of gray hair away from her eyes, tucking them behind one ear. *The currents of the Wisconsin River sure are moving fast today.* The line from her fishing pole catches on the fabric. She sticks one foot into the stream to try to release it, feels the tug of the current and steps back. She squints to make out the object tangled up in the tree branches.

It's probably a towel. I should cut the line. Whatever it is, it's nothing worth getting swept away herself for. And with her bad knees, that's just what would happen. But as she turns away, she stops. *Did it just move?* Of course it's going to move, water moves. She chuckles at her foolishness. *I'm a silly old bird.*

She squats on the riverbank and stares at the yellow cloth bobbing in the water. She breathes into her palms. *It's getting chilly out, time to head back to the house.* She presses her knuckles into the soil and stands. Wet leaves flatten and stick to the bottom of her boots as she begins to trudge up the hill.

And then she hears it. A splash. She turns toward the sound. It's unmistakable this time, fingers and a hand. Flailing around. Grasping. It's not a towel or loose trash tangled up in those branches. The old woman screams. No. It's a person.

"You okay, Madge?" Her husband races red-faced down the hill. It's not like his wife to shout.

"George, look." She points to the bare arm now resting still, atop the water.

"Good Lord," he says. "Call 911. Then help me fish this poor fellow out of the river."

Madge doesn't budge, her feet frozen from fear. She's never seen a dead body up close before and hadn't woken up this morning planning on changing that.

The hand moves again, fingernails scraping against the branches.

She screams once more.

"We need to hurry. I think he's alive," George says.

Madge races up the dock toward the house. George lies down flat on his stomach and stretches an arm out toward the body. But it is too far to reach from the riverbank. He's lived in Vintage his whole life and he knows better than to tread into the Wisconsin River alone, especially when it's moving this fast. He's known of too many unsuspecting folks who've been swept away by the currents, the force of which can knock over a grown man. He shakes his head. Each year there's at least one unlucky soul meeting a watery grave.

George wrestles a large stick out of the mud and extends it toward the body, hoping the man will wake up and grab a hold so he can be pulled to safety. He pokes and prods the body over and over. But there is no response. George climbs to his feet, looks over his shoulder for signs of help. Not yet. He stares at the river, at the gentle ripples covering the top, hiding the danger churning underneath. No, he wants to help, but he knows better than to do it himself. He brushes the dirt off his blue jeans as finally he hears boots scurry across the dock.

"Over here." George waves his hands high in the air, grateful the local fire station is nearby. He holds his breath as the paramedics climb down the hill.

The younger, fresh-faced one is the first to get to the riverbank. He spreads a tarp onto the ground and lays emergency supplies on top of it. When the second paramedic, a stocky man with a thick red beard, arrives he ties a weathered rope around his waist and wades into the water. White foam sprays onto his rust-colored beard as he moves through the churning ripples. He plunges his hands into the water, his fingers cold stung in an instant. He lifts the head of the submerged body to the side. Long strands of hair and delicate features, the face is swollen, bloated from the water, but this is not a man.

The paramedic works to get the woman free before she runs out of time. He loops his arms through hers and pulls her to the edge of the river. A nod and a thumbs up and the men hoist the water-laden woman out of the river and lay her onto the tarp.

He whispers in her ear, "I'm so sorry, ma'am," before flipping her onto her back. And that is when he sees it. He strains to find words as his partner rushes to her side. *Damn it. She's pregnant, all right.*

Just then he sees Madge coming from the house, down the slope of the hill. Wet leaves kick up from beneath her boots as she balances a tray of paper cups, steaming with hot coffee. He grabs a warm cup off the plastic tray and sips as his partner covers the pregnant woman with blankets and tries to breathe life into her. *The river is fierce, but the people in Vintage are kind.*

The pregnant woman coughs and gasps, a stream of murky water spilling down her chin. The paramedic kneels beside the pregnant woman and supports her as he sits her up.

George leans toward his wife. "What do you think, six months? Seven months pregnant?"

She shrugs her shoulders. "Yeah, about that. Poor dear."

"Looks like she's got a bullet wound near her shoulder. What do you think happened to her?" George's voice cracks as he speaks.

"I don't know." She squeezes his arm. He acts like a tough guy, but they both know she's the strong one. "We should pray for her."

The paramedics lift the pregnant woman onto a stretcher. She is barely conscious, but alive.

The paramedic turns to the elderly couple. He scratches his beard. "You guys know her?"

They shake their heads.

"Wait. There's something else over there." Madge points to a patch of orange flapping in the water, beneath a pile of leaves. Without missing a beat, she heads over to it.

"Be careful," George calls out to her.

Madge clutches a tree branch as she wades into the water and uncovers the orange item.

"It's a purse." She holds it up, water pooling out of the sides of the leather bag.

The paramedic helps Madge up from the edge of the riverbank. She walks over to where the pregnant woman now lies motionless on top of a rescue board. Madge removes a wallet from the purse and pries a state ID out of the plastic window.

"The picture looks just like her." She holds up the ID and reads the name. "Wanda Dellas."

The pregnant woman's eyes pop open.

Madge leans down and whispers into her ear, "Welcome back, Wanda."

PART ONE

Forget Me

Chapter One

Wanda After

He calls me Wanda. He tells me that's my name. Wan-da. But it doesn't feel right. Nothing feels right. I lie in this bed all day, in this run-down house in Chicago, shades drawn, and dream I belong someplace else. He tells me we were happy once and shows me wedding photos of a blissful couple smiling, beginning their life together. Wanda and Carl forever. But I can't remember that day. I don't recognize myself in the picture, a woman with round-apple cheeks and too much rouge. The face could be mine, minus the scar that now weaves its way from my eyebrow to my jawline. But I can't place myself in her shoes. Five years later and I still don't feel like I am her.

He tells me the same thing the doctors and investigators told me. They don't know how I got a bullet wound or who shot me. There are hunting accidents all the time where they found me. Heck, I may have even shot myself, or so they say. I was in an accident and that's why my face is all messed up. It's also why I can't remember stuff from before. I don't even remember the accident itself. Only a loud crack, like a firework going off inside my skull, and then water, water, wet, freezing into darkness, into nothing. There's a big black hole where my memories should be, a projector reel playing blank film stills, flipping by, one by one. Sometimes an image flashes across them and I try to grab onto it, but it fades away before I can catch it, fuzzy and distorted.

And I'm very suggestible. I once saw a billboard advertising for a company that manufactures fancy cheeses, and I was certain it was a clue to my past. But Carl told me it's just that I always liked cheese, is all.

I do remember some numbers. I even dream about them sometimes. But I rarely have dreams. If I do, they are filled with the blurred faces of strangers. But then again, everyone is a stranger to me. I'm even a stranger to myself.

9390. I like that number best. I don't know why; I just know it flashes hot across my consciousness with a familiarity of nothing else. The nines, the three, and the zero, I trace the numbers into the wrinkles of my comforter.

The bedroom door creaks open. In the hallway stands a little girl, barefooted, clutching a weathered stuffed bunny. Carl tells me she is our daughter. He says I gave birth to her in the hospital right after the accident, a premature baby. I don't remember being pregnant. So, to me it seems like she showed up out of nowhere, like everything else in my life.

"Mama, I'm hungry."

"Where's your father?"

"I don't know." She scratches her head.

She's only five years old. That's a number. I like that.

"Well, I can't take care of you."

She just stands there and shrugs, biting on the paw of her bunny. I look around the room and notice a half-eaten bag of potato chips sitting on the dresser. I lean sideways and grab them.

"Here, eat these. They taste good."

She scurries over to the bag and stuffs a handful into her mouth.

"Can I snuggle with you, Mama?"

"Okay." I agree even though I don't like to snuggle, don't like to be touched.

"Hooray." She giggles, a full-belly laugh, and I have to admit I love it. The sound awakens something in me, a memory just out of reach.

Maybe I wanted to have her. Maybe I wanted to be a good mother at one time, before the accident.

"Mama and Astrid," she says, potato chip crumbs falling onto the carpet.

Astrid. It's a pretty name, but sometimes I wonder why I chose it, where the hell did it come from? I swear it's a name I'd never heard of before, at least not that I can remember.

I pull back the covers and she climbs onto the mattress beside me. She rests her head against my collarbone. She smells like stale milk and is in dire need of a bath, but I am too lazy to give her one. And my meds sap all my energy. *Sorry, kid.*

I'd give them up if I could, but without the pills, there'd be nothing left to dull the ceaseless searing pain from where the bullet tore through my shoulder. And nothing to stop the electric migraines I get, ever since hitting my head as I tumbled into the water.

I run my fingers through the clumps of her dirty hair. I grab a brush from inside the dresser drawer and gently work my way through it, placing my hand on top of her head so I don't hurt her when I hit a tangle.

She reaches for the television remote control, and I ask her to push the number four. That's the local morning show on the news. A handsome man, clean-shaven and made up, speaks to an actress starring in a movie opening this weekend. I don't care about her movie. I am about to doze off when Astrid nudges me awake.

"Mama, Mama. It's you. You're on TV."

"I am? What are you talking about?"

She rolls onto her stomach and points to the television.

On the screen a woman dances in a blue sequined gown, her mouth pressed up against a microphone, singing.

"That is not me." Disappointment circles through me. But what was I even hoping for?

"It was there. A picture." She kicks her feet against the mattress and rests her chin on top of her fists.

I bat my hand in the air. "Well, it's not there now." My eyelids fall shut.

She nudges my shoulder. "I wanna watch cartoons."

I lift the remote and am about to change the channel when the television host's tone turns serious and a photo of a young woman blankets my TV screen. "The case of Claire Stanbrick is once again in the news."

"Mama. Cartoons." She raises her voice.

I stare at the picture. "Shush. I want to hear this."

Astrid slumps down on the pillow beside me and frowns as the newscaster continues, "Four years after financial giant Jack Stanbrick was convicted of the murder of his wife Claire Stanbrick, the defense is asking for a new trial based on the alleged mishandling of evidence in Stanbrick's original trial."

A new photo fills the screen. In this one, a woman stands on a beach with her husband, her skin tanned and salted from the ocean air. Her smile wide, a beach bag rests upon her hip.

"In addition, Mr. Stanbrick's lawyers assert there was insufficient evidence to support Stanbrick's conviction, given the fact Claire Stanbrick's body has never been found."

I wonder if they'll ever find her. I close my eyes and try to imagine what her life was like before the murder. I picture parties, diamonds, and five-star hotel stays. I imagine a life of ease and laughter. Bet she's not smiling now.

Astrid grabs the remote control and changes the station to a gaggle of puppets dancing out of step. The front door creaks open on the floor below. Damn, Carl's home. His unsteady footsteps echo through the hallway. I picture him scratching at his dirty blonde whiskers. Drunk again. Looking for a fight. Wasted and washed up at only thirty-five years old, like me. At least he knows how he got this way, unlike me. If only I could remember, maybe I'd know who I really am. Maybe I'd learn I'm meant for better things. Better than this. I grab the bottle of pain pills from my nightstand and pop two tablets into my mouth. *Night, night*. I pull the covers beneath my chin and begin to drift off.

Wanda. That can't be my name. Sleep pulls me deeper into its grasp. I feel like I'm more of a Juliette, Genevieve, or Victoria. An image of the missing woman flashes before my eyes . . . *Or maybe even a Claire*.

Chapter Two

Wanda After

There's a knock. It feels like it's coming from inside my head. I press my palms against my temples. Try to make it stop. It doesn't. Carl's face peers from behind the door.

"Go away." I throw a pillow at him but miss and hit the doorknob instead.

"You need to carry your weight around here," he says.

"Please leave me alone. I don't feel well." I pull the covers over my head.

"I'm tired of your lazy ass. Maybe I should leave. I don't have to stick around, you know."

"So don't. What do I care?"

"You will care when you lose your job." He points to a light blue uniform dangling from a hanger attached to the back of the bedroom door.

I can practically feel the starchy smock and stiff lace collar pressing against my neck. I cringe.

He notices my discomfort and grins. "It's 4:00 pm. You need to get into the city. Those offices aren't going to clean themselves."

"Where's Astrid?"

"Have you been taking the pain pills again?"

I nod.

He yanks the covers off the bed. "Cut it out. It makes you even more useless."

He towers over me, his brow furrowed, his eyes angry, and I can smell the stench of alcohol on his breath.

"Since I'm useless, why don't you go, and I'll stay here and sleep?" I roll onto my side, no longer facing him. Seems like a fair suggestion to me.

"You know I can't work since I injured my back."

Same old excuse, six months before my accident he got injured at his construction job. Or so he tells me. Then managed to lose all his worker's comp benefits on a bad investment. One bad investment and now we live like this. Dumbass. I prop myself up on my elbows and stare at his hairline. Receding, like my patience.

He grabs my shoulders, his speech slurred. "Get moving. You're running late."

"Fine." I swing my legs over the side of the bed and flip him my middle finger. He slams the door behind him, my uniform falling into a crumpled pile on the floor.

***

I walk along the pavement, slick from the day's rain. The air reeks of diesel exhaust as the 151 bus pulls in front of me. I hop on and ride it straight through the Loop. The brakes screech as the bus slows to a stop at the corner of Wacker and Michigan, two blocks from the Bursar building.

The Bursar building is old, with cracked brick lining the outside and warped linoleum covering the entryway. I swipe my plastic key card and ride the elevator to the eleventh floor. The janitor's closet on each level is narrow, only big enough to fit one cleaning cart and a weathered corkboard. The cart is heavy and smells of diluted chemicals. It makes me gag. I quicken my steps. The sooner I start, the sooner I get out of here. I clean the bathrooms first, emptying the trashcan and spraying the yellowed countertops. Then I'm on to the offices, the better part.

You can learn a lot about someone from tidying up their desk. Most people spend at least eight hours a day at work and leave remnants of themselves, shards of who they are, when they head home for the evening. I like to imagine what their lives are like. I stare at the pictures of their families in tidy frames, read the greeting cards propped up against their computers. It must be nice to know who you are, where you belong.

The door to the corner office is open. It's huge and overlooks Lake Michigan. I snap the blinds shut. I don't like to look at the water. Not since my accident, anyway. Don't like to be near it.

The lake now securely out of view, I slide onto the oversized chair. It's comfy and probably made of real leather. I take a deep breath. The smell reminds me of something. A man. But I can't remember who.

My limbs tired, I prop my feet up on the desk and turn on the radio beneath the window. I spin the dial, but stop when I hear the words, "Jack Stanbrick, owner of . . ." I turn the volume up and lean in toward the speaker.

"Stanbrick Financial, located on the hundred and twenty-third floor of the Creighton Building . . ."

At the corner of Madison and LaSalle. I sit straight up in my chair. *How did I know that?*

The voice on the stereo continues. "Is where Claire Stanbrick ran Stanbrick Marketing Group, the sister company to Jack's, Stanbrick Financial, under the umbrella company Stanbrick Worldwide, until her disappearance five years ago. Employees say they were shocked by Jack's arrest and subsequent conviction. They report that by all accounts Claire and Jack appeared to be happily married."

I close my eyes, tuning out the rest of the report and run my hand along the shiny lacquered wood of the desk in front of me. And I can picture it, my back against the wall, my legs wrapped around his torso. I inhale the smell of his cologne and feel his five o'clock shadow against my cheek. My fingers grasp the hair along the back of his neck, not wanting to let go, never wanting to let go. But I can't picture his face. Still within the memory, searching for answers, I press my palms against his jaw and try to turn him toward me to get even a glimpse. But it's a blur. I squeeze my eyes shut and think I remember his name. *Am I right? Could it be?* I can't be sure.

Chapter Three

Claire Before

I lean my hip against the cool glass of the tall conference room windows and look out across the city. Chicago is quiet this early in the morning. Only the rare blare of a stray cab's horn shakes the air. Sprinkles of light dot the windows of neighboring buildings like candle flames. I like this time of day best. The office is still. The secretaries aren't in yet. Phones haven't begun ringing off the hook. I inhale the crisp scent of my coffee, hold the mug cupped between my fingers and breathe in the steam. I run my thumb across the words on the cup, Stanbrick Marketing Group. My company. My future.

A woman needs a career, my mother always said. Her motto was, *a woman cannot rely on a man to take care of her.* She must be self-sufficient. Confident. Strong. She lived by these words after my father left us when I was three. Used them to amass a fortune through the sales of her paintings and carried that motto like a badge of honor, an achievement. An achievement that often eclipsed even me in importance in her life.

And I would do the same. I am doing the same. This company. This place . . . is where I belong.

The conference room door opens behind me. Jack's image is reflected in the window. I stand beneath the dim ceiling lights as he approaches. Broad-shouldered. Smiling, a wavy vein pushing out from his neck. He wraps his arms around me and kisses my cheek, the spice of his aftershave tickling my nose.

"You look tired." He turns me toward him.

I nestle my cheek against his collarbone.

"You work too hard." He runs his fingers through my hair.

"No such thing."

"Come with me to the river house this weekend. We'll drink some wine. Take the boat out onto the water." He pulls me in close to him, our bodies pressed against each other.

I cup his face in my palms. "As long as I finish the marketing plan by the end of the day."

"Deal," he says. "Do we need to shake on it, boss?"

"Nope. You have my word."

He presses his lips against mine. The kiss is soft. Sweet.

There is a tap against the glass conference room doors. Roger doesn't wait for us to respond. He just strides in, his tie askew, his shirt untucked.

He raps his knuckles against the lacquered wood of the table, frenetic, as he talks. "I need to talk to Claire about the Teason proposal."

Nate Teason, owner of Teason Dairy in Milwaukee. The largest cheese maker in Wisconsin, an account I've been hoping to land for months now.

"This account could be huge," Roger says.

"What kind of marketing research study is he looking for?" I ask.

"He's considering a quantitative tracking study on which cheeses consumers purchase most frequently and a qualitative study to see the viability of a new cheese combination."

"Excellent," I say. "I'm assuming he will want us to compile Teason's market share as well."

"Yes. And Claire, I'd like to be the head guy on the account." He fidgets with the cap of his pen.

Roger has proved himself at the office over the past few months. So I'm all right with it. "As long as Jack is okay being the number two on this one. Jack?"

Jack nods, signaling his seal of approval.

Roger exits the conference room a little less nervous and with a little more pep to his step.

"Thanks for letting him manage the account." Jack kisses my forehead.

Jack trusts him, believes the fraud charges against Roger at Roger's old investment firm were garbage. They never were proved, never substantiated. And he is qualified. Still, I've been a little leery about giving him too much responsibility too fast. But if Jack believes he's innocent, I believe it too.

Jack squeezes my hand and looks at the art deco style clock hanging from the wall, one of my mother's designs. "You better get to work on that marketing plan. Because even if you don't finish, you know I'm going to abduct you and make you spend time with me at the river house this weekend."

"That sounds scandalous." I let my fingers drift through his.

"You know I'll do it." He nudges my shoulder.

"I'm counting on it."

***

Rain falls in thick, wet drops against my office window, leaving long vein-like streaks upon the glass as I put the final touches on the draft marketing plan. I click save and email the document to my secretary, Marcia.

Excitement pools through me, proposed marketing plan for potential pharmaceutical company client, done. I stride down the narrow hallway toward Marcia's desk. I'll give her a head's up and tell her it's no problem to finish it on Monday. After that, I'm off to the river house for the weekend. Now that my work is done, I'm determined to go. Rain or shine. The wind picks up and thunder rattles the window. I stop in my tracks as I see someone sitting at Marcia's desk, fingers perched upon Marcia's computer, someone who is definitely not Marcia.

"Can I help you?" I ask.

Jittery, the woman swivels in her chair to face me. A paper napkin falls from her lap as she stands.

"Where's Marcia?" My eyes scan the desk. Marcia's family photos still line the cubicle walls.

"She's on leave for emergency surgery," the woman says.

"What? When did this happen?"

The woman rifles through a stack of papers. "All I know is I met with a guy named . . . hold on . . . Roger Lindsey this morning."

"Roger?" I scratch my head. I guess he has been helping out in HR lately.

"Yeah. I hope that's okay." She picks at her cuticles, one where a pink glue-on nail has popped off.

"I'm just surprised no one mentioned it to me."

"I don't know about that. The temp agency called me this morning and told me to show up here and ask for Mr. Lindsey."

"Well, as long as you're here, I'd like to go over a few things with you about how I format my reports. Do you have a couple minutes?"

"Sure thing." She smacks her bubble gum.

"I'm sorry, I didn't catch your name."

She wipes her palms on the front of her shirt and extends her hand. "Wanda."

"I'm Claire."

Chapter Four

Wanda After

It's after 9:00 pm when I spin through the revolving doors after my shift. The night sky is black and motionless, the stars invisible, their presence hidden by a thick mask of clouds. My stomach grumbles as acid bubbles up in my throat. I can't remember the last time I ate. The windows of darkened buildings line the street, their lights snuffed out for the evening. The stores are all closed except one. To my left, the flickering lights of a convenience store catch my eye. I pull the door open and head to the back of the shop where a row of hot dogs simmer on a bed of warm spindles. The smell of meat and plastic coats the air. Wax paper sits beside the rack, and I grab a slippery dog off the burner and press it into a bun. I take a bite. It's rubbery and burnt, but I don't care.

I walk through the store as I eat, stopping to read the labels of the shampoo bottles, opening their tops and smelling their fake floral scents. Nauseating. There is a turning rack next to the hairbrushes with beaded bracelets dangling from wiry rods. The bracelets have names printed on them in rainbow colors. I spin the rack, trying to read as many names as fast as I can and trying to see if any of the names feel familiar to me. I see a row with the name Astrid, and I think of my daughter. I pluck two of them off, and stuff them into my smock, one for me, and one for her. A present.

I head toward the door. A man with overgrown curly hair and a store manager pin stops me.

"You need to pay for that hot dog, ma'am."

"Right." I fumble in my jacket pocket for cash I'm not sure I have. I take my time looking, though, putting on a charade as I pop the last bite of hot dog into my mouth.

"I can ring you up here." He motions to the cash register at the front of the store.

I place the empty wax paper onto the counter.

"The bracelets too." He eyes my pocket. Right.

I place the bracelets next to the wax paper as I continue fishing for change. I am surprised when I find a crumpled up ten-dollar bill in my back pocket. Lucky day. As the store manager rings up my purchases, I grab a glossy magazine off the shelf.

"This too."

He pecks a few more numbers into the cash register and drops the change into my open palm. I stuff the coins and bills into my back pocket for next time. I roll one of the bracelets onto my wrist and head back out into the night.

The bus stop is nestled beneath a dimmed streetlamp a few blocks ahead. As I walk, a noise rustles behind me. I turn, no one's there. I take a deep breath and continue walking. But the sound of footsteps on the pavement echoes in my ears once again. I spin around and think I see a figure dart into the shadows of a darkened alley to my left. I pick up my pace. Run. The streets are empty. There are no cars on the road, no one to help. I am alone. My heart beats out of control within my chest as I approach the bus stop. I stand beneath the light of the streetlamp, and look this way and that, over my shoulder. A man comes up beside me, and I jump. He sees my face and takes a step back just as the bus pulls into the stop. I scramble up the steps. Once on, I look behind me to see if he is also boarding the bus. But as it pulls away, the man is gone.

***

I have barely caught my breath when I put the key into the door. But it is not locked. The door is not even all the way shut. I push on it, and it opens. Something's wrong. I race into the hallway and start screaming, "Astrid!"

There is no answer.

"Astrid." Panicked, I scramble through the first floor, skidding on pages of the daily newspaper scattered across the carpeting. I regain my balance and step over the antique lamp that usually sits on the living-room end table, its geometric pattern now splintered. The wooden blinds lay askew against the chipped paint of the window frames, their slats fractured.

"Astrid!" I call out my husband's name, "Carl!"

I feel a rough hand on my shoulder as a voice says, "Stop your shouting already, will you?"

I spin around. It is Carl. And at first, I am relieved. Relieved that maybe he can help. But then I notice the stench of alcohol on his breath and the pile of suitcases tossed against the wall.

"Where's Astrid?" My hands close into fists at my side.

"She's hiding in the closet. She's been in there since you left." He points to a slim broom closet beneath the stairs.

I pull it open and find Astrid cowering inside, her tiny legs curled up, her chin buried between her kneecaps.

"Come here, honey." I scoop her up into my arms and rub her back. "I'm taking her to Penelope's house. She shouldn't have to witness your drunken meltdown."

"Always running next door to Penelope's house. What's that nosey old neighbor going to do for you? She can't do what I can." He grabs at his crotch.

"You're disgusting." I turn Astrid's face away from him and pick up the telephone to call Penelope to see if we can crash there tonight. Carl is a mean drunk. I don't want either of us around him when he is like this. I am about to dial the first number when I hear a click and see Carl's finger pressing down the hook, ending the call.

"What are you doing?" With my free hand, I try to pry his finger off the phone. "You better let us be or I'm going to call the police."

"They won't believe you. You've called them so many times with your crazy conspiracy theories."

I hang up and try to make sense of what he is saying. Since the accident, there have been a few instances where I've reached out to the police because I think I remember something from that day, the day that erased everything. But my calls weren't baseless theories. Even though they never led anywhere. They always felt so real to me.

Carl interrupts my thoughts. "Where are the statements?" Spittle flies from his mouth as he shouts.

"What statements? I don't know what you're talking about." I sit Astrid down on the corner of the couch, out of the line of fire.

Carl hollers at me, red-faced, his nose practically touching mine. "You're useless. Before your accident, you were at least sometimes helpful. Now you're just a waste."

I try to shake off his words. Even though I hate this man, his words cut to the core because deep down, I believe them to be true. How can I have any worth if I don't even know who I am?

"That's right," he says. "You're a nothing and a no one. Can't even remember who the hell you are, let alone help me figure out where the money we invested went."

The sound of his footsteps on the wooden floorboards echoes in the hallway. He hoists his luggage over his shoulder and props the door open with the side of his shoe.

"You going somewhere?" I ask. I don't care about Carl, but I do need someone to help with Astrid. Penelope, with her arthritis, can only do a little of that.

"Yup."

"Wait, will you still watch Astrid while I go to work?"

He doesn't respond, but from the look on his face, I have my answer.

"But I can't take care of her on my own." I grab a hold of his arm.

He shakes my hand off and looks at Astrid. "Not my problem. I'm not even sure the kid is mine."

"Of course she is," I shout, although deep down I don't know for sure. I can barely remember giving birth to her. Let alone how or when I became pregnant with her.

He shrugs as if he heard my thoughts. "Bye, Wanda." His back muscles twitch as he marches out the door. He doesn't bother to close it behind him.

I kick it shut and turn my attention to Astrid, her head hidden beneath a couch pillow. I squeeze myself onto the sofa beside her and smooth her hair, wet from tears, off her forehead.

She looks up at me, her eyes large and hazel. She leans her head against my shoulder, and I notice the time. 11:00 pm. Way past bedtime.

I carry her upstairs and tuck her into her bed, carefully pressing the edges of the blanket underneath her feet.

As I am about to walk away, she grabs my wrist.

"Mama, your bracelet has my name on it. I like it," she says, her eyelashes still damp from tears.

I remember the matching one I have in my pocket. "You're in luck. I have one for you too." I slip it onto her wrist. She admires it in the soft glow of her nightlight.

"Everything okay now, Mama?"

Her words slice my heart. She's so innocent and I'm so helpless. Useless. That was the word Carl used. A waste.

But with her face so expectant, I know what to say, what she needs to hear. "Yes. We're going to be okay."

She smiles at me, snuggling deeper under her covers and I feel guilty, guilty because she believes me.

Chapter Five

Claire Before

We drive down Interstate 94 West toward the river house in Vintage, Wisconsin, my feet propped up on the dashboard of Jack's convertible, the new car smell circulating through the vents. The air tickles the bottom of my thighs as we head toward the river house. Tall, leafy trees hug the expressway as we make our way along the hills and curves of the highway. We pass the town's welcome sign and a sense of calm courses through me. Jack was right to bring me here. I do need a break from work.

The tires kick up gravel as we pull into the driveway. Jack parks and I step out of the car. I slip off my sandals and skip up the winding path to the front door. I pause to look over my shoulder at Jack and dangle the leather sandal strap on my pointer finger, motioning for Jack to follow. He drops the suitcases and chases me as I run up the steps toward the house. He catches me at the top and wraps me up in his arms. I laugh, flinging my head back as he spins me around.

"Gotcha." He rests his forehead against mine.

I kiss him and taste the salty sweat on his upper lip. "Don't forget the bags." I nod at the suitcases toppled over near the car.

"I'm on it, boss." He presses a key into my palm and curls my fingers around it. "Get settled. I'll be there shortly." He caresses the top of my knuckles before strutting back down the steps to retrieve our luggage.

The marble tile entryway cools the bottoms of my feet. I drop my sandals beneath the gilded hallway table and shield my eyes from the glare of sunlight peeking through the glass patio doors. I slide them open and step onto the wooden dock, still damp from the misty air. I curl up on a lounge chair as a yellow-crowned night heron swoops down and snatches an unsuspecting fish out of the water. Dinner.

Jack's footsteps creak along the dock. He slides onto the chair beside me. I readjust, rest my head in the crook of his arm, and watch the shadows of cattails dance along the water.

Jack weaves his fingers between my own and kisses my temple. "That's good news about the Teason account."

"Yes. I've been trying to get in there for a few years now."

"I know. You've done a great job building up Stanbrick Marketing Group."

"And this is only the beginning." I look across the river to where the rooftop of our neighbor's house pokes out among the tall trunks of maple trees, so many miles away.

"Was Roger helpful?" Jack rests his bare foot against mine.

"In what?"

"In landing the Teason account?" Jack props himself up on his elbows and turns toward me.

"He was." I trace my finger along the curve of his bicep.

"Good."

He slides back down beside me, but there is something in his tone that tugs at me. "Is something wrong?"

"No." He looks out onto the water.

I turn his face toward mine and peer into his eyes, a jeweled blue. "Tell me."

"I have an idea." A glimmer flickers across his features.

"Tell me." I nudge his shoulder.

"I've been thinking of starting an investment firm. I wouldn't have to leave Stanbrick Marketing Group. We could create a new entity that's made up of SMG and the investment firm."

"Oh." I spin the idea through my head to try and make sense of it.

He fans out his hands against the darkening sky. "Stanbrick Worldwide, encompassing your Stanbrick Marketing Group and my Stanbrick Financial."

"You don't want to work for SMG anymore?"

"It's not that. It's just with my credentials, I want to develop something of my own."

I can see the excitement in his eyes and I know how much he wants this. We've had similar conversations before, about his prestigious undergrad and business degrees, that he doesn't feel challenged enough at SMG. About his plans, before he met me, to start up a business of his own.

He takes my hands in his. "It was never the plan for me to work for you forever, right? You know that."

I want to agree right away, to jump up and sing out my approval. But something snags my enthusiasm. I'm just not sure.

He senses my concern. "We'll still be working in the same office building."

I nod. He's had other ideas before, and I've always put the kybosh on them. Not to be mean but because I've been so focused on my company, on making SMG successful, I didn't have time to help him start something new.

"And you won't have to do a thing." He interrupts my thoughts as if he were reading them.

"This sounds like a lot of work. Can you do this on your own?"

"Roger will help me."

"Oh." I pick at a loose thread in my jean shorts.

He brushes his lips against my shoulder. "Don't worry. He'll play a secondary role. He'll still have time to work on the Teason file for you."

But can Roger be trusted? The thought pecks at me. And yet Jack has worked so hard. He deserves this. I don't want my concerns about Roger to stand in his way. I don't. "So what's the benefit of having the companies under the same umbrella? As opposed to putting up your own shingle?"

"Because being attached to SMG will give the company credibility."

"I see." I rub my palm against a cramp forming along the back of my neck. "Linking Stanbrick Financial to Stanbrick Marketing Group will provide stability in the eyes of investors."

"And security." He rests his hands on top of my knees. He can see I am considering this one and drives his sales pitch home. "Plus, we'll be able to triple our income. At least." He knows me so well. "What do you say?"

A delicious breeze blows in off the river, the air clean and crisp from the afternoon rain, full of possibility. Jack has waited a long time for something like this. And it could be great, for both of us.

His eyes soften as he looks at me. He knows he doesn't need my approval, not really. He could start his own business any time he wants to. But he does want my approval and he is asking. I squeeze his shoulders as the words come out in a hopeful whisper, "Okay." After all, what harm can there be in giving it a try?

Chapter Six

Wanda After

A woodpecker pecks at the sill outside the bathroom window. My head rests against a damp towel on the tile, an empty prescription bottle lying at my side. I push myself to a sitting position and wipe my cheek dry with the sleeve of my nightshirt. My head hurts. Pounding. I place my palms upon the lid of the toilet seat and force myself to stand. The woodpecker spots me and flies away. Even he can't stand the sight of me.

I crank open the window and the smell of melting chocolate wafts into the room from the nearby confection factory. Astrid and I should go outside. Get some fresh air. Maybe it will help.

I step into the narrow hallway and rummage around in the closet for the stroller. It stands wedged in the back corner. Flimsy, but still big enough for Astrid to ride in. She climbs in.

It's late March and the Chicago wind still has a bite to it, but now, laced with the scent of springtime, it's more palpable. The streets are busy, and I have to wrangle the stroller between hurried pedestrians pushing past us. Astrid covers her face, thinking we're going to crash. We don't. I may have no memory, but I like to think I can see where I'm going.

After a hefty eight blocks, I pause and realize we are quite a distance away from home, in one of the fancier neighborhoods. The thought of it makes me uncomfortable. We don't fit in here.

"I'm hungry," Astrid calls to me from the stroller. She frowns.

I check my watch. It's 2:00. The nausea from the pill withdrawal erases my appetite. But Astrid needs to eat lunch.

"Okay, we can have cold-cut sandwiches at home." We have a package of turkey in the fridge.

"No. I want grilled cheese."

"We don't have that."

"Maybe they have it over there." She points to a deli on the other side of the street.

I didn't plan on eating lunch at all, let alone at a restaurant, so I didn't bring any money with me. Not that I have much anyway. I reach into my back pocket and say a quick prayer that maybe I have some leftover change inside.

"I'm hungry." Astrid starts to fuss.

I pull a five-dollar bill out of my pocket and roll it between my fingers. It's not a lot, but it's enough for a sandwich for Astrid.

A bell chimes as I tug open the glass doors of the deli. We step inside and the smell of dill pickles and baked goods welcomes us. The chatter of customers echoes in the air as I tear a number off the red dispenser and take my place in line. I scan the prices scrawled on a chalkboard above the counter, nervous the five bucks won't cover a whole sandwich. Out of the corner of my eye, I see a tall woman with long brown hair wearing designer exercise clothes rushing toward me. I step back and turn away from her.

Undeterred, she shouts in my direction, "Claire? I cannot believe it."

She spins me around. Confusion peppers her face as she tries to make sense of what she is seeing.

"Claire? Is it you?"

Startled and caught off guard, I can't speak. She stares at me, her eyes wide and hopeful.

I remove my sunglasses, revealing my scar.

Disappointment washes over her face. "You look so much like her, I thought maybe."

"Sorry." I crunch the five-dollar bill in my palm.

She looks at Astrid in the stroller, her hands tucked beneath her knees, her hair a messy tussle on top of her head.

"No. I should have known." The woman twists a hair tie between her fingers. Her face flushed. "The Claire I knew didn't want children."

My tongue scrambles to form words. There are so many questions I want to ask this woman. How does she know Claire? What made her think I was her? Maybe she knows something I don't, something that could help. My number is called, and I glance across the counter for a second. When I look back, the woman is gone.

***

That evening, I grab Astrid's backpack off a tarnished hook in our hallway. I stuff a coloring book and two sandwiches inside. With Carl no longer in the picture, there is no one to stay with her while I work. Penelope only likes to watch her during the daytime, and tonight I have the evening shift.

We arrive at the Bursar building and step out of the elevator onto the smooth carpet of a fancy law firm. We weave our way down the quiet halls. A huge conference room sits in the center, a large rectangle outlined with frosted windows. I get Astrid situated in a puffy suede chair and place her coloring books and a sandwich on the granite tabletop.

"How long?" she asks.

I want to say we can leave right now. I want to tell her we can hop into a shiny car and head to a fancy condo and never come back to this building again. But I can't tell her that. This job will not buy us a posh condominium, but it will allow us to eat.

"Not too long," I kiss the top of her head.

Unlike the others in the building, this law firm has a huge janitor's closet stocked with all sorts of cleaning supplies. I rifle through the various bleaches and cloths and dump them into a rubber bucket. As I stand up, I notice a job posting tacked onto a corkboard. It's from the company that manages the building cleaning staff. In bold letters it states they have signed on to clean the offices in the Creighton Building. *The Creighton Building.* Jack and Claire's building. I scan the rest of the notice. They are looking for people to clean those offices. Write your name below.

There are only two names scrawled on the sign-up sheet. I feel around in the pocket of my smock until I find a pen. It's leaking and stains the tip of my thumb blue, but I don't care. My fingers shaking, I print my name on the bottom line. I know it's silly. I don't even know Jack and he sure won't be there anyway. He's stuck in prison. Plus, that woman at the deli was probably just dehydrated from her workout. Confusing me with Claire? Yeah, right. Still, a wave of possibility washes over me. What if Stanbrick Financial holds some answers for me, answers about who I used to be, about who I'm supposed to be? I need to find out.

Chapter Seven

Claire Before

A loud clattering outside my office wrestles me from my thoughts. I look up and see Wanda as a flash of blue, racing away from her desk. Like the place is on fire. I don't understand why we use that agency. Their temps are never very good. I type a reminder into my cell phone to tell Roger not to use that company again. Only eight weeks until Marcia comes back from her emergency knee surgery. Can't happen soon enough.

An hour later and Wanda still hasn't come back from wherever she scurried off to, leaving me without the numbers or slides I need. This will not do. Frustrated, I dial Roger. It goes straight to voicemail. I leave a message, but too impatient and irritated to wait for him to get back to me, I walk down to his office.

Through the glass windowpanes beside the door, I can see his chair is empty. Does anyone work around here? Doesn't look like it. My blood curdling, I head back to my office to wait, but stop mid-way when the state of Wanda's desk catches my eye.

It's a complete mess. Sticky notes crumpled into balls line the walls of the cubicle and cover the stack of paper I gave her that morning. A wad of previously chewed gum sits in a nauseating clump on the edge of her calculator, and tissues are scattered like confetti around the perimeter of a tiny trashcan. With my pinky finger, I shimmy the mouse, awakening the computer. A document pops up on the screen. I squint my eyes trying to make sense of it, to organize the numbers. But the bar graphs and pie charts don't add up. They are in complete disarray. With the tip of a pencil, I brush the mess off the stack of papers I gave her earlier that day and compare them to those on the screen.

They don't match. Some findings are in the wrong columns and some answers to marketing questions from the questionnaires are misplaced. Frantic, I hunch over her keyboard and try to reorganize things when I spot a baggie lying on its side behind a pencil holder. The bag is filled with little pale, yellow pills. Drugs?

"Wanda?" A voice calls out from behind me.

The baggie slips from my fingers. "What? No." I turn around and Roger is standing behind me.

"Oh, it's you, Claire. Wow, I thought you were Wanda. She kind of looks like you."

"She does not." I fold my arms across my chest.

"I hadn't noticed it until now. But quite a bit actually."

I put my hand up, indicating he needs to stop.

"Okay, got your voicemail. What's going on?" He runs a hand along the top of his bald head.

"This temp you hired left me in a bind."

"What'd she do?"

"She flew out of here without finishing her work, and the work she did do doesn't look so good. I can't use any of it and I've got to get a report to Nate by tomorrow morning. I might have to fire her for this."

"Whoa, slow down."

I rest my hands on my hips.

"You're the boss, so you can fire her if you want, but I think you should give her a chance."

"Why?"

"Because first of all, she's new and I may not have given her good enough instructions on how to post the numbers. Second of all, it's a royal pain in the ass to go through the agency and hire another temp. Not to mention we'd have to pay an additional fee for breaking the contract."

Those fees can be high.

"I'm telling you they will defend her and charge us. You're the boss. So, it's your call. But for the few weeks she's going to be here, I'd give her another chance."

He has a point. Maybe she had a good reason for rushing out of here. Plus, if Roger didn't give her clear instructions, she's not entirely at fault. While I like to rule this place with an iron fist, I do try to be compassionate.

"Go talk to her while I finish writing the report. Find out where the heck she went and show her how to properly post the numbers in the charts." I close my eyes and exhale.

"Consider it done."

Before heading back to his office Roger scoops the papers off Wanda's desk. He makes a gagging noise as he points to the garbage scattered all around her work area. I can't help but laugh. I reassure myself that things will be okay. Take a deep breath, Claire. The work will get done. Nate will be happy. I close my office door behind me, and dive into the report I need to write.

When I look up, it's already after eight. A blanket of darkened sky fills the window in front of me. But I still have work to do. I pull up my email and notice one from Wanda. I open it and see it contains all the slides I had asked for. I check and cross-check the numbers. They all look correct. Excellent. Now I just need to finish my part.

I wrap my arms around my torso. Despite the chilly autumn air outside, the building still hasn't turned on the heat. I open the slim closet at the back of my office to grab the sweater I brought to work the day before. But it's not there.

Just then, there's a tap on my office door. A face pokes through the opening. My heart smiles. Jack.

"You ready to head home?"

"Almost. I'm putting the finishing touches on this monster report. You?"

"Just got off a conference call about the launch of the investment firm."

"How did it go?"

Jack comes up behind me and wraps his arms around my waist. "Brrr. You're ice cold."

His breath is warm against my neck. I lean into him, his shirt collar soft against my cheek. "I know, and you're warming me up. Have you seen my sweater?"

"Your sweater?"

"Yeah. I could've sworn I brought it in to work yesterday."

"No. Which one?"

"The blue one. Made of cashmere. My birthday present from you, remember?"

"You can't find it?"

"No, and I love that sweater."

"Don't worry. Once the money starts flowing in from Stanbrick Financial, I'll get you a hundred sweaters."

"Jack, we can afford a new sweater now."

His shoulders slouch, and I immediately regret my words.

"But the ones you buy will be so much better." I run my fingers through his hair.

A smile stretches across his face. "Come on. Let's go home. I'll make a cup of tea for you. That'll warm you up."

I bend over my desktop, type the finishing keystrokes into the report, and hit save.

Jack turns me toward him. We stand face to face, our foreheads touching. He wraps his jacket around my shoulders and pulls me in close. Snug. He tilts my chin up so our eyes meet and kisses me. I am ready for us to go home.

***

First thing the next morning, I look for Roger and see he is talking to Wanda. Her shoulders hunched; I feel momentarily guilty. After all, she did manage to get the corrected charts to me.

I wait outside Roger's office for a few minutes, cradling a cup of coffee, until I see Wanda exit.

I sit down in the armchair beside Roger's desk. "How'd it go?"

"As good as can be expected. She said she got sick yesterday and that's why she ran off."

I think of the pills I found on the desk. Maybe she has a medical condition or something.

He scratches at his chin. "She thinks she might be pregnant."

"Does she feel capable of doing the job?"

"She says she is."

"I hope so." Career before babies. That's my motto.

"She really wants to do a good job. Plus, she seems to like you and Jack a lot."

I shoot him a confused look.

"I mean she's taking a genuine interest in you guys. She wants to know everything from what Jack likes to eat, and how you guys met, to whether you have any children."

That last part catches in my craw. Why do people always assume that because I am a woman I want to have children?

I scowl. "What did you tell her?"

"That it's none of her business."

"Good." I don't want my personal business being broadcast to staff.

"And that she needs to focus on her work and not you and Jack."

"You told her she can't disappear like that again, right?"

"I did." He picks a fortune telling ball off the corner of his desk and gives it a shake.

My hands tense into fists. I have worked too hard to build this business to chance a careless mistake messing things up. "Okay. But one more slip and she's done."

Roger turns the ball toward me. *You can bet on it.*

Once in the hallway, I look back and notice a shadow crawl across Roger's features. I know Roger still struggles with the accusations of corruption from his last firm, and I can't help but wonder if maybe, just maybe, Roger would prefer to keep Wanda on board so he can feel superior to someone. He must feel if it weren't for his friendship with Jack, he wouldn't have a job at SMG at all. At the fork in the hallway, I make a sharp left toward my office, but stop mid-step as a thought pierces my ruminations. I shake my head, dismissing it. He didn't actually steal from a client at his old firm. He was wrongfully accused. No charges were filed. I wave my hand through the air, brushing the thought away. He wouldn't use the temp's lack of experience to hide behind while doing it again? No. I comfort myself. Roger is Jack's oldest friend. We can trust him. We can.

Chapter Eight

Wanda After

The telephone rings. It is the middle of the afternoon, but still, it wakes me from a sound sleep. I lift the receiver and place it against my warm cheek. A woman on the other end of the phone speaks, her words a jumble in my ear.

"Is this Wanda Dellas?"

I pause for a moment, my head fuzzy from sleep.

"Who works for Bengal Cleaning Services?"

"Yes. Sorry." I wipe a patch of drool from the corner of my mouth and try to steady my thoughts.

"You put your name down to change buildings? To clean the Creighton Building."

Right. I wriggle my finger into a tear in the fabric of the couch. An image of Jack, dressed to the nines, standing in a doorway, mugging for a photo, flashes before my eyes. It fizzles, replaced with Jack, sullen and in prison. The Creighton Building. Jack and Claire's building. "I did."

"Are you still interested in the position?"

"I am. You want me to go there tonight?"

"Not yet. There's one little matter we need to take care of first."

The tone of her voice, serious and authoritative, makes me nervous. My breath catches in my throat, and I force myself to speak. "What matter?"

"I looked through your file and noticed we do not have a drug test on record for you."

Crap.

"We recently updated our computer system and may have lost some data. So we need to get this squared away before you can start."

A drug test? This whole fantasizing about being Claire business is going to get me into trouble. Forget it. It's not worth losing the one job I've got.

"You know what? After thinking about it, I'm fine working at the building I'm already at. So, no need for me to switch."

"Even if you were to continue working at the Bursar building, we would still need an updated drug test for you. It's company policy."

"But I have a daughter and it's hard for me to come down to the office for the test."

"No exceptions. You can come by anytime. It won't take long. You have to pee at some point, right? Might as well make it count."

"I guess." I slide my toes beneath the weathered area rug and want to hide.

"Good. Once your test comes back clear, you can start working again."

"Wait, I can't work until it's done?" I sit straight up, my back arched at full attention.

"No. Sorry. Company policy."

"But I'll still get paid, right?"

"Not if you're not working."

Shit. "I'll come by today."

I hang up the phone and pace around the living room. The space is tight, and my shins keep bumping into the coffee table, but I barely notice. Drug test? What the hell am I going to do? As I am pacing, Astrid skips into the room, her green eyes wide with curiosity.

"What are you doing, Mama? Can I play?" She walks behind me, tracing my steps. I turn and almost trip over her.

"Stop it. I'm not playing." I say it harsher than I intend to. Her face turns red and scrunches up. She looks like she is going to cry. I place my hands on her shoulders and kneel in front of her.

"You hurt my feelings." She wipes her eyes with her sleeve.

"I'm sorry. I just need to think about something."

"About what?"

"It's nothing you need to worry about. You go play. It's nothing you can help with."

She plops down and starts picking at the loose threads of the fraying throw rug, sulking, when it hits me. Maybe she can help. No. It wouldn't be right. But what choice do I have?

I squat down beside her. "There may be a way you can help. Do you want to try?"

"Yes." She sits up straight, proud.

"It's all right if you change your mind, okay?"

"Okay." She grins and tilts her head to the side.

"Let me get you some cranberry juice."

***

We arrive at the front door of Bengal Cleaning services, located at the corner of Broadway and Wellington, at a little after 3:00 pm. A woman with a tattoo of a lizard snaking down her arm sits behind a desk. She reeks of cigarette smoke and all I want to do is grab Astrid by the hand and run right back out the door. But I can't. I need this job.

"Can I help you?" she asks.

"I'm supposed to do a drug test."

"Name?"

"Wanda. Wanda Dellas."

She pecks at her computer. A moment later she reaches into the desk drawer beside her and pulls out a small, plastic cup. "Here you go. The washroom is down the hall and to the right."

I hold Astrid's hand in mine, and we begin to walk toward the restroom.

"No, no, no. She can't go in there with you."

"Why not?"

"Because it's not allowed when you're doing a drug screen."

"But she's only five years old. I can't leave her out here alone."

"I'll watch her for you."

Astrid tucks her face behind my legs.

I decide to see if this woman has some compassion. "Any chance you can make an exception? We came all this way just to have this test."

"No. But you can leave and come back when you have a babysitter."

Crap. I change my tactic. Maybe if I make her feel like she's in charge, she'll help me. "Please. I need to work. I can't live without the paycheck. She'll just stand there with me. That's all. I promise."

She chews on the eraser of her pencil, and I can tell she's thinking about it. She likes the power, likes my supplications.

I place my hands together as if in prayer, really selling it.

She leans across her desk and looks right into my eyes. "No."

"Fine." I reach for Astrid's hand. "I'll be back." We march out of the office, through the glass doors. But my bravado dissipates as soon as my feet touch the pavement outside. Now what? We stand beneath the green and white Wellington Street sign, the wind whipping through Astrid's hair, and I have no plan for what to do next. I reach into my purse, pull out a rubber band, and fasten Astrid's hair into a ponytail. As I try to tame the tangled strands, I glance down the block and spot a big box superstore. I have an idea.

We enter through the sliding doors, the bright, artificial lights assaultive to our eyes.

"Can I get a toy?" Astrid spots a display of battery-operated dollhouses equipped with automated elevators.

"Not now." My heart aches. I so wish I could tell her it's okay. I steer her away from the toys and down the cleaning supply aisle.

"I'm bored. Can we go home?"

"Not yet. I'm looking for something."

"What?"

"I'm not entirely sure." We walk past rows of packaged diapers, then down an aisle filled with neon gardening hoses and supplies. I run my fingers along the spikes of a pointed rake. "I'll know it when I see it." And then I do. In a clear plastic bin, I see a cluster of travel acetaminophen containers on sale. Four for two dollars. I grab them. But I'm not done yet.

"Can we go now?" She tugs at the hem of her shirt.

"There's one more thing I need." I coax her down the paper goods aisle and pick up a bag of disposable cups, a hundred to a pack. I drop the top cup into my purse and place the bag back on the shelf. A pang of guilt shoots through me. Now I'm a thief. But there's nothing I can do. I can't afford to buy a hundred cups. I only need one.

Astrid and I approach the checkout counter, flanked on one side by a see-through heated oven displaying racks of oversized pretzels. The air smells of spongy dough and plastic nacho cheese. My stomach turns. I grab a roll of sticky tape off the shelf behind me and place it and the acetaminophen on the moving belt in front of the cashier, an old man with tufts of gray hair poking out from his ears. He looks like he'd rather be anyplace other than here. Just like me. I drop a couple bucks and some change into his palm and ask him where the ladies' room is. He doesn't reply, just points to a low-hanging sign along the left-hand wall. Restrooms.

The bathroom smells like rotten eggs and who knows what else. Astrid pinches her nose. We make our way to the large handicap stall and I tell her we'll make it quick. "Do you have to go potty?"

She nods her head.

I pull the disposable cup out of my bag.

"Do you think you can make it in the cup?"

Another nod.

"Okay. I won't look."

A minute later she calls out to me. "Did it." Proud.

I rest the cup on top of the toilet paper dispenser and fish the tubes of acetaminophen out of my bag. With a snap of the plastic seal, I twist them open. Each tube is filled to the rim with tablets. I am not sure what to do with them. I look around and then decide to dump them into the bottom of my purse. No reason to waste good medicine. Then with shaky fingers, I pinch the disposable cup, pour the urine into the tubes, and snap them shut.

"Close your eyes," I tell Astrid as I unbutton my jeans and tape the containers in a row along the sides of my upper thighs.

The tubes press against the denim of my pants, creating little bulges by the tops of my legs. I stretch my shirt over my hips to cover the evidence. I am ready to take the drug test.

A look of surprise blankets the face of the receptionist when we walk through the door. "I didn't expect to see you back so soon."

"I have a request."

"I already told you, the kid can't go into the bathroom with you."

"I understand. But what if you come in with me too?"

"Sorry but watching you pee is not part of my job description."

"No. I'd go into the stall by myself. You'd watch my daughter by the sink."

She spins her rhinestone ring in circles around her finger as she tries to picture what I'm saying.

"Please. It's a win-win. I won't be able to do any funny business because you'll be there, but I'll know my daughter is safe."

She twists a long strand of dyed purple hair as she thinks about it before giving in.

We head to the bathroom and I am about to close the door to the stall when she says, "I'll hold your purse. You can't bring anything in there with you."

"No problem." I loop it over her outstretched arm.

I lock the door and sit down on the toilet. First thing I do is flush to mask the sound of me peeling the tape from the top of my thighs. Then I pee into the bowl as I pour Astrid's urine out of the tubes into the sample cup. I breathe a sigh of relief as I tighten the cap. Water swirls in the bowl as I flush again and re-tape the now empty tubes back onto my skin.

With a smile, I exit and hand the woman my specimen.

"Yuck." She holds onto it with the tips of her fingers.

"Sorry. Company policy."

Astrid and I scurry out of the office. I let the door close behind us with a thud, grateful for the cool breeze of the early evening air that awaits us. I kiss her on the forehead.

"You helped Mama pass the potty test."

Her eyes glint in the waning sunlight. So innocent. So proud. And yet it's a punch in the gut. I vow to quit the pills. This is not the kind of mother I want to be.

Chapter Nine

Claire Before

Sweating water glasses sit in rows upon the conference room table. Bright orange and white napkins, Stanbrick Marketing Group colors, alternate in front of each seat. Pads of paper and pens bearing the bolded SMG logo rest beside each place setting.

I look up as Wanda taps on the glass door of the conference room before entering. She places a tray of cookies and pastries in the center of the table and a cup of coffee in my hands. The scent of roasted beans fills the room, sharpening my already heightened senses.

"I thought you could use a cup before everything started. Two creams, no sugar, right?"

"Right." I glance at the art deco clock hanging on the back wall. 8:30 am. Nate should be here any minute for the presentation.

"Do you need anything else before Nate arrives?" She places a pitcher of coffee on the table.

"No. This will do fine. Thanks."

She is about to walk out of the room, when I notice a bluish-purple bruise puffing out beneath her eye. "Are you okay?"

"This silly thing?" She presses her finger against the bruise, and I cringe. "I bumped right into a cabinet. Can you believe it?"

Actually, no. I place my hand on her arm beneath a bubbled-up red welt. "Wanda?"

She pulls away from me and giggles. "It's really nothing. Money is tight and with the baby coming, there are arguments. But we always make up. My husband and I, we have a very passionate relationship." She brushes a shock of hair from her eyes. "You should see his arms. I scratched him up good. It's going to leave some scars."

I look at her, unable to blink. The type of relationship she is describing is completely foreign to me. I don't know how to help her, but I wish I could. "If you need anything, you can talk to me, okay?"

She exhales and turns toward the door but stops. "Can I sit in on your presentation this morning?"

Her question takes me aback. I hadn't even thought of inviting her since she's only a temp. But I see no harm in it. "Sure." I grab an extra notepad and pen from the back of the room and hand it to her. "Can you check to see if Nate has arrived yet?"

She exits the room with a little more kick to her step, and I feel as if maybe, in some way, I've helped.

Jack walks in as Wanda walks out and a wave of relief washes over me. Jack, my husband, who would never lay a hand on me. That's not our type of passion.

"You ready?" He rubs his hands together and I can practically feel the heat emanating off them.

"I think so. I reviewed the preliminary findings so many times I have them memorized. But one never knows what can go awry during a presentation."

"Stop that." He pulls me into his arms and rubs my back. "Just do your best. It will be more than good enough."

I inhale deeply, the smell of his aftershave filling my lungs. That was exactly what I needed to hear.

Wanda's voice breaks in over the intercom. "Claire, Mr. Teason and his colleagues have arrived. They are waiting for you by reception."

I flash a smile at Jack. "It's show time."

"I'll be watching from the back. Hey, do you mind if I scatter a few of these on the conference table as well?" He pulls a stack of yellow highlighters out of his jacket pocket.

"What are they?" I give them a cursory glance and notice they have the name of Jack's company printed on them. Stanbrick Financial. Not wanting to leave Nate waiting too long in the reception area, I toss Jack a quick nod and hustle down the hall.

In the lobby, Nate sits with his hands folded neatly in his lap, a leather briefcase at his side. He rises to his feet as I march toward him, my hand extended.

"Thank you for coming. Did you get a chance to look over the preliminary report I sent you?" I ask, confidence lacing my words.

Nate, a tall, older man with broad shoulders and kind brown eyes, smiles back at me. "I did, but I am looking forward to hearing your interpretation of the results. From this initial report, it appears as if Teason Dairy is kicking Daylen Farm's ass in market share."

I laugh. "True, true. But follow me and I'll tell you why that is and how to keep it going."

"Excellent. I can't let that jerk Daylen beat me." Nate pats my arm. "It's been a family rivalry for decades. Old grandfather Daylen once tried to murder my grandfather, or so the story goes."

"My goodness." I chuckle and place my hand on his arm.

We arrive at the conference room. Jack holds the door open for Nate and his colleagues. Everyone takes their seats as I make my way to the front of the room. I am ready to begin. I breeze through the slides, explaining the differences between Teason Dairy and its competitors, making sure to crack only appropriate cheese-related jokes at the exact right moments. I keep a close eye on Nate throughout the presentation, watching for his reactions, tailoring my comments to keep everything running smoothly. I am about to reveal the reason for Teason Dairy's edge over their rival when the look on Wanda's face distracts me. She is staring at me. Her eyes squint into almost a line, her lips pursed, and suddenly I don't feel so good.

"Excuse me for a moment. I'm so sorry." I race out of the conference room, down the hall, past reception and into the women's restroom. I don't even bother to close the stall behind me and I am already throwing up.

A moment later, I pull myself up off my knees and straighten my skirt. I wash my hands and splash water on my face. What the hell? I didn't think I was that nervous. Just finish it up. Make the sale.

I walk back to the conference room where everyone is waiting for my return. Nate's colleagues put away their cell phones when they realize I am back in the room. Jack leans against the conference table, chatting and shaking hands with Nate. They stop talking when I approach.

"You okay?" Jack asks.

"Yeah, I don't know what happened. Maybe I ate something bad. But I'm good now."

"Nate gave us his new office information. Wanda is going to update his contact data in our system," Jack says.

Wanda scribbles on her notepad, highlighting the words with one of Jack's pens so it glows.

"We're moving offices," Nate says. "To a bigger facility. It's just down the block, but the move is still going to be a hassle."

"I bet." I force a grin and gesture toward the whiteboard. "Should we get back to the presentation?"

Nate smiles at me, kindness in his eyes.

"It is Teason Dairy's presence in the more rural markets that is making its market share shine."

Nate's features light up with recognition. "It is imperative that Teason continues to court those rural markets."

Nate turns and whispers something into his associate's ear.

I continue speaking with confidence, selling it. "And Stanbrick Marketing Group is just the company to help Teason Dairy do so."

A smile spreads across Nate's face.

***

An hour after the presentation, I am sitting at my desk, my head in my hands, still nauseous. I hear a tap and am happy to see Jack standing in the doorway.

"You nailed it."

I don't respond.

"Still not feeling so good?"

"Nope. I don't know what it's from."

"Did you eat anything different today?"

"Not really. I had my usual breakfast and some of the coffee from the conference room."

"Want me to take you home?"

"Please."

Jack grabs my coat and drapes it across my shoulders. He kisses my cheek.

"Do I feel warm?" I ask.

"No. My husband thermometer is telling me you don't have a fever."

As Jack leads me toward the elevator, we pass Wanda sitting at her desk. "Can you put together those papers for Teason Dairy?" he asks.

"What papers?" I stare down at the wavy lines in the carpet and try to keep my balance despite the nausea.

"Nate is going to be one of my first investors." Jack puffs out his chest.

"That's wonderful." I try to steady my words.

"Yes. He likes my credentials and the fact that the company is linked to yours. He's very impressed with you, you know. But then again, who isn't?"

Chapter Ten

Wanda After

Stanbrick Financial is located on the top floor of the Creighton Building. Astrid and I ride the elevator to the 123rd floor, our ears popping on the way up. Anticipation courses through me as the doors to the elevator slide open. I can't believe I'm here. But as soon as Astrid and I step out, my hopes deflate. I can hear it, a vacuum cleaner. Another member of Bengal Cleaning Services is on the floor. This will not do.

"There must be some mistake," I say, smiling at her, pretending we are teammates.

"What? Can't hear you." She tugs at her ear, points to the vacuum cleaner, and I already can't stand her.

"This is my floor," I shout.

She shuts off the vacuum. "Nope. I got this one." She turns the vacuum back on.

I place my foot upon the end of it, stopping her from moving forward.

She turns it off again. "Do you mind? I've got work to do."

My eyes focus on the thick black mole above her top lip as I formulate my next move. I can't do what I need to do if she is here. I won't be able to look around the offices. I inhale, taking in the scent of her too pungent perfume, smooth my hand over the sweaty strands of hair by my temples and decide to try a different strategy.

"My friend used to work at this company. So it's important to me to be the person cleaning it."

"Oh really, who's your friend?"

Without thinking, I say it, "Claire Stanbrick."

"The missing woman? You know her? You know where her body is?"

Crap. "No, no. I don't know her. I'm just interested in her case. I think she might still be alive."

"So you're a detective, is that it? Well, guess what? I got here first, so beat it. You're not the only one who wants to get their hands on that reward money."

"Reward money?"

"Her convict husband put up a reward for information leading to her whereabouts and it's still up for grabs."

Jack wanted help finding her.

Astrid covers her ears as the woman turns the vacuum back on. I've got to come up with something. I take a few steps toward the elevator when she calls out to me over the hum of the vacuum cleaner, "Hey super sleuth, what's it worth to you?"

"What?"

"If I trade floors with you, how much are you willing to pay?"

"I don't have any money. I have nothing to give you."

"Oh, I think you do." She shuts it off. "There's always something."

"Like what?"

"If you give me half of what you make each night, I'll let you have this floor."

She stands, hands on her hips, smug, and I think about Astrid. On the one hand, we really need the money. On the other hand, this could be our ticket out. If I can learn something here that helps prove who I am, that would be worth way more to me than my hourly salary. Invaluable.

"Come on, yes or no? I don't have all night."

I search her eyes for some shred of decency, some hope that she'll back off this position and let me have the damn floor.

"Do we have a deal?" She pressures me.

I am about to agree when Astrid reaches for something on the woman's cart. "Astrid, no. That's not ours."

Astrid tugs a slim thermos hiding behind a bag of paper towels off the cart. In that moment, I have a hunch and a hope for a last-minute Hail Mary touchdown to help me save the day. I take the thermos from Astrid and hold it out of the woman's reach. "What's this?"

"None of your business. Give me that." She grasps at the air.

"Nope. What do you have inside here?" My fingers grip the plastic as I unscrew the top. As soon as I lift off the lid, I have my answer. I don't need to taste it. The acrid smell of alcohol wafts from the thermos as the woman's once pompous features turn pale.

"Give that back. It's not what it looks like."

"I think it's exactly what it looks like. We're not allowed to drink alcohol while we're on the job. That's grounds for termination." I speak these words as confidently as possible, even though I'm not actually sure if it's a policy or not. But it sounds good and she seems nervous, so I drive it home. "Now I have no choice but to report you."

"Please don't. My husband lost his job over a year ago and we need the money to pay for my son's school."

"I need the money to care for my daughter and you were fine trying to take half of it. Maybe I should do that to you."

"No, please don't." Beads of sweat form a line above her mole.

"I'm not going to do that to you, because unlike you, I'm not a jerk. But here's the deal. Pack up your things and let me have this floor. Permanently. And I won't report you."

She fumbles for her keys, then grabs her belongings off the cleaning cart. She scurries toward the elevator without even bothering to unplug the vacuum before she goes.

"Pleasure doing business with you," I call out. If uncovering what happened to Claire can possibly help me figure out my past, I can't chance letting anyone get in my way. No one.

***

From that night on, Stanbrick Financial's floor is mine to clean every evening. Astrid rides on the back of my cart as I push it from office to office. She giggles as I make wide turns, veering through the doors. We pretend we are the rulers of the floor, that it is our kingdom. I am the queen in search of her king, and she is the fair, maiden princess. She places her tiny fingers upon her chin as she tries to decide which office would be her suite if we lived in this castle.

Sometimes we take a break and dance in the conference room, spinning around the upholstered chairs as if they were our dates to the royal ball. She often fades out early, being so little and all. So I draw up a makeshift bed on the sofa in the employee lounge and tuck her in, her doll beside her. She smells fresh and enjoys her baths now that I'm off the pain pills and have the energy to give them to her. She loves the clean strawberry scent of the kiddy shampoo I pick up at the dollar store. It's the generic kind, not the fancy brand version, but she doesn't care.

I check the time. I am behind schedule. I vacuum, dust, and empty the waste baskets in the various offices along the way, gagging occasionally at the smell of stale salad dressing and hardened cheese left decaying in garbage cans by company employees. But cleaning the coffee maker in the kitchen is even worse. Soggy filters caked with grounds remain jammed in the top of them. Sometimes I dream of leaving it there, letting the lazy employees deal with it. As if they'd even notice.

From the kitchen, I head to the main receptionist's desk at the front of the office. With a dry cloth, I polish her computer screen. Dust particles stick with static to the glass. I straighten the items on her desk: a vase of plastic colorful flowers, the day's old tea bag dried and staining the pile of napkins it rests on. I scoop it up with gloved fingers and pitch it into my garbage bag. A picture of a dog in a Halloween costume is tacked to the corkboard cubicle walls. My elbow knocks the photo loose from its pushpin. It falls onto the desk in front of me. I am about to stick it back in but stop short when I notice a sheet of paper pinned to the wall behind where the picture used to be. Yellowed at the edges, the paper appears to have been long ago forgotten, until now.

It's a map of the office. On it, little squares line up in rows corresponding to where each office is located on the floor. But what really catches my eye are the extension numbers listed inside each box, extension numbers and names of the people who used to inhabit each office. The list is old. Outdated. I know this because Jack's name is clearly marked. Corner office. I scan the page, the words a blur until I come to the spot located at the opposite end of the hallway from Jack's. Claire's office.

Without bothering to remove the thumbtack, I tear the map off the wall, and make my way along the carpeted hallway. I arrive at Jack's old office first, my pulse doing flip-flops. Anticipation courses through me. And excitement. But a sick feeling smacks me when I spot the nameplate on the wall outside the door: Roger Lindsey. I back away, bumping into my cleaning cart, and hustle down the hallway in the other direction.

Breathless, I pause. This is it. Claire's old office. I can't believe I'm actually here. The nameplate has been removed. No reminders or identification remain to signal this office was once where Claire spent her days. Just a smooth brass panel of metal. Blank and nameless.

I spray glass cleaner onto a cloth, the lemony scent tickling my nose, and polish the plaque. I take a deep breath and reach for the doorknob. Locked. Crap. Two panels of frosted glass line each side of the door. I press my face against one and try to get a glimpse of what's inside. But I can't see a thing. Out of nowhere, a panic comes over me. I need to get into the office. Now. I pull and tug on the door but it refuses to open. Disappointed, I slump down against the cleaning cart. I drape my arms across my yellow bucket and am suddenly keenly aware of the pain from my injuries. My head throbs, my jaw aches, and all I want to do is rest. Just for a minute. I press my palms against my eye sockets.

A moment later, I am startled by the sound of coins jangling. In someone's pocket? Someone's coming. My bucket tumbles onto the floor beside me. A bottle of multi-purpose cleaner glides to a stop against the boots of a person standing in front of me. Tall and beer bellied, a security guard.

"You okay, ma'am?"

"I'm fine. Sorry." I scramble to pick up the toppled-over supplies.

"What are you doing here?"

"I'm part of the new cleaning crew." I stretch out my smock so he can see the logo.

He squints as he reads.

"I was trying to get into this office. To clean it." I point to the basket of cleaning products.

"There's no need to clean in there."

"Why not?"

"Because it's not an office anymore."

"It's not?"

"Nope. After the arrest, the new boss insisted the room be closed off."

"Why?"

"It used to be that woman's office. You know, the one they think was murdered. He doesn't want anyone snooping around in there. So the new boss turned it into a storage room. Shame though, it's one of the bigger offices."

"A storage room?"

"Yup. Everyone's used to it now. It's almost like no one had ever been there at all." He rubs his forehead with his fingers, as if he's as confused about it as I am.

A wave of sadness curls through me. Claire. Erased and forgotten. It doesn't seem right.

"You kind of look like her. Anyone ever tell you that?"

An image of the brunette woman at the deli flashes before me. "No."

"There's definitely a resemblance." He strokes his beard. "You know, they say he did it, her husband. But I'm not so sure."

"Why not?"

"Because he always seemed like a decent guy. Seemed to really love his wife. Gave big holiday bonuses too. I always liked him."

Generous. Loved his wife.

"Now the new guy, he's stingy. Just gives us crummy five-dollar coffee shop gift cards. Roger. He took over Jack's company when Jack went to prison. I don't trust him at all."

"No?"

"Nope. I don't trust a guy who's cheap like that, lousy five-dollar gift cards for keeping him safe all year. Pfft."

"I hate cheap bosses too."

"He liquidated her business, you know."

"Who?"

"Roger, after Claire went missing and Jack went to prison. No more Stanbrick Marketing Group. Only Stanbrick Financial."

"Why?" My head pounds.

"Not enough money in the business to run both. And apparently, no one could run Claire's business like she could."

"Why not?"

"I didn't know her much, but I hear she was pretty talented."

My face blushes, as if he's talking about me. But, of course, he's not.

"You okay?" he asks.

"Just tired."

"You better get going now." As he walks away, I see a ring of keys dangling from his belt loop.

"Wait."

"You need something?"

"Any chance you could open this door for me?"

"I'm not supposed to do that, ma'am."

"Seriously? But they told me to clean the whole floor. All the offic-es."

"I'm sorry, ma'am."

"But if I don't clean it, I could lose my job. My cheap boss will toss me right out."

He scratches his graying beard.

"I'm just going to dust a bit, and vacuum. Anyway, it's not healthy to let mites and dirt accumulate. It'll get in the vents, people will breathe it in." I place my hands upon my chest as if the air quality of the building were my number one priority.

"You're only going to clean, right?"

"Just dust and vacuum. That's all."

"I guess there's no harm in that." He turns the lock on the doorknob, and tugs at the door. It doesn't open. "Oh, right." He puts his key in a deadbolt higher up, beside the doorframe. He chuckles.

I fake a laugh, exhaling for what seems like the first time since he showed up.

"But don't move anything. Clean around whatever is there, got it?"

"Got it." No one will know I was ever here.

Chapter Eleven

Claire Before

A copy of the day's newspaper is fanned out across my desk when I arrive at work the next morning. Open to the business section. Across the top of the page are the words, "Showing Up: Out of Nowhere Jack Stanbrick is On the Scene." A full-color photo of Jack blankets the front of the business pages, a proud grin stretching across his face.

I lift the paper up and begin to read.

"Jack Stanbrick, husband of marketing maven Claire Stanbrick, is making his mark in the Chicago business landscape by starting his own investment firm. Mr. Stanbrick says that by opening this firm, he is realizing one of his lifelong dreams, helping others reach their financial goals through thoughtful, personalized investment strategies. When asked about the relationship between his Stanbrick Financial and Claire's Stanbrick Marketing Group, Jack shot this reporter a wink and a smile, and stated that, 'like any solid marriage, Stanbrick Financial and Stanbrick Marketing Group are mutually supportive in terms of growth. Clients investing in Stanbrick Financial can feel reassured that their investments will be safe as they are guaranteed by the financial success of Stanbrick Marketing Group. If anything were to go awry with Stanbrick Financial, which of course it won't, the profits of Stanbrick Marketing Group would serve as collateral to guarantee the treasured investments of our clients. If our clients lose, we lose. And Stanbricks are winners.'"

The heat from my morning coffee burns my fingertips through the paper cup. I am proud of Jack's accomplishment and am glad that he is doing all he can to market his company, but I am not sure I agree with some of the claims he is making. I fold up the newspaper and tuck it in the crook of my arm. I need to talk to him. I know he has good intentions, that he is only trying to engender confidence. I've been running a business for a lot longer than he has and I can't say I feel entirely comfortable with him using SMG as collateral for his clients' investments.

I walk out into the hallway and spot a woman sitting at Marcia's desk, with auburn hair, the same vibrant red shade as mine. Not brownish, like Wanda's. Roger must have decided to replace her after all.

"Excuse me." I tap the woman on the shoulder.

She spins around in her chair. "Good morning, Claire."

I take a step back. Not a new temp. It's Wanda, her hair colored like mine, and twisted up into the same bun I wore mine in yesterday. She brushes a few crumbs of cranberry muffin off her sweater, blue cashmere, just like my missing one.

She runs a hand across the top of her bun. "What do you think?"

"Nice."

"My hairdresser thought if I went redder, it would be very becoming on me. Don't you think?"

"I like your sweater. Where did you get it?"

"A discount shop near where I live. It's totally a knock off. You can't tell, can you?"

"No." I purse my lips. It looks an awful lot like the real thing, like the one that went missing from my office, my real cashmere one. But unless I'm sure, I can't just accuse her of stealing. I look at the calendar pinned up on the wall of Wanda's cubicle. October 12th. Marcia's scheduled to come back on the 19th. It can't happen soon enough. I know Wanda's got it rough with her husband, but she's beginning to creep me out.

"If you're looking for Jack, he just stepped out with Roger for a meeting with some potential investors." She points at the newspaper still tucked under my arm. "You saw it? Great. I left it on your desk."

Inside I cringe. I'm not sure I feel comfortable with her being in my office when I'm not there.

"Isn't it amazing? Jack Stanbrick, owning the city, one client at a time." She looks out into the distance, a dreamy look sliding across her glassy eyes.

I want to smack her. "That's quite a slogan you got there. Did you come up with it yourself?" I'm wondering if I should be impressed.

She covers her mouth with her hand and giggles. "No, no. Wait. I should say yes. But that would be a lie and I would never lie to you."

I'm not sure what that means. "So you didn't come up with it?"

"Nope. Roger did. Look." She scoots her chair away from her desk and turns her computer screen toward me.

My breath catches in my chest. Covering her screen is the remains of what used to be the Stanbrick Marketing Group website. My website. Only now, it says Stanbrick Worldwide and has both Jack's and my company listed.

"What do you think?" she asks.

"Excellent." There is not a chance in hell I am going to discuss my feelings about this with a woman who says she'd never lie to me while wearing a sweater she likely stole out of my office. I roll back my shoulders. "I have a report to finish. When Jack comes in, please tell him I'm looking for him."

My head held high, I close my office door and pull up the new website on my computer. Photos of Jack, his arms crossed, his chin out, flash across my screen. There is also a picture of Roger, mugging for the camera in an expensive, neatly pressed suit. I scroll down to the text beneath his photo. Vice President. Jack's number two.

I click on the link beside Jack's name and read his credentials. Trained at elite universities for his undergraduate and business degrees. He should list those accomplishments. He earned them. Located beneath Jack's credentials is a quote from a prestigious investment-rating firm lauding their approval of Stanbrick Financial and giving it a five-star rating.

A silhouette moves in the corner of my eye. I look up from my computer and see Jack leaning against the doorframe to my office. "We did it."

"Did what?"

"Stanbrick Financial is officially launched and thriving."

"That's great." I strum my fingernails against the lacquered coating of my desk.

"What's wrong?"

"Nothing." I look away from him. I don't want to, but I can't help it.

"Hey." Jack kneels in front of me and pulls my desk chair close. He rests his hands on my lap. "I thought you'd be excited about this. Did you see the newspaper article?"

"I did."

"That was Roger's idea. The clients are pouring in. I cannot believe it." He drums his palms against my thighs.

"I see. I wish someone had cleared it with me first."

"I thought you were on board with linking our companies. You're still okay with it, right? If not, I'll undo it. I'll find a way."

I can see the concern in his eyes. "That's not necessary, but I do worry about promises of using SMG as collateral. That feels risky." I slide a garbage can out from under my desk and toss my coffee cup inside.

"Our companies are now incorporated under one umbrella conglomerate. They are somewhat dependent on each other. Like you and me." He squeezes my knee.

"Like you and me?" I sit up straight. My mother's warning that a woman must be self-sufficient pings in my mind.

"That's not a bad thing. We support each other and are stronger united than if we were separate. It's the same with our company. If Stanbrick Marketing Group ever hits hard times, profits from Stanbrick Financial would be there to help keep it afloat too."

I know this, I do. I'm just so used to the independence of having my own company, unfettered to anyone else's, that this makes me uncomfortable.

"I'm sorry I didn't show the copy of the article to you beforehand. I honestly didn't think there would be anything in it that you wouldn't approve of." He lifts my hand toward his lips and kisses my palm. "I thought it would be a happy surprise."

I reassure myself that this is in fact a good thing. Our businesses are growing. "So how many new clients are there?"

"Thirty accounts this morning alone." He claps his hands. "We've already received investments in the hundreds of thousands."

"Already?" I open my eyes wide.

"This is going to be huge. My dream is coming true." He rests his hand on my shoulder and the warmth of his touch calms me.

I look into his eyes and am proud of him. He's going for it. And why shouldn't he? I always do. I brush my fingers against his cheek, his whiskers scratchy and familiar. "I'm happy for you, Jack."

He kisses my forehead. "I'm happy for us."

Chapter Twelve

Wanda After

My nerves fire hot beneath my skin as I wait for the security guard to vanish. I loop my cleaning bucket over my arm and inch the cleaning cart toward the door, nothing to see here. I'm nonchalant, until I am certain he is out of sight. Then I rush in, leaving the door slightly ajar behind me. The room smells of mold, of dust and mothballs, but mostly of secrets. I breathe in the air, the same air Claire used to breathe, and wonder what discoveries await me.

The office has a presence to it, of life lived, of love. The familiarity of the space butters my skin. But I'm not sure why. I feel warm and bubbly. I want to dance. It seems as if I've seen it all before: the desk chair with the wobbly arm, the triangular table wedged into the corner, the half-bookcase standing against the back wall. But have I?

Piles of files and folders litter the floor. Old computers sit in a mound, crammed in a heap against the back wall. A desk sits at an awkward angle in the center of the room, stacked high with boxes. A thick layer of dirt coats the desktop from end to end. I run my pinky through it. This place hasn't been cleaned in years. I pull out a can of wood cleaner and wipe the desk down with a cloth, polishing the sides, pressing dust out of the carved crevices. But I can't just spend my time cleaning. I need to see if there's any information I can find that will shed light on whether or not I am Claire.

My fingers trace the base of the desk drawer. I tug it open. Inside, two picture frames rest folded up. One with a photo of Claire and Jack, facing each other laughing, the tips of their noses covered in buttercream, a wedding photo. I giggle and wipe at my own nose. But of course, there's no frosting there.

The other contains a picture of Claire in a graduation gown, shaking hands with a dean, receiving a diploma. In the photo, she is beaming, her dimples peppering her cheeks, her red hair bright against the black cloth of the gown. I squeeze my eyes shut and try to remember something, anything about that day. The smell of flowering spring leaves in the quad? Shielding my eyes as the sun reflects off the tops of the program covers? The sound of applause as graduates cross the stage? But I've got nothing. Even the name of the university evades me. I flip the frame around, slide the metal tab to the side, and pry the picture out. The photo crinkles between my fingers as I read the words on the back. "Class of 2000." I spin the year around in my mind, to see if it triggers something. My shoulders fall. Nothing.

I stuff the photos back into the drawer when a box, its top partially open, catches my eye. Inside are stacks and stacks of notepads and pens, each with an orange and white SMG logo printed across the top. SMG, Claire's now-defunct company. I grab a fistful of pens and stick them in my smock. Souvenirs.

The room suddenly feels suffocating. I walk over to the window, press my palms against the glass and look out. The city is peaceful. Most offices are still dark and only a scant few cars make their way along the empty streets below. I rest my hands on top of the ledge, the marble smooth and cool beneath my fingertips. The answer to who I am is not out there.

I am shaken from my thoughts when footsteps shuffle into the room. It's Astrid, sweet, sleepy Astrid, rubbing her eyes.

"Is it almost time to go home, Mama?"

"How did you know where I was?" I ask.

"I looked in all the rooms. I'm an explorer."

A panic washes over me as I think about Astrid roaming the hallways by herself. "Astrid, please. Next time you have to stay put. You can't go wandering around. It isn't safe to do that. Someone could see you. I'm not supposed to bring you with me. I could lose my job or worse, you could get hurt."

She pouts at me. I've bruised her feelings. But that's too bad. I would die if anything happened to her. Die.

I rest my hands on her shoulders. "You're not in any trouble. Just promise me you won't wander off again."

"Promise." She chews on a strand of hair.

I kiss the top of her head. I'm a horrible mother. It's my fault we're even here. She should be at home sleeping securely in bed. But she's not. She's stuck here with me. I'm going to get to the bottom of this. I just need to find out what happened to me. How did I end up shot and in the Wisconsin River? The answer to those questions lies somewhere with Claire and this company. It's got to.

***

Home from my shift, I collapse into bed and close my eyes. But sleep evades me. The light from the hallway reflects onto the magazine I bought the other day, peeking out of the wastebasket. I crawl across my bedspread and grab it. A lamp sits upon the nightstand beside the bed. I flick it on as one of the bulbs burns out with a crackle and flash. The remaining bulb emits only a dim glow, but it's enough, enough to read the article about Jack and Claire.

I flip through the magazine's silky pages and stop when I see a picture of Jack standing proudly next to a slain deer, a rifle at his side, Jack, a hunter and gun collector. Beneath the photo, in bold print, the article mentions that casings were found at Jack's house on the bank of the Wisconsin River. Casings that were the same caliber as a gun missing from Jack's collection.

I run my fingers along the words of the head juror from Jack's trial. "That was among the most damning evidence. The murder weapon was never found, but the casings located at the crime scene were a .45 caliber. The same caliber as the semi-automatic pistol missing from Stanbrick's collection. To us jurors, that pointed to a guilty verdict." A glossy photo of a semi-automatic pistol follows the juror's words, an exclamation point. The article goes on to say, "The defense emphasized the inherent doubt. 'Lots of guns use that caliber of ammunition. Without the gun, the casings can't be linked definitively to Jack.'" I nod my head. Makes sense to me.

I turn the page and land on a photo of Jack beaming, leaning against a sports car. A convertible. Cherry red. I laugh out loud at the sight of it. I have no idea why. I slap my hand over my mouth to stifle my laugh. Confused. The photo is not funny. But it's triggering something in me, a memory just out of reach. As I stare at it, the memory of a scent flutters through my mind, vanilla with musky undertones. Jack's cologne?

The next page features a photo of Claire wearing a light blue cardigan. It looks soft to the touch, expensive, yet somehow familiar. I can't shake the feeling I've seen it before, felt it.

I swing my feet over the side of the bed and shuffle to the closet. The light bulb chain is old and rough against my fingers. I give it a quick tug and begin fishing through my closet, digging, tossing clothes out onto my bedroom floor: crumpled up t-shirts, wrinkled blouses, old faux-leather heels, weathered and cracked. I am about to give up when my palm brushes up against something soft. Something gentle. I push a pair of stockings and sweatpants aside and there on the floor of my closet is a light blue sweater. Claire's?

I pull it over my arms and run my fingers across the mother-of-pearl buttons. It smells dirty, like damp shoes, but I don't care. The delicate material beneath my fingertips fills me with hope. If only I were her, I could fill up my memories once again. I could know who I am supposed to be. Be the mother I want to be. I curl up on top of my mattress and flip through the pages of the article, looking for clues, some sign that it's true, that I really am Claire. But a cold chill slices through me as I read the words, "Jack is currently serving two life sentences for the murder of his wife and unborn child." A photo of a pregnant Claire fills the page. Claire was pregnant? An image of Astrid dances before me. There's no way Jack committed this crime. And if I'm Claire, I can prove it. I can save us all.

***

The harsh light of the morning sun snakes its way through a hole in my window shade. I rub my hand along the smooth fabric of the sweater and shake my head at my foolishness. Me? Claire? Please. I look around the bedroom, cringe at the peeling wallpaper and question whether this is truly my fate. I twist my legs around to the side of the mattress and spot the magazine lying open on the floor beside my feet. There is a photo of Jack in an orange jumpsuit, his hands shackled behind his back. Incarcerated. I wrap the sweater tight across my chest.

A moment later, there's a knock at the front door. I slide my feet into my slippers as Astrid races barefooted into my bedroom. She runs into me so hard I lose my balance and have to steady myself against the nightstand.

"Who's here, Mama?"

"I don't know." I bite my nails. We aren't expecting anyone. "You stay here."

"No. I want to come with you."

"Stay here. I'll go check it out."

She doesn't listen and follows close behind me as I tiptoe down the stairs. We get to the landing, and I can see the outline of a person through the etched glass framing the door. I approach the window as Astrid calls out, "Penelope. Penelope's here."

Even though I really appreciate her help most of the time, I am not in the mood for her right now. I pull the door open and stare at the scrawny woman with pocked skin and a wrinkled, skeletal neck standing in my doorway. Irritation bubbles beneath my skin as Astrid rushes into her arms. She unzips her purse, weathered at the seams, and fishes out a bright green lollipop. She places it in Astrid's outstretched hand. Astrid unwraps it.

"Wait." I cover Astrid's hand with mine. Nosey neighbor bribes my daughter for affection with candy and I haven't even been able to give her breakfast yet.

"What's the matter with you?" Penelope steps into the front hallway.

"I didn't say you could come into my house." I place my hands on my hips.

"An open door is an invitation. That's what I always say." She peels off her coat and hangs it on the railing.

I grab it and toss it back to her. "The door wasn't open."

"Don't start this again. You used to like it when I came over. Before."

Before the accident, a time I have no recollection of.

"That's right." She peers into my eyes. "Remember? We used to talk for hours about Carl and your marital woes."

I sigh. I've heard this all before. She tells me we were friends. That ever since the accident, I'm not the same.

"By the way, have you found my gun yet?"

And she always asks me about that stinking gun, and I always tell her the same thing. "I don't have your gun."

"You do. I lent it to you before your accident. I'd like it back."

I tell her what I always tell her when she brings this up. "I've searched the house and I've never found a gun anywhere."

She squints her eyes at me.

"And I'm glad for that. Trust me, if I ever find it, I will give it right back to you. I don't want something dangerous like that around with Astrid in the house."

Her eyes soften. She hangs her coat back up and tousles Astrid's hair. "All right, I'll let it go for now. But I'm not letting you go. No, I'm not giving up on you, Wanda."

Sometimes I wish she would.

She hugs me, her overly floral perfume making me nauseous. "When you had your accident, I was worried you weren't going to make it."

"You were?" My guard weakens. She means well and she does care.

"I was sure that deadbeat Carl was behind it. All he cared about was trying to collect insurance benefits or see if there was someone he could sue."

I laugh, not because it's funny, but because it's sad. "Now he seems to think I made some investment with his worker's comp benefits. He thinks he's due some big payout."

"Figures. So, where is that no-good husband of yours?"

"He left."

"Again, huh. Bastard. He'll be back. When he runs out of money, he'll be back trying to sniff out any you've got."

"I don't have any money."

"But you've got a roof over your head."

I look up at the paint peeling on the ceiling beside the rusted-out light fixture and shrug. The weight of the conversation is getting to me. I am about to ask her to leave, politely this time, when Astrid tugs at Penelope's pant leg, the polyester crinkling between her fingers.

"Will you play with me, Penny?"

"Of course I will." Penelope cups Astrid's chin in her hands, then picks her up. Astrid fluffs Penelope's hair, covering and uncovering her face with the staticky strands.

A jolt of jealousy over Astrid's affections toward Penelope courses through me. "We'll stop by later, okay? I'm not up to company right now."

Astrid begins to cry as the woman sets her down.

Penelope takes a step closer to me. "You need me."

"I'm fine."

"You don't look fine."

I run my hands over my hair, tucking the fly-away pieces behind my ears, suddenly self-conscious.

"Have you been taking those pills again?"

"What pills?" I play coy.

"Answer me. I'm the only friend you've got. Are you still taking them? The pain pills?"

"No. I'm clean."

"Good. We need to keep you that way." She pulls me into her arms. I twist away. "Why do you care?"

"Because you remind me of myself. After my husband died. I was tied to the past. Couldn't get over the loss. But the past isn't where I am anymore. I needed to move on. And so do you."

I scowl. What does she know? At least she still has her memories. I lost my entire self.

She rests her hand upon my wrist, her fingers bony, her skin paper-thin. "You look so tired. Didn't you sleep last night?"

I think about how I stayed up reading and re-reading the article about Claire and Jack. "Not much."

"Come, let's get you to bed."

As she speaks the words, I realize she's right. I am exhausted. Maybe this idea that I could be Claire Stanbrick is just a distraction, a diversion from my miserable life. Goodness knows getting lost in a fantasy is so much better than facing my reality. Who could blame me for that? Who could blame me for wanting more? I glance back at Penelope and Astrid. Astrid happily chomping on the lollipop. They smile at each other. A searing pain throbs behind my cheekbone, a souvenir from my accident. I miss my pills. I follow Penelope into the living room, and per her instructions, lie down on the couch. She pulls the bunched-up threadbare blanket off the armrest and covers me.

"That's right, you rest," she says. "Astrid is going to help me in my garden."

Penelope's garden, full of vibrant flowers, and life.

Astrid bounces on her heels and nods.

Penelope strokes my hair. "It's a new day and we're going to make the most of it. Come join us when you are ready to be part of it."

Chapter Thirteen

Claire Before

Having been up throughout the night, tossing and turning, my stomach cramping and tight, I decide to work from home the following morning.

"Are you sure you don't want me to stay home with you?" Jack kisses my forehead, his lips cool against my sweaty skin.

"I'm sure." I tuck the covers beneath my chin. "It's probably some kind of stomach bug. You probably shouldn't get too close to me."

He peels off his suit jacket and sits on the edge of the bed.

"What are you doing?"

He kicks off his dress shoes. "I'm worried about you. You haven't been feeling well since the presentation with Teason Dairy."

"I'm fine. This is different. That was nausea. This is stomach cramps. It's probably from the olive oil in the pasta I made last night. I put too much into the sauce."

"But it was so good."

I think about the *linguini aglio e olio* and I feel like I can still smell it, the garlic, the oil. A cramp cinches within my abdomen but I keep my face still. Jack's been so excited about Stanbrick Financial and there is so much work to do. I'd hate for him to take time away on account of me. I'll be fine. I'm Claire Stanbrick. I'm always fine. "You should go. Seriously. I'll call you if I need something." I sit up in bed to prove I'm all right. "In fact, maybe I'll even head in this afternoon."

Jack shakes his head. "You are one tough lady."

"And you love that about me." I flash him a smile.

"I love everything about you."

My heart bubbles with warmth inside my chest. "Now go to work. That's an order."

"Yes, ma'am." Jack salutes me before his face turns serious. "But promise me you'll call if you need me." He props a stack of pillows behind me as I give him two thumbs up.

He is about to leave as a sharp pain slices through my abdomen, a pain even I can't hide. I race into the bathroom, doubled over. My underpants wet, I peel them down and see thick spots of blood. I press my palms against my stomach to ease the cramps. A trail of clots fall to the floor. I tally in my mind the last time I had my period. Almost two months ago. How did I lose track? I never lose track. I call out to Jack as I type my symptoms into my cell phone.

He bursts through the bathroom door. "Are you okay?"

"I need you to take me to the doctor."

His eyes widen as he stares at the blood splattered on the white bathroom floor tile.

"I think I'm having a miscarriage."

"But I didn't even know you were pregnant."

"Neither did I."

***

The doctor said there might be some cramping after the procedure. Still, I didn't expect to be in pain the following morning. But then again, I didn't expect to be pregnant in the first place. I wrap my arms around my stomach and bend forward, but the aching persists. I hobble down the hall to our master bedroom, press a button next to the bed to lower the blinds, and pull the covers over my head. Even with the shades drawn the room still feels too bright for me. I want to sink into the mattress, disappear. Melt away.

Miscarriage. I hate that word. As if I 'miss' carried her. As if I did it wrong. And I don't do things wrong. The baby was a girl. A simple test on the tissue confirmed it; too much information, though. Now I get to picture dressing her up in pink onesies, clipping bows to her baby-fine curls. I roll up into a ball beneath my bed sheets as the image vanishes.

Stop it, I scold myself. This baby was never meant to be. How can I long for a pregnancy I didn't even want? Didn't even know I had? Career before babies. Period. All these years trying to avoid getting pregnant, taking the occasional pregnancy test, always hoping for a negative, and now look at me.

It's true that I never wanted a baby. Is that why I lost her? Did my feelings cause this? I squeeze my eyes shut. And now I can't stop wanting hcr.

My cell phone buzzes on the nightstand beside my bed. I reach a blind hand out from under the covers and feel around for the phone. I bring it into the cocoon I've created for myself beneath my comforter.

It's a text from Jack. I forced him to go into the office, if only for a few hours. No need to stay here with me. I can take care of myself.

"Heading home soon. Bringing wine."

I laugh, but quickly stifle it. Caught off guard. Even in my darkest moment, our darkest moment, Jack can still make me smile. I text back a heart emoji and distract myself by looking over my emails. But for some reason, they are not coming through on my phone. My last email is time stamped the evening before.

Frustrated, I fling the covers off and make my way into our home office. The blinds are open and sunlight bounces off the windows of the condo building next to ours, casting a reflection across the office's dark oak desk. I squint in the sunlight at the boats tethered to the dock below, bouncing to the hypnotic pulse of the Lake Michigan waves. I rotate the window crank, let the breeze blow into the room, and pause to smell the crisp, autumn air.

My computer hums to life. I log in, but when I click on my emails, they still refuse to load. I grab the phone and dial Marcia's extension.

The phone picks up on the first ring.

"Marcia?"

"Nope. Wanda here."

Crap. "I thought Marcia was coming back today."

"She said she needed an extra week. Her knee is still sore and she's enjoying getting to be home with her kids. Having trouble separating from them."

This I understand. A pang of sadness courses through me. I am having trouble separating from my baby too.

"What can I do for you?" she asks.

At first I think, nothing. I swallow down a bubble of jealousy. Wanda's still pregnant and I am not. I run my palm along the smooth wooden surface of the desk and force myself to focus. There's work to be done. "I need you to log into my computer and read my emails to me."

There is silence on the line, and I can't tell if she's still there. "Wanda? Hello? It's not working remotely, so you'll need to go into my office."

"Okay. Putting you on hold." Light elevator music plays in my ear. A minute later, she picks up again. "What's your login and password?"

"The username is just my name. So, Claire.Stanbrick."

"Got it."

"The password is . . ." I hesitate. Unsure if I should give it to her. It's not that I dislike her. It's just something about her makes me uncomfortable. I tap my knuckles on my desk. Maybe I should check my mail when I get in tomorrow morning.

She interrupts my thoughts. "The password is?"

But then I think about all the important client emails I could be missing. "I'll tell you, but don't write it down or anything, okay?"

"I'll type it right into the computer."

I picture her fingertips at the ready, poised on the keyboard. "It's 'Red Roller.'"

She repeats the words out loud, "Red Roller," and I cringe hearing the sound coming from her lips. These words are private, intimate to me, an inside joke between Jack and myself. Although I can't explain why or how, I feel violated.

"We're in." Her voice sounds happy, chipper.

"Can you read my emails to me, please?"

She goes down the list, reciting the headings of each one. Most are either junk or non-urgent, until she gets to one from Nate Teason regarding the Teason billing statement.

"Stop," I say. "Read that one to me."

"It says, 'Claire: We have received the most recent billing statement sent to us and are concerned as to how you derived the balance due for the upcoming project. The balance in the account appears to be off by $9,898, as if we never made the preliminary payment. I'm assuming this is either a misprint or a miscalculation. Please look into this and report back to me immediately."

My blood steams beneath my skin. My account statements are never off. Never. And I won't have anyone from my office sending out inaccurate statements either. I try to control my anger. "Connect me to Roger, please?"

Once again, I am on hold listening to that ridiculous music.

After a few minutes, Roger picks up. "What's up?"

"I got an email from Nate Teason that their account balance is off by almost ten thousand dollars."

"What? I checked those numbers myself before the bill went out and they were perfect."

Doubt's knuckles needle me. "The client says they are off. Do you have the file in front of you?"

"Hang on."

Papers shuffle as he rifles through documents on his desk looking for the file. Meanwhile, I pace around my home office, tugging at my nightshirt, sweat pooling, sticky, beneath my armpits.

"Got it."

The sound of more pages flipping and fingers typing upon the keyboard echoes in the background.

"I see the problem," he says. "When Nate signed on with Stanbrick Financial, money that was supposed to go to his SMG account went to his Stanbrick Financial account instead. That's why it looks low."

My breath pulses into the phone.

"Don't panic. It's an easy fix. I'll make sure the accounts are squared away," he says.

An error like this never should have occurred in the first place. "How did this happen?" I choke out the words and wipe a line of sweat from my forehead with the back of my hand.

"It was an error Wanda made. Damn."

"Why was Wanda even handling account balances? That's the project manager's job. Which, by the way, is you."

"I know, I was swamped, and her resume indicates accounting experience. I'll change it and send a revised document to Nate."

"No."

"What do you mean?"

"Before you send it to Nate, email it to me. I want to look it over before it goes out to him. I've got damage control to do now." I cringe as I say it, the words acrid on my tongue.

"Want me to have another talk with Wanda?"

"Is Marcia coming back next week?" I ask.

"Yes. Monday."

"No, and you are also to blame for this one. Connect me back to her, will you?"

Wanda picks up. The sound of her smacking her chewing gum reverberates through the receiver. Every muscle within me aches to shout at her to let her know she shouldn't take on tasks she is unqualified to do, to emphasize to her the risk she has put the firm in, but I decide not to. It's not worth it. A few more days and she'll be gone. Instead, I ask her to put me through to Jack's office.

The phone rings, looping over and over again with no answer.

After a few minutes Wanda picks up the line. "Didn't he answer?"

"No. Can you walk down to his office and see if he's still there or if he's left already?"

I wait and wait, and wait, listening to the obnoxious hum of the hold music. I crouch down onto the floor and watch the minutes go by. Five minutes. Then ten.

Wanda comes back on the phone. "Looks like he is gone for the day."

I hang up. Maybe he's in his car on the way home. I dial his cell phone. But it goes straight to voicemail. I leave a message. Where is he?

***

A half hour later, I feel the gentle weight of Jack's hand upon my shoulder. I wipe my cheeks with my sleeve and look up at him, my eyes puffy and swollen.

"My poor girl." He squats down on the floor beside me. "For you," he says and places a brown paper bag in my lap.

I peek inside and see it is a bottle of my favorite wine. Riesling. It's cool to the touch, the glass already frosted from the heat in the condo. I unscrew the top with my bare hands, bring the bottle to my lips, and take a few large gulps.

"Whoa. Slow down. You're going to make yourself sick." He pries it out of my hands.

"Where were you?"

"On my way home."

"I tried calling you. I couldn't reach you." My voice cracks as I speak.

"You tried calling? But my phone didn't ring." He pulls his phone out of his jacket pocket, and sure enough no calls from me are shown.

"I don't understand. I know I called you. Can I see your phone?"

He hands it to me. I pull up my information in the contacts and have my answer.

"You blocked me."

"What? No. I didn't."

I hand him the phone.

"How did that happen? How do I undo this?"

I scroll down and press the "unblock" button.

"I don't get it." He shakes his head, incredulous. "Actually, you know what?"

"What?" I rest the bottle of Riesling on the floor beside me.

"Now that I think about it, I did misplace my phone today. Wanda found it in the office kitchen. Which is odd since I don't remember being in there today."

"Wanda found it?" I clutch the neck of the wine bottle.

"She seemed very proud of herself when she waltzed into my office with it. You don't think she played around with the contacts, do you?"

I furrow my eyebrows. "She's a little loopy, and she should never have her hands on client account statements, but I don't think she'd do that."

Jack tucks a loose strand of hair behind my ear. "I'm sorry you couldn't reach me."

Tears cloud my vision. He pulls me close to him, and somehow, just being beside him, I begin to feel better.

"What can I do to help? Tell me what to do, and I'll do it." He kisses my forehead.

"Baby. I want to be a mother." I blurt it out without thinking, surprising even myself.

Jack's eyes open wide. "You do? Now you do?"

I exhale. "Yes."

A smile spreads across his face. "I've always hoped you would change your mind about this. But I never thought you ever would."

I laugh through my tears. "Me either. How can I want something I always insisted I didn't want?"

"People's desires change sometimes." He squeezes my knee.

"When my mother was building her career, a single mother trying to support us, I felt like a burden, like I was holding her back. I thought I'd never want a child to hinder my career opportunities."

"But unlike her, you don't have to do it on your own. You have me." He pulls an argyle handkerchief out of his coat pocket and dabs at my eyes.

"We have each other." I rest my head against his chest.

"Your mother wasn't all bad. She left you quite an inheritance, right? Made sure you would be set for life."

"But what I really wanted was her time, her affection."

"You have my time and my affection." He lifts my chin and kisses me.

I turn away. "But I'm not pregnant anymore." I hug my knees to my chest. "Wanda is."

"Who cares about Wanda? You've got so much more going for you than she does." He presses his palm flat against my own.

I smile.

He wraps his arm around my shoulder. "Listen to me. One day, you will be a mother. I promise."

I shrug away from him. "You shouldn't make promises you can't keep."

He nudges back closer to me. "I never do."

Chapter Fourteen

Wanda After

That evening, I am back at work, cleaning the offices in a daze. Just going through the motions, wanting to get my shift over with. Penelope's right about one thing. I do need to move on. I'm just trying to escape from reality by entertaining the idea that I could be Claire. It's no different from my pills, allowing me to live in a fantasy world. And yet the idea that I am not Claire, that I am simply plain old miserable Wanda, leaves me feeling like a balloon with the air let out of it, deflated and limp.

Astrid lopes along beside me, the excitement of our evening adventures fizzled out for her too. I pack up my cleaning supplies and tell her to come with me. I have one more office to clean for the evening before we can head home. She follows me down the hallway, whining and kicking at the carpet the entire time, until we arrive at Roger's office.

Once inside, I glance around the room. Even though I've cleaned his office before, tonight there's a feeling of familiarity that I can't deny. Can't shake off.

No. I'm being ridiculous. I dust the shelves lining the windowsill.

"Look at that." Astrid points to the computer sitting on top of the desk.

"Yep, a computer." No surprise there, an office with a computer. Damning evidence that I must be Claire if I might say so. Yeah, right. I get back to work straightening a scattered pile of file folders before giving a final dusting to the window ledge.

"Can we get one?" She looks up at me, hopeful.

"No, honey. Too expensive."

Disappointment colors her delicate features.

“After I empty the trash can, we’ll leave.” I dump the contents into a black garbage bag: an old sticky note and a crumpled-up napkin. Not much to see here.

I tie it up and am about to leave when I notice a file cabinet with a lock on it. I tug on the drawer. Locked. My interest piqued, I kneel beside the cabinet and notice it is not completely closed. I grab a letter opener off the desk and slide it in the lock. Anticipation beats through me. What are you hiding in there, Roger Lindsey?

My shoulders drop with disappointment as I look through the contents of the drawer, nothing but empty multicolored file folders. Figures.

Astrid skips over to the desk and calls out to me. “Can I play with it?”

“Play with what?” I wipe my forehead, exhausted and ready to leave.

“The computer.”

My eyes track to where she is pointing. The computer is on. A screensaver of a clock bounces from one end of the monitor to the other. Tempting me. No. Except for dusting the computers, I’m not supposed to touch them.

Astrid’s face falls as I shake my head no.

I turn away from the computer and begin to pack up. But a voice in my head pecks at me. Maybe there is some information on the computer that can help me find out what happened to Claire. Stop it. If I’m not Claire, then it doesn’t matter. “Come on, Astrid. Let’s go.”

In an attempt to get one quick touch of the computer in, Astrid reaches for the mouse and rolls it across the desk. As she does, the clock screensaver disappears. A login page pops up in its place. I stare at it, the blank lines calling to me.

Don’t do it. I turn toward the door. “We’re going.” But my feet don’t move.

Instead, I bend over and press the letter 'C' into the top line for the username, as if I were logging in as Claire. The phrase *Claire.Stanbrick* autofills the space. I type the word "Jack" into the password line and hit enter. A red message pops up, telling me I have the incorrect password. I try again, "Claire+Jack." Again, I get a failed login message. I try a few more times, combining their names in every possible combination. But with each attempt, I get it wrong. Astrid plays with her untied shoelace, twisting it around her fingers. This is silly. It's late and this is a waste of time.

I am about to leave when it hits me. A flash of words dances through my mind, I turn back to the keyboard and type them in. "Red Roller." Jack's sports car? I laugh. The Red Roller. I wonder if Jack called it that as he rolled around town on summer nights, top down, Claire in the passenger seat beside him. I want to say he did. I bet that would be something he would do. In the upper right-hand corner of the screen, the words "Hello, Claire" greet me.

My reflection smiles back at me in the screen. "Hello." I am logged into Claire's computer.

Without taking my eyes off the monitor, I grab the desk chair and scoot it beneath me. I click on the mail icon. My breath catches in my chest as over a thousand emails download. When the downloading stops, I scroll through the messages, scanning them one by one. Impatient, I head to the bottom of the list. It's the older ones that matter, the ones from right before Claire went missing. Most are spam, but I stop as one in particular catches my eye. It is marked *urgent* and is addressed only to Roger Lindsey, but Claire is blind copied on it. Someone didn't want Roger to know she was seeing it too. I read the subject line, "re: Teason account."

I spin the name Teason through my mind, to see if it sparks something. But there's nothing.

I need to read the body of the email. Maybe something in it will jog my memory. I pull it up but am only able to read the first few words when I hear footsteps in the hallway. I click the *X* in the top left corner of the screen and close the email. I turn to Astrid. “Hurry. Someone’s coming.”

Oblivious, Astrid lies on the floor, tapping her shoes against the leg of the desk.

“They can’t know you are here with me.”

The worried tone in my voice gets her attention. She clambers to her feet, the anxious look on her face mirroring my own. I’ll lose my job if they see I brought her with me. Panic jolts my nerves to full attention. I notice a skinny closet wedged along the side wall of the office. “Quick. Climb in.”

Astrid does as she is told.

“You too, Mama.”

“No, no. They just can’t see you.” I guide the closet door shut, grab my feather duster out of my cleaning bucket, and wipe at a bookcase. I count the seconds for the screensaver to pop up again, to cover my tracks. I’m allowed to clean the offices, but not to snoop on the computers. My heart knocks in my chest. The screensaver isn’t appearing.

I jump as a tall man with a bald head flings open the door to the office.

“Who’s there?” he asks.

“Cleaning service.” I smile innocently.

“Who are you? What are you doing in here?” He pauses and does a double take, as if he knows me.

“Just cleaning, sir.” I roll up my sleeves.

“Well, you need to leave. I don’t want anyone in here unless I’m in here too.”

"Okay." I eye the closet. I can't leave without Astrid. "I'll just finish dusting and be on my way."

"No. You need to leave now."

My palms sweat. What am I going to do? I take my time, replacing the duster into the bucket, buying time to think, when suddenly I feel hands upon the back of my shoulders. He spins me around, his fingertips pressing into my skin. I gasp and see the closet door creak open a crack.

"Why is this computer logged on?"

"I don't know." I shake my head at Astrid. She closes the door.

"Were you on it?"

I whisper, "No." But he doesn't hear.

"Answer me."

"No. I didn't even know it was on. Is it on?" Just then the screensaver pops back up.

"You're lying. Who are you?" he shouts at me.

"No one. Just the cleaning service."

"What are you looking for?"

"Nothing. I don't know what you're talking about. I swear."

He is still squeezing my shoulders when the security guard enters the office, his hand pasted onto his holstered gun.

"What's going on here?" The security guard looks at me. "It's okay, I spoke with her the other day. She's part of the cleaning crew."

I nod, my face hot.

The man releases me and takes a step back. He bends over his computer and clicks the "sign out" button. "No one should be in here. There is confidential client information in this room. Don't clean this office again, got it?"

"Okay." But all I can think of is Astrid. How am I going to get us out of here?

"I think she understands now. It won't be a problem again, Mr. Lindsey." The security guard assures him.

Roger? This is Roger Lindsey? I pictured him differently. He is more wiry, less stocky than I imagined, but just as intimidating.

"Funny, though," the security guard continues. "It's almost like déjà vu, seeing her standing here in this office. I told her before that she sort of looks like Claire. Don't you think?"

His mouth straightens into a tight line. "She doesn't look like anyone I've ever seen before."

The security guard shrugs, "Let's go. I'll lock up."

The guard puts his hand on the small of my back and leads me toward the door. Inside I am screaming. Astrid. I can't leave without her.

My thoughts a tangled web, I can't think straight. I don't know what to do. I try to form words, to come up with something, anything, any excuse to have them leave so I can get to Astrid without them seeing her.

The security guard closes the door behind us. He seems jovial as he tries to make friendly conversation with Roger. "How's the hip?"

"Same as always. Shitty." Roger traipses off ahead of us and for the first time I notice he walks with a limp.

"Wait." I turn and face the security guard. "I left some cleaning supplies down the hall. Can I just grab them and meet you outside?" Maybe it will be okay. If the security guard leaves, maybe I can grab Astrid and get out.

"Sorry, ma'am. No can do. It's time for you to head home for the night."

"But it'll just take a second." Blood pounds in my ears. I am panicking.

"Nope." He points in the direction of the exit. "No one is going to miss a few cleaning supplies. But I'll lose my job if I let you mill around here any longer."

He takes a step away from the door and then stops. "I almost forgot." He pulls out his key and locks the deadbolt. "There, now we're all secure."

Panic stings the back of my eyes as he leads me to the elevator. He guides me on board and climbs in beside me. The numbers flash, hitting me like bullets, as we head down to the first floor, and I know I have got to get back up there and fast. In my mind, I weigh my choices and really there is only one. I have to tell the security guard what I've done, that I've been bringing my daughter with me to work each night. I'll probably lose my job, and while that's a big concern, it's not my main one. My biggest fear is that they will take Astrid away from me, force her to live with Carl. The thought pierces my heart. What argument could I make? An irresponsible, until very recently drug addicted mother who keeps her child out at all hours of the night while she cleans office buildings? I wouldn't stand a chance. Words fail me. Before I know it, I am pressing through the revolving doors, the security guard's eyes fixed on me. The cold night air assaults me. All I can think about is Astrid, up there, frightened, trapped and alone. I need to get to her. I picture her, her face buried in her hands, her eyes puffy, her lips stung from crying. Astrid.

No, I won't. I won't go home without her.

***

I stand on the curb outside the Creighton building, my love trapped inside. The tall building stretches out long and ominous before me like a fortress. Impenetrable. But I have got to get back inside. Now. The wind whips at me, stinging my cheeks. I wrap my scarf tightly around my neck. Crazy thoughts race through my mind. What if Roger goes back to his office now? What if he finds her there? He's such an angry man. If he hurts her, I'll kill him. I will.

From where I stand, I can see the security guard pacing back and forth along the marble floor of the entryway, stopping occasionally in front of the window. There's no way I'd be able to get past him. And what excuse would I give for going back into the building? I can't think of anything. But what choice do I have? None. I have to tell the truth. Her safety comes first. She comes first.

I inhale the crisp late-night air and start to walk toward the door. I place one foot into the street and immediately jump back as a garbage truck barrels along in front of me. Loose papers fly off the back of the truck, landing in crumpled bundles at my feet. I shake one off the top of my foot and am about to resume my death march when it hits me. The dumpsters. Dumpsters are usually located at the rear of a building. Which would mean there's got to be a back entryway.

Without missing a beat, I race across the street and around to the other side of the building. I see the dumpsters, two of them, filthy, the stench of garbage enveloping them like a putrid cloud. I run past them and see the back door, tucked away beneath a single caged-in light bulb.

Worried about the possibility of a security camera, I cover my head with my hood and bury my face into the folds of my scarf. When I reach the doorknob, I say a little prayer. "Please, please, please, open." I twist the knob and it doesn't budge. No. I have to get this door open. I try again, turning the cold metal in the other direction. But it remains shut.

I head over to the dumpster, hold my nose, lift the top, and look inside. Disappointment is bitter in my mouth, nothing but stacked-up garbage bags. There's got to be something. I drop the lid and walk around to the side of the trash container, and that's when I see it: a gas station just across the back alley. From where I stand, the lights of the service center behind it are out, that area closed for the evening. But maybe there will be something there that will help.

In the dark, I dash over to the garage door of the service station. I press my hands against the glass and peer inside. Along the side wall of the service shop is a cart full of tools. If only I can get to them. The garage door is sealed tight, a car needed to trigger it to open. I try the door beside it. Not surprisingly it is also locked. Shoot. What am I going to do now? I am about to leave when I see it. In the dim glow of the moonlight, nestled in the mud behind a neglected row of bushes, there is a crowbar. It's not a perfect solution, but maybe, just maybe, it will work.

I wrestle the crowbar out of the dirt, twist it from under a tangle of branches. The grainy metal of the bar feels cool against my palms and leaves a rusty stain upon my fingertips. Determined, I race across the alley. But once I reach the back door of the Creighton building, I am not sure exactly what to do. The aggressiveness of it all feels foreign to me and yet thoughts of Astrid urge me forward. I look up. The sky is beginning to lighten. A few of the streetlights have turned off. I am running out of time.

I notice that one end of the crowbar is beveled and thin, like teeth. I wedge that part in the slim opening where the door meets the frame and tug hard. Part of the frame loosens and I think I might be getting somewhere. I nestle it in a few more times, but the door won't open.

Damn it. The scratchy metal of the crowbar scrapes my skin raw as I slam it against the doorknob. Again and again, I hit it with the metal of the bar until the knob dangles warped and disfigured against the door. Fear fueling my every move, I bash the remains of the lock with the blunt end of the crowbar. The door pops open.

I sprint inside. Not knowing where I am going, I dart toward a door that I hope is the stairwell and fling it open. I take the steps two at a time, my breath catching in my throat, my lungs on fire.

The floors are marked with painted numbers on the cement walls of the stairwell. I have only reached the eighteenth floor when I realize I can't climb anymore, my legs weak rubber bands. I fall out of the bowels of the stairwell and scamper onto an elevator. My heart hammers within my chest. I just need to get to Astrid and get out. The elevator opens onto the 123rd floor. I sprint out and race up to the glass doors guarding the entrance to Stanbrick Financial. They are unlocked, but when I arrive at Roger's office that door is still shut tight.

I tap on the frosted glass that outlines the door.

"Astrid? Astrid?"

A moment later I see her beautiful face, the sight of an angel. Love surges through me and I feel as if I could break down that door with my bare hands if I had to.

"Mama."

"Shush, shush. We have to hurry."

"Mama." She covers her ears with her trembling hands.

"I know, honey. I'm scared too. But I'm here now. We're going to be all right. I just need you to do what I tell you, okay?"

She nods. Wet streaks run down her cheeks in dirty smudges and all I want to do is cradle her in my arms. Comfort her.

"Can you open the door?"

She tries the handle. "I can't. I can't. It won't open." She's panicking.

"Okay, is there a button or a latch somewhere?"

"What's a latch? I don't know." She starts tugging at the door.

And in that moment, I don't care anymore about anything but her. Not my job. Not Claire. Not my past. "Stand back. All the way back."

She does as she is told.

I raise the crowbar and smash the glass, shattering it into pieces. I untwist my scarf from around my neck and lay it on top of the shards of glass, scattered like confetti upon the carpet. I scoop Astrid up and help her through the opening. Once she is safely out, I stuff the scarf into my bag.

With her securely in my arms, my second wind kicks in and I dash back into the stairwell. But we are not in the clear. Voices are approaching, feet climb the steps from the floors below. Still cradling Astrid in my arms, I jump into an open elevator. With security likely stationed on the first floor, looking for who broke into the building, I figure our best bet is to try to blend in. Sneak out later with a crowd. There is a cafeteria two floors down. It is probably our best place to hide.

The cafeteria is just opening for the day, but already there are employees waiting in line for their morning coffee. The smell of orange-scented disinfectant spray permeates the air. I place Astrid down on the sticky floor beside me, pull my hood off my head and stand in line behind the other patrons. Act naturally. Blend in. We're just like anyone else getting their morning dose of caffeine. We walk along the rows of help-yourself food items. Astrid grabs a cookie. I pick up an apple, a chocolate milk, and a pair of paper plates.

The woman at the checkout counter peers at me from beneath her beehive hairdo. She gives me a funny look when I approach, sizing me up, trying to figure me out. Does she recognize me? I smile at her and show her my employee badge.

She looks at Astrid. "Is she going to the daycare?"

"Yes." There's a daycare in the building?

She checks her watch. "You know it doesn't open for another hour, right?"

"Of course." I have no idea what she is talking about, but I play along.

"Well, you can't hang out here. My manager says kids are not allowed to wait around in the cafeteria."

"Not a problem. We'll be on our way as soon as we pay. Hey, the weather seems to be warming up finally, so that's good."

She looks at her cash register, uninterested in engaging in small talk with me. "That'll be $4.99."

The cool facade I present to her masks my fears. As usual, I have no idea if I have enough money in my bag and Astrid has already begun eating the cookie. Crumbs sprinkle from her lips onto her windbreaker. Not wanting to call any attention to myself, I try to remain calm. I scrounge around a bit, blindly thumbing through the interior folds and pockets of my sweat jacket and am grateful when I feel a crumpled-up piece of paper. A five-dollar bill. The cashier is indifferent as I drop my change, a penny, into the plastic tip cup beside the register.

Astrid's grip tightens around my fingers. I follow her gaze to the entrance of the cafeteria, where two police officers stand next to the security guard, weapons drawn.

"Put your hands up," they shout from across the room.

Astrid's fingers loosen from my own. I raise my arms in the air as the crowbar falls from my bag and vibrates against the unforgiving linoleum floor. The jig is up.

Chapter Fifteen

Claire Before

The weight of the loss of the baby still heavy in my heart, I decide that maybe going back to work will serve as a helpful distraction. On my way out the door, I tiptoe past a still-sleeping Jack, his bare arm dangling off the edge of the mattress. When I arrive at the office building it looks deserted. The sound of my heels clicking against the polished lobby floor echoes in my ears. Paranoid, I spin around thinking I hear someone behind me. But when I look, no one is there, just the wind outside brushing against the paneled windows.

Through the glass I can see the sky is still dark. Streetlights cast shadows on Madison Street. I press the up button on the elevator and arrive at my floor to a blackened hallway. I flick the switch and squint, my eyes unadjusted to the fluorescent brightness. I take a deep breath, grateful for the isolation.

My computer hums to life with the shake of the mouse. I tap my fingernails against the maple wood of my desk and wait for the emails to load. Right away, the one from Roger to Nate Teason pops up. In nervous anticipation, I skim through the note, unable to slow myself down. Please be okay. Reassured by my first perusal, I read it again more slowly. It looks good. Roger included the requisite mea culpa and, most importantly, a correction of the statement. We dodged a bullet. This time.

I spend the rest of the morning pecking away at my keyboard, analyzing marketing data, creating colorful charts that compare one brand to another. The halls of the office are once again alive with employees and the cadence of business-as-usual cradles me in a sense of security. By the time I look up it is already lunchtime.

My stomach grumbles and I realize I haven't eaten anything all day. I save my work and head down to Jack's office. Maybe we can grab lunch at the Italian restaurant on the corner. I could go for one of their salads. The door to his office is closed. I tap against the frosted glass windows beside the door. Laughter emanates from behind it as Jack calls "come in," followed by a waterfall of giggles.

I pull the door open and find Wanda sitting on the chair across from Jack's desk, a notepad and a salad-filled cardboard carton balancing on her lap. She opens her mouth wide and stuffs a forkful of lettuce onto her tongue, dressing drips from the plastic utensil and lands on her knee. More laughter. The smell of her perfume stings my nose. She's wearing too much.

"That's enough dictation for now," Jack says. "Wanda, can you excuse us?"

She places the notepad under her arm and scrambles to gather up her lunch.

Once she has left the office, Jack walks over to me. "I wish I could open up a window in this place. Her perfume is killing me." He waves his hand and fakes a cough. "Did Roger get the discrepancy in the Teason account worked out?"

"He did."

"Phew." Jack wipes his palm across his forehead.

"No thanks to Wanda. I am so ready for Marcia to come back."

"I am too. Thankfully, Wanda's only temporary. She's also terrible at dictation."

We both laugh and it feels good.

"I think she's been trying to dress like me. It's just weird," I say.

Jack looks at the calendar on his desk. "When is Marcia scheduled to come back?"

"Monday. I swear she is irreplaceable."

Jack leans toward me and kisses my cheek. "No, you are. Wanda may try to look like you, but no one could ever take your place."

***

Even though he already ate, Jack accompanies me for a long lunch, complete with a heaping bowl of pasta and a small glass of wine. I arrive back at my desk and notice that Wanda is nowhere to be found. I check out her workspace and see that her purse and her coat are gone. Only her salad is still there, the dressing congealing on top of the produce. Has she left for the day early again?

I tug my cell phone out of my briefcase and pull up Marcia's contact information. After two rings, she answers.

"Marcia? It's Claire. How's the knee? I've heard the first couple months after surgery are the toughest."

"What do you want?"

Her response catches me off guard. But I press forward, maybe she's just worn out from her surgery. "I wanted to double-check that you are planning to come back to work on Monday. We miss you around here."

"What? You've got a lot of nerve."

"Is something wrong?" Worry weaves its way through my words.

"What do you think is wrong? I was planning on coming back on Monday, but . . ."

A baby cries in the background, one of Marcia's three children.

"But what?"

"You called the other day and . . ."

The baby's shrieks get louder.

"Wait. What? No, I didn't." I can't help but raise my voice.

"Hold on." She puts the phone down and comforts the baby, cooing in his ear, and I feel an ache, physical and piercing, in my abdomen where I no longer carry a baby. When she returns to the phone she says, "You did call. You told me I wasn't needed at SMG anymore and not to worry about coming back."

"No. That's not right."

"I know it's not right. My husband was so mad. He wants to sue for discrimination, but I told him I didn't want to do that to you. I've always liked working for you, Claire. I just don't understand why you'd get rid of me."

The baby starts screaming again.

"I didn't get rid of you. You're not fired." I am practically shouting so she can hear me. "Please come back on Monday."

"I'll think about it." She hollers over the baby's cries. "When you told me you didn't want me back, I pretty much made my peace with being a stay-at-home mom. Honestly, I can use more time for my knee to heal anyway. So now I don't know what I want to do."

"But I did want you back. I do want you to come back."

"I've got to go feed my youngest now. I'll let you know in the next couple days."

The line goes dead.

It takes me a few minutes to compose myself. I pace around my office, swearing under my breath. The question I can't shake is, who would call Marcia behind my back and essentially fire her? I know I didn't call her. I've been counting the days until she returns to work. And I would never expose the office to that kind of liability. Firing someone when they are out on disability leave? It's unacceptable.

I stand at the window and look out at the street below. From this height all the people look like chess pieces sliding up and down LaSalle Street, turning onto Madison Avenue. They look like toys, not like real human beings with stress and problems of their own. And dreams. I think about how hard I have worked to grow this business and how easy it would be for it all to go away. It would just take one financial slip, one bad lawsuit. I square my shoulders and take a minute to compose and comfort myself with the fact that, even if Marcia decides not to work for us anymore, I will be able to find another assistant. I inhale and head down the hall to talk to Roger. Maybe he knows something I don't.

When I arrive at Roger's office, he is hunched over his laptop typing away, his brows furrowed, deep in thought. I don't wait for him to say "come in" before barging through the door. He jumps. I don't care. I'm too worked up.

"What's going on?" he asks.

"So when exactly is Marcia coming back to work?"

"Monday."

"Nope. She said someone called her and told her not to come back. That we don't need her anymore."

"Wait. Slow down." He pushes his chair back and meets me at the front of his desk. "Who called her?"

"She says I did."

"Whoa, I hope that's not true. Marcia's on disability leave. That's a lawsuit."

"I know." I chew on my lip.

"Did you tell her not to come back?"

"No, of course not. I want her to come back. I want her to come back now."

"Good. Don't call her again until I figure out what our next move is."

"Okay." I twist a chunk of hair around my finger, pulling out a few pieces. "You don't think someone called her pretending to be me. Maybe Wanda."

"No. I actually think it's more likely that Marcia, possibly not wanting to work anymore, but still needing a source of revenue, made this whole thing up to try to milk some money out of the company."

"What? Marcia wouldn't do that."

"People make up lawsuits all the time to try and get money. Then the company has to spend money to either defend itself or settle and make the thing go away."

I shake my head.

"Yep. It's a dirty practice, but people will try to do it. People will do almost anything for a buck."

I rub my temples, trying to imagine Marcia doing something like that. It didn't fit, but I guess you never really know who someone is, who you can trust.

Just then Wanda appears in the doorway. Roger jumps and moves away from me, as if we were just caught doing something we shouldn't have been doing. We weren't.

"Am I interrupting something?" She looks at us with suspicion.

No. "Not at all." I smooth the wrinkles on the sleeves of my blouse.

Roger chimes in. "Claire, I'll circle back with you later and we'll come up with a game plan on . . . that issue." He looks at me all shifty-eyed as he talks and I want to say *stop it*, to tell him to cut it the heck out.

But there's nothing I can say. Anything will either make me sound crazy or make us appear guilty of something. And someone is guilty, but it sure as heck isn't me.

Chapter Sixteen

Wanda After

My wrists handcuffed behind me, I am forced to duck as they guide me into the patrol car. "You have the right to remain silent," an officer with a spiky blonde crew cut and mint-scented breath tells me. But I don't stop talking.

"You can't take my daughter. Where is my daughter?"

The police officer doesn't answer me.

"She's only five."

The officer's voice spins past me, a jumble of legal jargon.

"Please, I'll answer any questions. I just need to know that she's okay."

He finishes reciting my Miranda rights and it's a blur, a blur of words that mean nothing to me. I sit in the patrol car, and stare out the window as it drives, lights flashing, south on Michigan Avenue. I can't believe this is happening to me. How can this be happening to me?

We arrive at the station and the officer leads me into a holding cell, crowded with other women, some shaking, detoxing, others dressed like whores. I wrap my fingers around the bars and press my face against them, trying to look down the hall to see if I can spot Astrid. But I can't see anything except the soles of the arresting officer's shoes propped up on his desk.

"Excuse me." I try to get his attention.

"Yes?"

"Do I get a phone call?" I'm pretty sure I'm entitled to my one phone call, like on television shows.

"Are you going to call your lawyer?"

"No." I think for a moment, not knowing who to call. And then it hits me. "My neighbor."

The officer makes me wait for what seems like forever and when I finally get the chance to make my call, I punch Penelope's number into the pay phone as fast as I can. But there is no answer. My call goes straight to voicemail. I leave a message while praying she actually will listen to it.

A thin metal bench lines the wall of the cell. I slump down onto it and try to figure out what to do. I lean against the brick wall, its ridges rough and uneven. Uncomfortable. The back of my shirt sticks, attached to the wall by a wad of pre-chewed gum.

Graffiti scribbled in pen covers the walls of the cell. All swear words and profanity, except for one set of initials with a heart around it. An image of Jack flashes through my mind. I don't belong here.

"Officer?"

"What?"

"I need to talk to someone. Is there someone I can speak to?"

"About what?"

"I think I know something about a case. The wrong person was convicted of a crime."

"Is that so?"

"Yes."

"And are you the person who should be convicted of the crime?"

"What? No. But I think I have some information."

"All right. I'll get you someone." He chuckles as he walks down the hall.

As soon as he is out of sight, a hand grips the back of my neck. "What info do you have? Can it get you out of here?" A tall woman with emaciated arms marred with needle marks stands behind me.

"No. It's not like that."

"Tell me what it is or I'll snap your neck."

Goosebumps form upon my skin. She doesn't look that strong, but she does look that desperate. I have to tell her something. "I'm going to rat out my husband. I don't think he pays taxes."

"Taxes? Shit, they don't give a damn about stuff like that."

"I thought maybe they'd want to know." I lie.

"Only the Inside Revenue Service cares about that crap."

Internal Revenue Service. "Then I guess I'm screwed."

"Yep. Just like the rest of us. You're no better."

Just as I am losing hope that I will ever get out of here, an officer approaches the cell, his keys jangling on his belt.

"Wanda Dellas?"

"Yes."

"Come with me. Officer Harper will talk to you."

The officer leads me into a closet-sized room with yellowing chipped paint and what I imagine to be a two-way mirror along the opposite wall. A female plainclothes officer sits at a metal desk waiting for me. Her pink lipstick is two shades too bright for her complexion. She flashes me a knowing smile as I enter the room, and despite the sprig of parsley wedged between her teeth, I feel a glimmer of possibility that maybe she can help me.

"What can I do for you?" she asks.

"First, I need to know where my daughter is."

"I don't think you're in a position to be making demands, dear. Do you have some information you want to share with me about a case?"

"I do."

"Then I suggest you tell me what it is. We'll talk deals after I hear what you've got."

"I'm not looking for a deal. I just want to help someone, someone who's been wrongly convicted. But I can't think straight unless I know my daughter is safe."

She folds her hands and rests them on top of the table. "She is perfectly safe. She is with the social worker right now."

"Here?"

"Yes, at the precinct."

I exhale and it feels as if it's the first time I've done so all day. It's not a perfect solution, but at least I know Astrid is okay, for now.

"Ms. Dellas, Wanda. Can I call you Wanda?"

If you must. I nod my head.

"Wanda, you are in a lot of trouble. Do you know that?"

"Yes, but—"

She interrupts me. "Do you know what the charges are against you?"

"No." But I can guess.

"The officer read you your rights, correct?"

"Yes, but I don't remember the charges. I was too nervous to pay attention."

"You are being charged with trespassing and destruction of property."

"I wasn't trespassing. You can't trespass on your own property."

"Are you saying you own the Creighton Building?" She raises her eyebrows, so high they blend in with her hairline.

"No." I drum my fingers against the top of the table. I can't think of the words. I can't think of how to explain this personal, crazy notion of mine to this stranger sitting across the desk from me. *Just spit it out. You've only got this one shot.* I gulp down some air. "No. Stanbrick Financial is my company. I am Claire Stanbrick."

Her eyes widen. Expectant. And I think that maybe she believes me, that she can feel it too, can see the resemblance. But a moment later she slaps her hands against the splintered table and begins to laugh. "No sweetie, you are not."

I wipe the sweat from my forehead. It suddenly feels very hot in the enclosed room. "But I am. I am Claire Stanbrick and Jack is my husband. He has been charged with my murder, but he couldn't have killed me because look, I'm alive."

"And what makes you think you are Mrs. Stanbrick?"

"I can feel it."

She shakes her head. Incredulous.

"But it's more than that. I feel like I know things, things about Jack, things about my life with him, about my work. There's so much."

"Listen, I believe you."

"You do?" A weight lifts. I feel buoyant. "Thank you."

"I believe that you genuinely think that you are Claire Stanbrick. But if I can offer you any reassurance, it is this: You are not her. You are Wanda Dellas. We have a file on you here. You have some significant mental problems."

"A file? What's in my file? Can I see it?"

She slides the manila folder across the table. "It lists your prior arrests."

I flip open the flap and start rifling through the pages. "Prior arrests?"

"Yes, for assaults, disorderly conduct, most occurring during domestic disputes."

This doesn't feel right. This doesn't feel like me. "Did I go to jail?"

"No. Charges were always dropped by your husband, Carl." She stretches out Carl's name, emphasizing it, as if to say *your husband's name is Carl, not Jack.*

This can't be right. I can't be her. "Stop it. Those are Wanda's actions, not mine. They all date back to before my accident."

"Your chart indicates that you have trouble processing reality." She nods her head and purses her lips.

"If I'm wrong and I'm not Claire, then how do I know the things I know about her? About Jack? Answer that for me."

"For one thing, you've been cleaning the offices where they used to work. I'm sure if you spend enough time snooping around, which is what I'm told you were doing just prior to your arrest, you can discover a thing or two. Things that could influence someone with your problems to make conclusions that are not true."

Just then a uniformed police officer pokes his head into the room. "Her neighbor posted bail."

Penelope. Thank goodness.

"You are free to go. For now."

The officer motions to the door where, just outside, Penelope is standing, her arms draped across Astrid's shoulders.

"Astrid." I bypass Penelope and scoop Astrid up into my arms, burying my face into her neck. She is safe. That's all that matters.

Penelope walks up to the front desk at the station and asks a short rotund woman with long stringy hair when I can expect to get my hearing date and whether there are any free legal services we could apply for. The woman hands her a form with a list of legal aid agencies that offer pro bono services.

We exit the station and have barely stepped foot onto the sidewalk outside when Penelope grabs my arm. "What were you thinking?"

"About Jack."

"Jack? Who's Jack?"

"He's been wrongly convicted. I can save him. I can."

"You're talking nonsense."

"I'm not. Jack is a man who holds the key to my identity. And he is sitting in jail for a crime he did not commit."

"Tell me, how is that so?" She slides her glasses onto the bridge of her nose, her gray hair poking out of her bun.

"I am Claire Stanbrick." I place my hands on my hips.

"The wife of that financial guy? Not a chance."

"I am. I feel it in my bones. He didn't kill her because I am her." I plead with Penelope as if she is the arbitrator in my case.

"It's kind of a moot issue at this point, dear." Sympathy laces her words.

"Getting to the truth is a moot issue?" My cheeks burn.

"You clearly haven't been following the news today."

Obviously. I've been stuck in jail.

"Jack Stanbrick is about to be released from prison."

"What? That's incredible." Excitement courses through my veins.

"He has a hearing in two days where an Alford plea is on the table."

"An Alford plea?" I spin the words over in my mind. I don't know what that is, but if it means Jack is free, I'm not sure I care.

"It's a plea that allows him to be released from prison."

Released. "That's great news. That proves even more that there's a possibility that I am Claire. They're offering him that plea because they know he didn't do it."

"No. If he takes the plea, he's basically saying he did do it."

"I don't understand." A plea that lets him out of prison but means he killed Claire? My hands shake.

"The Alford plea is a guilty plea."

***

Later that evening, I can't fall asleep. The sheets suffocate me, tight around my torso. I can't breathe. Penelope's words bounce back and forth through my mind, reverberating, leaving ripples of question marks floating without answers. She can't be right. Jack wouldn't admit to killing Claire. He wouldn't. And the officer, she is wrong too. I knew things before I started working there. And the things Officer Harper said about me, that I have a file at the station. Prior arrests? None of it sounds like me.

I kick the covers off the bed and pace around the room. What am I going to do? I can't let Jack take the fall for something he didn't do. I am alive and I am Claire. I have to be. This can't be my life. All messed up, delusional, and practically a criminal . . . with an arrest record. The pieces don't fit. But how do I prove I am Claire when no one believes me?

And what about Astrid? This is not the kind of mother I want to be for her. A thought hits me like a thousand bullets. I have a hearing date. I could go to prison. Forced to be away from Astrid. It is more than I can bear. And now I need a new job too. Bengal Cleaning Services will never allow me to continue working for them after this. The blue digital numbers on the clock burn bright, illuminating the room. 2:00 am. I walk down the hallway, tiptoeing so as not to wake Astrid. I sneak into her room and watch her as she sleeps.

Eyes closed, her long lashes rest upon the tops of her cheeks. She breathes in and out, with little snores interrupting the rhythm from time to time. The sound soothes my consciousness, a balm against the turmoil swirling within me.

I sit down in the rocking chair opposite her bed and close my eyes. The words "I will keep you safe" play on repeat in my mind. We're going to be okay. I'm going to make everything better. Jack taking a guilty plea? It's not right. It can't be true. I am Claire Stanbrick and I'm going to prove it. I will. Even if it's the last thing I do.

I awake the following morning to a tugging upon my nightshirt.

"Mama. Did you sleep in my room?"

My back aches as I realize I spent the remainder of the night sleeping in her chair.

"I'm hungry." She clutches her belly.

I lift her up onto my lap. "We better do something about that. What would you like for breakfast?"

"Pancakes." She hops off my lap and scurries down the stairs.

I follow her into the kitchen and open the freezer. Penelope went grocery shopping for us again. I hate that she does it, and at the same time I am grateful because, while far from full, the fridge does have a few essentials inside. One of which is a box of frozen chocolate chip pancakes. I pull out the carton, its cardboard sides cold and flimsy, and slide two hardened spheres onto a ceramic plate. The microwave whirs as the room fills with the scent of chocolate and dough. I let the pancakes cool for a minute before placing them in front of Astrid. As I wait, I read over the ads on the side of the pancake box. There is a picture of a girl smiling, her hair in pigtails, her teeth healthy and white. She has a book propped up on her knees. A reader. Astrid can't read yet. But then again, she's only five.

"A is for?" I call out as she stuffs a huge bite of pancake into her mouth.

She stops chewing and looks at me, her eyes blank.

"Apple," I say. "And Astrid."

She smiles at the mention of her name.

"B is for?"

"B."

Did she mean *B* or *bee*? I have my work cut out for me. Once I get this Claire situation figured out, I'll be able to send her to the finest preschool around. Right now she doesn't go to any preschool at all. But that doesn't mean she can't learn.

"Do you want to go to the library today?"

She raises her hands in the air, pumping her fists up and down.

"We'll go after breakfast." It sounds like a reasonable plan until I realize I have no idea where the library is. I've never taken her there.

We don't have a computer in the house, so I rifle through the cabinets until I find the yellow pages. I scan the listings until I spot a library that's close by, a simple bus ride away.

The first two bus drivers who pull up to our stop tell me they don't go anywhere near the library. But the third says he has a stop two blocks away. That will do. I feel a bit refreshed, the spring air awakening my senses like a jolt of caffeine. The library is a good choice for both Astrid and me.

We arrive at the columned entrance to the public library and walk through the automatic doors. The building smells of disinfectant and old books. We walk past an indoor fountain. Astrid giggles at the metal frogs resting on top of floating brass lily pads. The sound of splashing water droplets echoes through the air.

"Look, Mama. Money." Astrid points to the shiny coins coating the bottom of the fountain. "Can I take one?"

She reaches her hand toward the water, but I stop her. "No, that would be stealing."

"Why are there pennies in the water?"

"People throw them in and make a wish."

"A wish." Her eyes light up. "Can I have a penny?"

I unzip my purse and fumble around, but my hand comes up empty. The disappointment on Astrid's face cuts through me as my heart sinks. I don't even have a single penny to give my child to make a wish. I run my sleeve across my forehead and cringe as the button scrapes my skin. I have an idea. I place the button in my mouth and bite down. Already loose, it comes off easily.

"Here, use this. Who says you can only make wishes with pennies?" I place the button into Astrid's hand. "Go ahead. Make a wish and throw it into the fountain."

Astrid closes her eyes and mumbles as she tosses the button into the water. "I wish for a daddy."

My heart wrenches inside my chest. "A daddy? What about Carl? Isn't he your daddy?"

"Whenever you fight, he always says he's not."

That's true. I squat down in front of her and place my hands on her shoulders. "He wouldn't make a very good one anyway." I imagine Astrid, Jack, and myself as a real family. Claire was pregnant when she went missing five years ago, and Astrid is five. The timing matches up. "One day, Astrid. You're going to have the best daddy there is. I promise." I squeeze my eyes shut and make my own wish that it's true. It has to be true.

"If you can't get me a daddy, can you get me a bicycle?" she asks.

I laugh. I can't help myself. "Yes, if I don't find you the perfect daddy, I'll get you the perfect bicycle."

"A pink one, with a white basket?"

I pull her into my arms. "A pink one with a white wicker basket."

From there, we make our way to the back area of the library, the children's section. At the entrance a child-sized statue of a giraffe with a welcome sign around its neck points in the direction of the books. Astrid pats the fuzzy patch on its head and we both giggle. A woman with a pinched face waves us in. She's the librarian. We've arrived just in time for story hour. Astrid and I find two round beanbag chairs and sit on them as the librarian begins to read. Astrid loves the first story. She laughs in all the right places.

Before reading the second story, the librarian sings a song about the seasons and her precious flowers dying in the winter and how, to her, they are like her heart. My stomach twists into a strangled knot when she belts out the last line. "Please don't keep my heart from me."

I squeeze Astrid tight. The words hit me like a baseball bat cracking my skull. I push the thought of a hearing date out of my mind and instead turn my attention to getting a new job.

Some of the other mothers have left their kids with the librarian while she reads. As she begins the next story, I spot an empty computer a few steps away and decide to sign in as a guest. I do a quick job search, scrolling through the postings, looking up every few minutes to make sure Astrid is still in my line of sight.

Despite my searches, no job seems to fit. Frustrated, I take a break and scan the library home page. But I bore with that quickly and on impulse type the words "Alford plea" into the search bar. A long list of articles pops up. I click on the first one and see Jack's face staring back at me, his head bowed in shame. "Financial Giant Scheduled to Plead Guilty." My stomach sours within me. I scan the article.

> Jack Stanbrick, owner of investment firm Stanbrick Financial, is likely to accept an Alford plea offered to him by prosecutors. The Alford plea is a guilty plea, which means Mr. Stanbrick will be admitting to the murder of his wife and business partner, Claire Stanbrick. But why would Mr. Stanbrick be released from prison if he accepts a guilty plea? The answer to that lies in the intricacies of the Alford plea itself. While the Alford plea is a guilty plea, it is also a plea that allows the accused to assert their innocence.

"Assert their innocence." Yes.

> Alford pleas are often offered in cases where the defendant realizes the prosecution had enough evidence to convict, as they did in Mr. Stanbrick's original trial, but where appeals have arisen allowing for a new trial. In the case of Jack Stanbrick, his appeal for a new trial based on the mishandling of evidence in the original trial has been granted.

Why would he plead guilty now if he's been granted a new trial? I read on.

> But as is often the case with Alford pleas, Mr. Stanbrick would likely rather forgo waiting in prison for a new trial date, which could take years, and instead accept the plea and be released immediately. Accepting the plea also prevents him from running the risk of a second guilty verdict at the new trial. Although inherent in the Alford plea is the defendant's assertion that he is innocent of the crime for which he is charged, by accepting the Alford plea, he is in fact pleading guilty.

The gears whir in my brain as I try to make sense of this. He is pleading guilty but insisting he is innocent at the same time. My thoughts catch on the second part. He is insisting he is innocent.

The article continues:

> "In addition, because of the assertion of guilt in the Alford plea, Mr. Stanbrick will not be able to inherit any money from his wife's estate. Illinois law prohibits a person from profiting from crimes that they commit."

I bet he doesn't care at all about the money. If he were after her money, he probably would wait in prison and fight for that not-guilty verdict in the new trial. To me, this proves even more that he is innocent.

I scroll further down. The article continues:

> "Ever since news of his hearing broke, protesters have gathered outside the federal prison where Stanbrick is incarcerated, calling for prosecutors to withhold the plea. To make matters worse, Stanbrick Financial stock has taken a severe nosedive since news of the potential plea deal was revealed, making some wonder about the financial sustainability of the company."

Hasn't he lost enough without losing his company too? Like me, Jack is on the verge of losing everything. I can't let that happen.

Without thinking, I open a new window and type the words "Stanbrick Financial" into the search bar. The website pops up. I do a quick check on Astrid. My heart warms as she claps her hands along with the librarian's alphabet song. Given that she is happily occupied, I take the opportunity to tool around the Stanbrick Financial site. I click on the "Our Story" tab and a photo appears of Jack and Claire in business suits, grinning, their arms around each other.

Next to the picture is a paragraph of text describing how Claire started Stanbrick Marketing Group from nothing and built it up, later inviting Jack to join the firm. It goes on to state that Jack eventually started Stanbrick Financial, at which point she and Jack incorporated both SMG and Stanbrick Financial under the corporate umbrella of Stanbrick Worldwide. At the bottom of the webpage there is a photo of a tiny bouquet of flowers and the words, "in memoriam" next to Claire's name.

But I'm alive. The words screech through my mind. Adrenaline coursing through me, I click on the "Who We Are" tab. A huge photo of Roger Lindsey blankets the screen, a mischievous grin on his face, the title CEO under his name. A chill etches its way through my spine.

I force myself to read the description beneath his picture. It's all praise and gratitude to him for keeping the company going after the unfortunate events that took place involving Claire and Jack. This guy, this bully, he gets to be the hero? It can't be right. I need to get in touch with Jack.

Anger pulsing through my veins, I continue searching the site. I click on a drop-down arrow and discover a bookmark that says "Login." I look over my shoulder to see if anyone is watching. Astrid catches my eye and waves. The librarian dances in step to a silly rhyming song. I sit up straight, blocking the computer from view, and wave back at them. I click on the line that says *username* and fill in Claire's name just as I had the other day. But what was the password again?

I look around the library as I toss ideas in my head. I am about to give up when I notice a boy playing with a toy car. And it hits me. That's right. Red Roller. I type it in, and a moment later I am logged into their server. But it's better than that. I pull up Claire's email and click on a button that says "Compose." I can send emails from her account.

Uncertain what to do next, I stare at the blank square on the computer screen, taunting me. My heart drops in my chest with a thud as I realize I don't have a current email address for Jack. I type his name into the "to" line and his Stanbrick Financial email address fills in. But he hasn't worked at the company for years. If I send the email to his Stanbrick Financial account, he may not even get it. Does he still check his old email account? Will he be checking it now? I don't know.

I am playing a risky game here, I know it, doing this on the library's computer, privacy being nil. I toggle back to the article and stare at the picture of Jack, his face sullen, and I can't stand it. If I can prove that I am Claire, we can both get our lives back. I flip back and forth between the photo of Jack and the Stanbrick Financial web page, where my blank email waits for me. I have to try. But when it is time to type the text of the email, my mind goes blank.

What do I write to him? "Hey, remember me? Sorry you've been stuck in jail and are now facing public scorn and a guilty plea, all for murdering me. But great news, turns out I'm alive. My bad." No. Obviously, that won't do. A headache forms above my right eye. What am I going to say?

As I am trying to figure out what to write, a finger pokes my shoulder. A young mother, her dark hair in a messy bob, a baby fastened to her belly by a teal scarf stands behind me. She takes one look at my scarred-up face, steps back, and covers her baby's head with her hand.

"I was in an accident," I say. "You can't catch it."

"Oh. I wasn't . . ." She places her hands on her hips. "It's 11:00. Your turn at the computer is up."

"My turn?"

"There's a spreadsheet at the information desk where patrons have to sign up for slots to use the computers."

"I didn't know that."

"I signed up for 11:00 and it's 11:00 now. So . . ." She taps her fingers against the fitness watch on her wrist.

"I'll be off in a few minutes."

"No. It's my turn. Parker has to go down for his nap soon."

The baby, zoned out, dangles from her midsection. "Looks like he's already napping." I shrug.

She peers into the scarf. "Shoot. You need to get off the computer now or I'll report you to the library staff."

I laugh. I know this is supposed to sound threatening, but after just being sprung from the county jail, the idea of a "talking to" from the librarian almost sounds like fun.

"Just give me two minutes." I keep my fingers perched on the keyboard.

"No. Now." She pesters me.

I don't move. Can't move.

"That's it," she says and waves her hands, attempting to flag over the librarian.

"Just chill." I begin closing some of the windows on the browser.

"Oh my gosh." She gasps, her face pale with fear as she spots the article about Jack and the beginnings of an email addressed to him. "Are you emailing him? He is a murderer."

"Relax. I'm a law student." I bat my hand in the air as if she is the nutty one.

She squints her eyes in disbelief.

"And if you don't give me just a few more minutes, I'll sue you for harassment." I point my finger in the direction of her face, selling it.

She grumbles under her breath. "Fine. You've got two minutes. Rule breaker." She mopes across the library carpet in a huff.

I need to hurry. Despite my best efforts not to let that woman derail me, I feel uneasy and unfocused. Rushed. I look at the clock and begin to type. Already only a minute and a half left until she comes back, possibly with the librarian.

Subject line first. For lack of a better one, I go with, "Remember Me?" I figure I'll circle back and change it later. Then I begin to type, my fingernails clicking shakily against the keyboard.

Dear Jack, I can only imagine.

No.

I can't even imagine what you must be thinking, receiving an email from me. Well, fortunately it is not an email from the beyond. Nope. I'm sitting at a computer typing this right now. Alive. Yes, alive. I don't know how we got into this mess, but I promise you I am doing everything I can to figure out how to get us out. What I do know so far is that I was in an accident, a very bad accident. But I survived. Somehow, I survived. That's the good news. The bad news is I lost my memory. I can't recall hardly anything about myself before the accident. I just know that I woke up one day and couldn't remember. But some things are coming back, like my memory of you, of us. And all I'm trying to do now is get back to you, back to myself, back to where we were before all of this happened. I know you are in trouble. Big trouble. Wrongfully convicted of killing me. Forced to take a guilty plea and ruin your reputation over a crime you didn't commit. But you couldn't have killed me. Because I'm alive. Please write back to me so we can reclaim the truth about our past, together.

Your Beloved Claire

I am in the middle of scanning over the note, when the woman with her baby in a kangaroo pouch comes up to me again.

"Times up." She smirks.

"Wait. I just need one more minute." Frantic, I try to check the last few sentences.

"No. Now."

She motions toward the librarian. And despite my earlier bravado, I do not want to call attention to myself. So without thinking, without allowing myself the time to re-read, let alone build up the necessary courage, I hit send. A red sentence pops up on the screen indicating my message has been successfully transmitted. My hands fly up and cover my mouth. What did I just do?

Chapter Seventeen

Claire Before

Two pink lines. I peel back the layers of paper towels and stare at the plastic stick. I don't know how to tell Jack this time. I don't know what to say. Last time I told him at the same time as I lost the baby. In that moment, it just felt like a crisis we were going to have to deal with. But that was before. Before I realized how much I want to be a mother, after all. Before my heart broke from the pain of losing her. I squeeze my eyes shut and push the memory out of my mind. I rub the plastic stick between my fingers.

In my brave moments, I imagine making a whole production out of it tonight. I can make a fancy dinner and scatter baby bottle–shaped confetti all over our granite kitchen countertop. This time the news is so exciting, so full of promise. A baby. A new life. I can hardly wait.

A jolting thought wipes the smile off my face. But how can I trust this? How can I trust my body to hold onto the baby this time? I don't know if I could handle it if I lost this baby too. Maybe I can convince myself that I am not pregnant until the baby is born. I've heard stories of teenagers who've done it, denying they are pregnant, convincing themselves they are just gaining weight until one day a baby pops out. Voilà.

No. I rub my hand across my abdomen. Even though I am only five weeks pregnant, it's already too late for that. I'm hooked. This baby inhabits my heart, a permanent resident.

I head down to Jack's office. I'll just tell him. I'll just say, "Hey, how about that football game last night? Oh, and by the way, I'm pregnant." My heart flutters in my chest just thinking the words. Maybe it's a girl. If it is, I'll name her after my mother.

Slow down, Claire. If I learned anything from the last time, it's that it is way too early for all this excitement, for any excitement.

I am about to head out of my office when I notice that the picture frame that usually sits on top of my file cabinet is turned over. I flip it upright and slice a gash into my index finger. The glass is shattered. Instinctively, I stick my finger into my mouth, the metallic taste of blood curling my stomach as I question how this happened. Maybe the cleaning service knocked it over accidentally. Except the top of the cabinet is coated with a thick layer of dust. Well, they certainly aren't cleaning the darn thing. But more troubling than the frame being broken is that the photo that used to be inside, a picture of Jack and I dressed to the nines at our casino-themed charity auction in Chicago last summer, is missing.

I scratch my head and peek behind the cabinet, nothing but a few loose papers there. I am about to crawl beside my desk when I think of the baby. Nope. Not worth it. No contortions for me. The thought of the baby reignites my excitement. The picture is simply not that important. I turn on my heels and strut down the hall toward Jack's office.

As I round the corner, I see Jack talking to Roger. They're laughing and I can't help but chuckle as I approach them, even though I am not in on the joke. Just hearing Jack laugh, just anticipating his reaction to the news, makes me smile.

He turns to look at me, his eyes affectionate and gentle. I stuff the pregnancy test deep into my pocket. Roger is there. I don't want an audience.

Jack motions for me to join them. He wraps his arm around my waist. I lean in, resting my head against his shoulder and breathe in the shaving cream scent of his cologne. Jack.

He kisses me on the temple before he speaks. "I need you to be a witness."

"A witness? For what?" I ask.

"A document I'm signing," he says. Confident.

"What document?"

He turns to face me and rubs his hands along my bare arms. My skin bubbles into goose bumps. "I think I should sell the river house."

"Really?" A wave of sadness washes over me as I think of the smell of pine trees and the hiss of the early autumn sun setting on top of the Wisconsin River. I don't want to sell it. I want to go there now, even though we were just there last weekend. "Why?"

"Housing values are dropping rapidly. We're losing money on it practically every day."

"Oh." I hadn't realized. I curl my fingers around the stick still hidden in my pocket and decide he is probably right to sell the place. I'm not sure babies and rivers are a good mix. "If you think it's best, I guess I'm on board."

"It's buggy and it's starting to get run down. It'd cost a fortune to rehab."

Money that will be better spent on the baby. My nose itches as I remember the starchy smell of the citronella candles and the sting of the mosquitos that bit me up anyway.

"This document gives Roger the power to show the property, et cetera," Jack says.

"It allows me to act as your realtor. I've had my realtor's license since right after I passed the bar. You know that," Roger says.

I did not know this.

"It can be a good gig for attorneys," Roger says. "Plus, it'll save you guys a bunch of dough and it's a way for me to make some extra money."

Is Roger having financial problems again? I wonder.

Jack interrupts my thoughts. "It's great because Roger isn't going to charge us the usual realtor fees. Isn't that nice of him?"

I don't respond, still somewhat disappointed about selling the house. But then again, it really is Jack's decision since he owned the house prior to our marriage.

Roger motions for Jack and me to follow him back to his office. We trail behind him, arm in arm, and stand shoulder to shoulder as he slides the document across the shiny maple wood of his desk.

I skim through the pages but stop short when I see an additional document beneath the first that states, "Revised Estate Plan of Jack and Claire Stanbrick."

"Wait. Why is this in here?"

"You guys have been talking about rewriting your will for a while now, haven't you? I thought that since you're selling the river house, it's a good time to make any other changes you both had in mind," Roger says.

"I didn't authorize that," Jack says.

"I'll do it for a reduced rate. It really is the perfect time."

"If Jack wants to sell the river house, I'm fine with that, but I'm not prepared to change the will at this time and we're definitely not changing the terms of my inheritance." I run the tip of the ballpoint pen across the pages that state "revised will," leaving a trail of blue smudge marks etched into the page.

"The way it is now, if you and Jack have a child, the child automatically gets it all if something happens to you," Roger says.

Jack looks at me, his eyes sympathetic. He doesn't know about the baby yet. "That's enough, Roger. If Claire doesn't want to revise the will, we're not going to revise it."

I mouth the words *thank you* to Jack. "It's all I have from my mother. Maybe we'll change it in the future. But not now." The pen in my hand feels heavy; my hands shake just holding it.

Jack takes it from me. "Are you okay?"

"I'm fine. I need to sit for a minute."

Jack loops his arm through mine and leads me to a chair. Then he turns to Roger. "Can we finish this later?"

I look at Jack. "I would appreciate that. I'm not up to signing anything right now."

"That's okay. We can deal with this later." Jack pats my arm.

"We only need her as a witness," Roger says. "It would be good to get started trying to sell the house. Maybe Wanda can serve as the witness instead."

Jack looks at me for approval.

I nod as a wave of nausea courses through me.

Roger presses the intercom, beckoning Wanda to come down to serve as a witness. She enters the room in a tizzy, her hair a staticky mess, a chocolate stain on her blouse. She stares at Jack until Roger points to where to sign. Jack goes first, then Roger. Although I've seen Roger write his name dozens of times, this is the first time I notice the way he makes the "i" in his last name, like an upside-down check mark.

Before I let Wanda have the papers, I flip through the pages. Even though the river house is not mine, being property Jack brought to the marriage, I still want to make sure this contract seems legitimate. I shoot Jack a pout as I read the address of the river house out loud, "9390 Riverside Drive." I sigh, breathing out nostalgia.

After Wanda signs as a witness, Roger pats Jack on the back and shakes his hand. "I'll take care of this right away."

"Back to work," Jack says and points at Roger and then Wanda. She walks out of Roger's office ahead of Jack and I, but pauses briefly to look back at us, and then keeps going.

Once Jack and I get to his office, I reach for his hands. I hold them tightly in my own, and don't even need to say a single word. He just knows. Baby.

***

I settle in at my desk and see the message light blinking on my telephone. It's Nate asking me to call him back. I hope everything is okay with the first quarterly report I sent to him. A worm of worry slithers through my stomach as I dial him back.

"Do you have any questions on the report?" My palms sweat as I wait for his answer.

"No. The report looks good."

I sigh, relieved.

"I have a question about Stanbrick Financial."

"That's really Jack's area, but I'll try to answer as best as I can."

"I happened to be researching something on the Security Exchange Commission website this morning and I decided to look up Stanbrick Financial and its advisors."

I am confused as to where this is going.

"There's a place on the SEC website where you can verify the legitimacy of an advisor and neither Stanbrick Financial nor Roger Lindsey are listed there."

"That's strange. What about Jack?"

"Jack is, but under the name of a different firm. Beagle and Cranston, I think it was."

"That's the firm Jack worked for before he started working for me." A memory flashes before me, of Jack quitting that job and deciding to work at Stanbrick Marketing Group temporarily while he developed a game plan for opening his own investment-banking firm.

"It did appear to be an old listing from many years ago."

"I'm sorry for the confusion. I know Jack just got the new Stanbrick Worldwide website up and running. He and Roger probably haven't updated their information with the SEC yet."

"I wanted you to be aware. It's important that they take care of it as soon as possible. That's the kind of thing that can make an investor nervous."

I hang up the phone. I need to talk to Jack about this. I buzz his office, but there is no answer. He must be in a meeting. I leave a voicemail. While I wait, I distract myself and pull up the spreadsheets detailing the project balances for a few clients who asked for financial breakdowns.

I prop my elbows up on my desk and take a deep sip of the decaf vanilla hazelnut coffee I picked up on the way to work this morning. It tastes bitter and burnt, and cold from sitting too long on my desk. I crinkle my nose and look out the window at the buildings staring at me. I take a breath and tally the columns.

But something is wrong. The numbers, they are not adding up. The balances look like they are slightly off, by $100 here and there. I run my fingers through my hair and squint at the screen. What's going on here?

Roger's words echo in my head, that doing real estate is a way for him to make some extra money. Is Roger stealing from SMG clients?

I need to double-check the numbers. I don't want to accuse him unless I am sure. Normally, I can fix this type of thing by just looking at it, by rearranging the amounts in my head. I try, but I can't seem to get the numbers to add up properly. Maybe if I look at the physical files, it will make sense. Sometimes there are notes jotted down of time spent, of work done, that doesn't get recorded correctly.

I search my desk for the files containing the hard copies. But they are not there. I look under a stack of lined yellow notepads and beneath a tower of accounting books. Nothing. Maybe they are in the file cabinet. It wouldn't be the first time I outsmarted myself by trying to clean up, only to make matters worse when I can't remember where I tidied the thing up to. But when I peek into the drawers, the files are not there either. I head out into the hall to see if they are by Wanda's desk.

The sour smell of old milk punches me right away. I stuff my nose into the neck of my top and try to hold my breath as I spot a container of curdled yogurt, open and unattended, balancing beside Wanda's telephone. But it is a tipped-over purse, the contents spilled out across her desk and onto the floor below, that catches my eye. I gasp out loud. Is that my purse?

I dart over to it and notice that it is practically identical to mine. Same tangerine leather, same brass-buckle across the back and front. But as I look closer, I can see that it is not exactly the same. The name etched into the metal keychain dangling from the strap is off by one little letter. Other than that, the bags are identical.

The contents are different too. I can't help but stare at the open tubes of lipstick broken and smashed against the carpeting, the clusters of candy wrappers and piles of safety pins scattered beside her cubicle.

I shake my head and am about to walk down the hall, to see if the files were placed in our office library, when I spot what seems to be the edge of a photo peeking out of a notebook. Only a third of the picture is showing.

I bend down to look at it when, without warning, Wanda appears beside me, angry. "Were you going through my purse?"

"No. Actually it looks an awful lot like mine."

"You have no right to go through my things."

"I didn't."

"Then who did?" She slaps her palms together, making a loud clap.

"I have no idea, maybe you."

"I'm going to tell Jack that you were snooping into my things."

That's a non-threatening threat if I ever heard one. I look at her over the rims of my glasses. "I wasn't snooping. Try to settle down."

She drops to her knees and starts scooping items up off the carpet and tossing them back into her purse. I squat down beside her to help and pick up a folded piece of paper. There is a yellow sticky note attached with what looks like instructions on how to make an investment through Stanbrick Financial.

"Don't touch that." She grabs it out of my hand.

As she stuffs it into her skirt pocket, the handwriting on the sticky note catches my eye. The 'i's' in particular, little upside-down check marks.

Chapter Eighteen

Wanda After

I am lost in thought as Astrid and I walk to the bus stop, her little hand a squishy sponge in mine. She chatters away about the fun she had at the library, talking in fragmented exclamations about how much she loved listening to the stories, playing with the mini chalkboard, and being with the other children. But I am too distracted to hear her, too fully absorbed to enjoy what she is saying. My thoughts blocked by one phrase. I emailed Jack. I e-mailed Jack? What was I thinking?

It must be true what everyone is saying about me. I am delusional. What would lead me to believe he would take my email seriously? Worse than that, I already have criminal charges pending against me for trespassing. What if he thinks I'm harassing him? Could Jack press charges against me now? More charges? That means a greater chance I could lose Astrid. This madness needs to stop. We pause at the corner and wait for the red light to change before crossing. Think of Astrid.

But I was thinking of her. She deserves a better life. If I were Claire, I would know who I am. I could fully be a mother to her instead of an empty shell searching for answers. I would have the answers.

My heart races as we walk, and I move faster than I intend to.

"Slow down, Mama." Astrid double steps to keep up with me.

It is only then that I realize she is practically jogging beside me. I stop, stoop down beside her, and pull her into my arms. She giggles.

"I love you so much," I say.

She looks at me with a wide grin and tugs at me to keep moving. I pick her up and twirl her around, before placing her back on her feet.

The sky is overcast. Threatening. As if the clouds could open up and pour down on us at any moment. Astrid kicks a pebble into the gutter as we walk. We're almost at the bus stop.

It was only one email. Jack's probably not even going to see it and if he does, it's not a crime to write to someone. The rain starts, pelting down hard, as the bus pulls in front of us. We climb the steps, our shoes soggy, and head home.

Astrid presses her palms against the foggy bus window. We lunge forward and watch the rain run down the glass in wavy rivers.

The bus makes a left turn at Clark Street. The tires splash dirty rainwater onto the sidewalk as a wave of worry washes over me. Technically, I did hack into Claire's account.

By the time Astrid and I hop off the bus and walk the two blocks to the house, we are soaked through and through. Astrid shivers as I push open the front door and a burst of cold air greets us. I turned the heat off before we left to save a few bucks.

"Come on, let's get you into some dry clothes." I follow her up the stairs to her bedroom.

The air in her room is only a hint warmer than on the first floor. I reach for the thermostat in the hallway outside her door and dial it up. The furnace hisses and moans, and emits a foul burnt smell as it gears up. It's on its last leg. But this heater is the only one we've got and I need it to last through the chillier months of spring. I'll just have to figure something out after that.

I pull open the bottom drawer of her dresser and see there are no warm clothes inside. No long pants. I open the drawer above it where I keep her long-sleeved shirts. Empty.

"Astrid, where are your warm clothes?"

She shrugs, water dripping from her sleeves.

I open the hamper. All her fall and winter clothes are jammed inside. Even though I'm off the pills now, I've been too distracted to do the laundry. I pull a sweatshirt and a pair of sweatpants with a strawberry on the leg out of the hamper, and hand it to her. "Here, wear these."

With armfuls of dirty laundry in hand, a tape plays on repeat in my mind, reminding me of what a horrible mother I am. I bet Claire Stanbrick would never let her daughter run out of clean clothes. Then again, Claire Stanbrick would probably pay someone to do her daughter's laundry. No. No she wouldn't, she would want to take care of Astrid, just like I want to take care of Astrid.

The laundry room is filled with cobwebs. In the corner a spider circles a fly caught tangled in its web. Dinner. The scent of mildew assaults me as I open the lid of the washing machine. I stuff Astrid's clothes into the washer and open the cabinet above, looking for detergent. A spiral notebook sticks to the bottom of the bottle. I peel it off and toss it onto the ground. Garbage. I pour a cup of old, too-thick detergent on top of Astrid's clothing.

Just then, Astrid pads into the room, her bare feet pale against the dark cement floor. I spin the dial on the machine around until water begins filling the basin.

"What's that?" She points to the notebook.

"Junk."

"Can I have it?" She chews on the collar of her sweatshirt.

I give her a nod of approval.

She picks it up off the cement floor. As she does, the notebook fans open revealing a page covered with newspaper ads, yellowed at the edges, taped inside.

"Can I see that for a minute?"

"It's mine." She stomps her foot.

"Please, it could be important. Maybe it holds the key to who I am."

“But you are Mama.” She wraps her arms around my legs and my heart thumps, bruised within my chest. Why is knowing I am her mother not enough for me?

She rifles through the notebook. Then, losing interest, she drops it on the floor. I begin flipping through where she left off. Not much to see here, just a bunch of random job ads. I skim the pages again. A cloud of dust billows out, scratching my throat. I cough as the washing machine clanks and hums beside me. I wave the dust through the air, and as I do, something falls out of the spiral.

Astrid laughs, chasing it, trying to catch it on its way down. She claps when it lands on the laundry room floor. A picture. A picture of what looks like Jack and Claire at a casino charity night. In it, Jack grins holding a fanned-out deck of cards. I tuck the picture into my bra, for safekeeping.

The photo remains pressed against my chest even when I take Astrid back to the library the following morning. My one goal is to look for a new job. No more logging into Claire’s email. Too risky. I am here for a job search and for Astrid to be around other children. That’s all.

And yet, as I sit in front of the computer, a question pecks at me. Why do I have this photo of Jack and Claire? I pull it out from under my shirt and stare at it. Creased at the corners, the picture resembles a photo taken with instant film, snapped and developed in minutes. Not a mass-marketed shot from a magazine. This is an original.

A librarian with her hair piled in a bun on top of her head taps on my shoulders and asks me how much longer I plan on using this computer. I point to my name on her clipboard and the time period I signed up for, a full hour. She smiles at me before heading over to the college student sitting at the computer across from me. I’m learning how this library thing works. I don’t want to call any attention to myself, nor do I want to make careless pressured decisions, like last time when I emailed Jack.

I scroll through the want ads and try to imagine myself doing the jobs I'm potentially qualified for. The problem is I don't really know what my skills are. I have no recollection of what I was capable of before the accident, and none of the postings appeal to me in the slightest.

Astrid plays a game of Duck, Duck, Goose with the librarian and a group of other children. I chuckle as Astrid chases another child around the circle, their giggles a joyful symphony. And I want that, more of that, more joy. But in order to have happiness, I need to get a new job so we can eat. There is no joy in starving.

I close my eyes and remind myself I am Claire. What positions would she look for? I open my eyes and type in the words, "marketing account manager." *You're not going to understand a single word in these job ads*, I chastise myself as I wait for the computer to load. A moment later, a list of postings fills the screen.

'Seeking Marketing Account Manager. Responsibilities include the preparation of marketing research studies, including the creation of tabulation plans, the pulling of tables, the analysis of study findings, and the presentation of study results to clients."

My brain cells begin to buzz: tabulation plans, pulling tables, presentation of results. I imagine spreadsheets dotted with numbers, organized into formulas and charts, indicating study findings. I picture bar graphs and pie charts with different slices representing various products. This sounds like the type of job Claire would do. The type of job I want to do.

But I am snapped back into reality when I see the words, "send your resume and list of references to human resources." I have no resume, no references. I can't imagine the folks over at Bengal Cleaning Service would have anything good to say about me after that stunt I pulled the other night, breaking into Stanbrick Financial. Plus, all these jobs require a degree, and to the best of my knowledge Wanda Dellas does not have a college degree. It makes me wonder, what credentials does Claire have? Suddenly, I have an intense craving for cheese.

I push my hunger away and pull up the Stanbrick Financial website. I'm just going to see if it lists what degree she got in college. That's all. No hacking for me today. I click on the home tab and the drop-down button where it says, "About Our Firm." There, once again I see the dedication page to Claire. But this time, I scroll down further and spot where it talks about the history of the firm.

Beneath a huge gold star are the words, "Stanbrick Marketing Group was a top-rated marketing research corporation prior to Claire's disappearance. She began the company immediately after receiving her MBA. Claire's vision was to create a no-nonsense marketing research firm that worked tirelessly for its clients' best interests while still maintaining a gentle and personalized touch. Always recognizing the human beings behind the products and making sure both her clients' and their consumers' needs were met."

Genius.

I scroll down to where the page attempts to gloss over the tragedy of Claire's alleged murder and stresses in bold letters that Stanbrick Financial is still in business. On the website it is emphasized that while Claire's business, Stanbrick Marketing Group, is now defunct, the best way to "honor Claire's vision and her memory is to invest in Stanbrick Financial."

I should close the page, shut down the browser, and resume my job search. I should click on the *X* in the upper left-hand corner and type in "cleaning service jobs" or "maid services."

But I don't. Instead, I pop a lint-covered mint from the bottom of my purse into my mouth and open the login page. I promise myself as I click the mint against my teeth that I'm only going to look, just a peek. I'm not going to write to Jack again. No harm can come from looking. The emails load, one by one. New junk: a sale at this store, a giveaway at that. You'd think with Claire missing for over five years, these stores would take her name off their subscription lists.

I debate whether to print out a coupon for a free ice cream cone when the ding of a new email chimes. And that's when I see it. As clear as the sky on a June morning, I see it. An email from *jStanbrick@Stanbrickfinancial.com*. An email from Jack.

Chapter Nineteen

Claire Before

Still shaken from my encounter with Wanda, I head to Jack's office. He is at his desk, hard at work, telephone cradled between his shoulder and his ear. He smiles at me, and my muscles relax, my tension dissipates. He hangs up and motions for me to enter.

"What's up?" He kisses my palm.

"Where do I start?" I scratch my head.

"What's going on?" He furrows his brow. Concerned.

"Nate called me. He says Stanbrick Financial is not listed on the SEC Website."

"I know. I just got off the phone with him myself and my next step is to get all of Stanbrick Financial's information updated on the site." His tone is positive, upbeat. My worries dissipate.

"Good, because he's my client too and I don't want him to feel insecure about any of the work we are doing for him."

Jack jingles some coins in his pants pocket. "Me either."

There is a knock on the door. Roger's face pokes around the side.

"Sorry to interrupt, but I wanted to let Jack know I left the draft client statements on Wanda's desk. She is going to make the changes you asked for and send them out." Roger runs his fingers along the wood of the doorframe.

"You're having Wanda handle the client statements for Stanbrick Financial?" I ask.

"She's only typing in the information we give her. She's not compiling any of it. I wouldn't let her do that," Roger says.

I look at Jack. "Still, you should double-check it to make sure there are no errors."

Roger shoots Jack a sympathetic look and I worry I've overstepped. After all, Stanbrick Financial is Jack's business. Not mine. And there I go, taking control, like I always do.

"I'm not trying to tell you guys what to do, but I've noticed some discrepancies in my client account balances lately. I'm not sure what's going on."

"If that's the case, Claire is correct. We need to make sure those statements are accurate. We're just getting started and we don't want to erode client confidence right out of the gate." Jack runs his hand through his dark hair.

"I'll check her work before anything goes out," Roger says.

"While you're at it, see if you can get to the bottom of why my client accounts are off." I direct this at Roger. "Was Wanda working on those too?"

Roger nods.

"Why is she still working here?" I place my hands on my hips.

"Because it would be difficult to fire her at this point," Roger says.

"Why?" I ask.

"As an attorney, I can tell you if you get rid of her now, we would be exposing the company to a lawsuit."

"For what?" Heat bubbles up behind my eyes.

"Because she is pregnant. She could claim that is why we are terminating her."

"But she's incompetent."

"We'd have to prove it, which could end up costing a mountain of money in legal fees. Not to mention what she might try to seek in damages," Roger says.

"But she's only a temp," Jack says, supporting me.

"Yes, but if she puts forth accusations and the court gets a whiff of Marcia's termination while she was on family medical leave, it's not going to look good for us."

My hands clench into fists. "I didn't fire Marcia."

"I know, but Marcia thinks you did," Roger says.

Jack rubs his jaw. "Before we put ourselves at risk of any legal mess, I think Roger should talk to her about her performance and see if it can be improved."

I clench my teeth.

Roger is halfway out the door when Jack calls to him. "I'm a 'no' for the fantasy sports league draft."

"I'll count you out." Roger tosses a salute in Jack's direction before closing the office door behind him.

I turn and face Jack.

"Don't worry. I'm not doing it. I don't believe in gambling." He pulls me toward him.

"I know."

"I'm not my father." Jack stares at his shoes. His father, a gambling addict, put his family in insurmountable debt when Jack was a child.

"Of course not."

"You know how I feel about gambling. It starts with just a little, a bet here, a fantasy sports league there, and then it snowballs. It can get out of control fast. No way I'm doing that to us." Jack presses his lips against my cheek.

"And what about Roger? He doesn't have good judgment when it comes to these things."

"I can't control Roger. He's a big boy. He makes decisions for himself." Jack kicks at a renegade thread of carpet with the ball of his shoe.

"How can you be sure he isn't gambling in other venues, isn't in over his head?"

"He's not. He's clean. I can tell," he says.

"Just be careful. I don't want you, us, getting dragged down along with him."

"Not going to happen." He tucks a loose strand of hair behind my ear. "Everything's going to be okay. It won't affect you or me." He rests his palm on top of my abdomen. "I'm not going to let anything bad happen to us. Ever."

***

Two huge stacks of tabulations are waiting for me when I arrive back at my desk, the data from Nate's most recent study. Preparing to dive in, I recline in my desk chair and rub my pregnant belly, already beginning to show. Stay with me, kid. I take a deep breath and begin rifling through the numbers, looking for patterns, a lofty task, but one I enjoy.

The hours pass and the sky begins to darken. Closing time. I am about to pack up my things when my phone rings. It's Jack.

"I need to work late tonight. There are a few calls I have to make with clients on the west coast."

"How late will you be home?"

"Not too late. I'll be home for dinner. Want me to pick something up on the way?"

"I can do it," I say. "How about Ana Olive's?" It's a new Greek restaurant, one Jack and I have been wanting to try.

"Ana Olive's sounds perfect."

"It's at the corner of Washington and State Street, right?" I ask, already craving tzatziki and stuffed grapevine leaves.

"Is Ana Olive's at the corner of Washington and State Street?" Jack asks Roger. "Yep, Washington and State."

An hour later, my stomach grumbling, I decide to close up shop. I phone in the order to Ana Olive's so the food will be ready when I arrive, nice and hot.

Once outside, I pull my coat tight, and brace myself for the cool autumn air. As I walk along the darkened pavement, an image of Wanda frantically cleaning up the mess from her purse fills my mind. Her purse. Sure looks an awful lot like mine. Except hers is a knockoff. Still, if one wasn't careful, they could easily mistake it for the real deal. But it's not the purse that bothers me, it's the picture poking out of a notebook. Was that the photo from my office? I didn't get a good look. But if it were, why would she be keeping a picture of Jack and me? Not to mention notes on how to make an investment with Stanbrick Financial. The company really focuses on investors with large sums of money, not small individual investments. And in Roger's handwriting? None of it makes sense.

I scratch my forehead, the wool of my hat itchy against my skin, and make a left off Washington onto State Street. The outline of the restaurant's sign, neon letters above a sea blue awning, is in sight. But as I get closer, I hear voices. Angry voices. To my right, a cluster of people argue beneath a streetlamp. One man pushes another. They are shouting, but I can't make out the words. Is that Roger? Behind him, I see a pair of legs, sculpted and panty hosed. Female.

The arguing stops as the shadow of faces turn in my direction. I snap my head the other way, pick up my pace, and continue toward the sign. I don't want to get involved. The shuffle of loafers quickens on the sidewalk behind me. Footsteps. Two sets? One? I spin around, but no one is there.

I keep moving. Faster. The wind whips my face with each step. I look over my shoulder. A figure with a black umbrella darts into a darkened alley. I run toward the sign, away from I don't know what. Maybe nothing. But I can't shake this feeling, that I am being followed.

After what feels like an eternity, I arrive at the fogged-up door to Ana Olive's. I press it open and am greeted by a friendly hostess asking me if I'd like a table.

"No." I try to catch my breath as I speak. "I'm here for carryout. Stanbrick."

The smell of pastitsio and spanakopita warms my skin. The rhythmic sound of clanking utensils emanating from the kitchen steadies my breathing. Safely enveloped within the familiar smells of gyros and saganaki, my muscles begin to relax. I rub my palm against the glass of the door, wiping away the condensation and peer out. No one is there, just a couple strolling arm in arm, enjoying the landscape of the city.

My skin clammy from running, I walk to the back of the restaurant in search of the restroom. The bathroom is tiny and cramped. I splash some cool water onto my face and pat it dry with a scratchy paper towel from a roll resting on top of a chipped ceramic sink.

Back at the hostess stand, a man wearing a white jacket and a tall chef's hat stands looking like he'd rather be in the kitchen than at the front desk. He points to a stapled brown paper bag on the counter. "Stanbrick?"

"Yes." I slide a couple bills across the countertop and am about to leave when I notice there are words scrawled in black sharpie on the back of the bag.

I mouth the words "Curiosity killed the cat."

The paper bag slips from my hands and onto the floor. The man in the chef's hat scurries from around the counter, picks it up, and asks me if everything is okay.

Panic floods my eyes as all the crazy things that have been going on flash before me. The answer to that question crashes down on me, a thousand bricks heavy. It burns the back of my retinas. Is everything okay? The answer is no.

PART TWO

Remember Me

Chapter Twenty

Wanda After

An earthquake of excitement shoots electricity through my veins like defibrillation paddles shocking my heart. A response from Jack. An email from him to me.

I am resuscitated, brought back to life. Yet no one in the library seems to notice. Everyone is just going about their business, their heads buried in their laptops and books. But I am jumping out of my skin.

I look at the subject line, "Re: Remember Me?"

Hello, Jack.

The large digital clock on top of the librarian's desk flashes the time, scolding me, in red-hot numbers. I am keenly aware I only have five minutes left on the computer. I must hurry. I close my eyes, breathe in courage, and click on the email.

The first sentence tears through my heart like a bullet.

> Due to the large volume of emails Mr. Stanbrick has been receiving since news of his potential release from prison were leaked last week, I am screening them. After I finish reviewing each email, I will pass the legitimate ones along to Mr. Stanbrick. If you would like to make an investment through Stanbrick Financial, someone from our office will be in contact with you shortly. We are thrilled to announce that Jack Stanbrick will be resuming employment at Stanbrick Financial. However, I will remain the acting CEO of the firm as I have for the past four years. Please be advised fraudulent or harassing emails will be passed along to the proper authorities for investigation. Mr. Stanbrick has been through enough.

Regards,
Roger Lindsey

The air in the library is suddenly thick. I'm suffocating. I open my mouth and try to breathe, but I can't get any oxygen in. I begin to wheeze as one by one, the heads of the other library patrons pop up, out of their books, to look at me. Now they're interested. I wave my hands and shake my head, which seems to satisfy them that I'm okay. But I am not okay. My email went to Roger Lindsey. If he thinks my email is a prank, he will report it to the police. What if they trace it back to me?

The numbers on the clock taunt me. Time's up. But I'm not done. I need more time. I need to re-read Roger's email, digest it, dissect it.

Without taking a moment to think, I press print, sending the email to the library's printer. I regret it immediately. What if somebody sees it? What if someone reads it and turns me over to the police? I scroll through Claire's other emails and click "print," "print," "print." I have no idea what I am printing, and I don't care. I log out of Claire's account and type in the word "Target." Print, print, print. "McDonald's." Print, print, print.

I clear the search history just as an elderly man with a monocle and a paisley handkerchief steps up behind me.

"All yours." I force a smile and race toward the printer, bumping my hip and an elbow into a chair and table on my way over.

Once there, I scoop the papers off the tray and scan them for the email from Roger. I stuff it and every other page from the tray into my purse, even though I'm sure some of them are not mine. I don't care.

Frustration courses through me. My email didn't even make it to Jack. It went to Roger. Roger, who is already on the lookout for me, who already had me arrested once, who if he wanted could have someone trace where the email came from. Send more legal trouble my way.

Astrid clutches the bottom of her Mary Janes, rolls back on the rug, and laughs. It's a dagger through my heart. She loves it here. But I can't chance someone tracing that email back to me. Another thing I've ruined for her. We won't be coming back.

The whole way home, I scold myself for wasting the time I had at the library researching Claire when I was supposed to be looking for a job. I remember the notebook I found the other day in the laundry room. The listings inside are many years old so they won't help much with a job search. But maybe they will point me in the right direction.

Once home, I find the notebook right where I left it, resting on top of the dryer. I brush a thick layer of dust off the top and open it. It smells like old newspaper. The chemical scent of ink permeates the tiny laundry room.

All the postings are for temp agencies in the Chicago area. But what's strange is beneath each ad are notes about where the companies tend to place their temps. Some companies are crossed off, with big black x's covering them. I scan the ads looking for a reason. And then it hits me. In addition to being in Chicago, each of these companies have another thing in common. They all place people at Stanbrick Marketing Group.

I fan through the pages of the notebook. As I do, an article pasted inside catches my eye, its edges bumpy, dried glue pressing through the warped paper. The article is from a prominent Chicago-area business magazine, dated six years earlier.

"Chicago Heiress Gets Her Due," reads the title. My eyes jump from paragraph to paragraph, skipping from one highlighted sentence to another. I pause when I get to a chunk of text circled in bright yellow and read.

When Claire Stanbrick, founder of Chicago's own Stanbrick Marketing Group, was only three years old, her father abandoned her and her mother, Florence. For many years after, Claire's mother struggled as a single mother to provide for Claire and herself. Through sheer grit and determination, Florence managed to make a name for herself in the art world, amassing a huge fortune due to sales of her famous paintings. In interviews, Claire acknowledges how hard her mother worked, often leaving Claire to care for herself while her mother traveled from country to country for her art shows. "But I know she did it for me, for us. As a single mother, she provided everything I could possibly want and taught me the importance of financial security. Sure, it was lonely sometimes, but the role I played in our lives was to step aside and let her provide." When Claire's mother passed last spring, she became the sole heir to her mother's artwork, artwork valued in the millions of dollars.

The article goes on to discuss the travels Claire's mother took while promoting her artwork. I skip over those sections and jump to another highlighted paragraph.

However, instead of keeping all the paintings to herself, Claire chose to auction a number of them off at a charitable function with proceeds benefitting abused and homeless children in the city, making her not only one of the youngest and wealthiest entrepreneurs in the city, but one of the most generous as well.

> But Ms. Stanbrick did not auction off every painting, and she noted there is one painting she will never auction off or sell. That painting, titled "A Portrait of a Mother and Her Child," hangs above the mantle at the Stanbrick couple's riverside home in Vintage, Wisconsin. When asked why she would never part with that painting, she replied, "It portrays a deep kind of love. A child's love and dependence on their mother."

I stare at the image of the painting, and I don't see it the way Claire did in the article. To me, the painting shows a mother's love for her child, not the other way around. I flip the page of the notebook to finish reading the article. It ends with a photo of Claire and Jack at the charity auction, just like the original I found the other day in the notebook. The one I've been carrying around with me in my bra.

Except the one from the article is slightly different. Jack's head is turned a bit more to the left. Looking at something? Someone? And it clearly has been tampered with. Claire's face and body are cut out of the picture and a snapshot from one of my wedding photos to Carl is taped in its place, the words "Wanda and Jack" scribbled in erratic marks beneath the photo.

Crap. I slap the notebook shut and toss it into the corner. It lands upside down, its cardboard backside facing up. Something is taped onto it. I crawl over to the notebook to get a better look. And that is when I see it. A photocopy of a pay stub for $500, made out to Wanda Dellas. I squint my eyes, trying to read the smudged name of the company. I can tell it is a temp agency, although only the first letter and last name of the agency is legible: "B . . . Temps." Typed in the memo section at the bottom of the stub, in print as clear as freshly washed crystal, are the words, "For work at Stanbrick Marketing Group."

I do a double-take, my breath hitched in my throat. A pay stub from Stanbrick Marketing Group. My fingers graze my lips. Did I intentionally look for a job at Stanbrick Marketing Group? To be close to Jack? To Claire? When did my obsession with the Stanbricks start? My cheeks flush with embarrassment.

Who is this Wanda Dellas who worked for the Stanbricks? Me? I pace around the enclosed space of the laundry room.

Maybe if I can find the temp agency, they can give me some information. Maybe there's something they can tell me that will clue me in to who I am? My heart stalls on that last thought, fish hooked in my chest. What if they recognize me as Wanda? What if they tell me I really am her? On the other hand, what if they have information that shows I am not Wanda? That I am Claire. My heart pumps possibility through my bloodstream. I need to find out. Now.

The smudged-out name of the agency taunts me. "B . . . Temps." This tells me nothing. I peel the pay stub off the cardboard back of the notebook and hold it up to the light bulb dangling from the laundry-room ceiling. But even through the light, the words are no more defined.

I grab a red pen from a cup beside the dryer, and once again start flipping through the notebook's warped pages, marking every temp agency that starts with the letter "B." But there are too many. I'll never figure this out. I cradle my head in my hands. This is ridiculous. Silly. Even if I were to find the correct agency, what do I think they are going to say? "Oh Wanda, we're so glad you called. We've been so lost without you." Or "You can't possibly be Wanda Dellas. You must be the missing, presumed dead, Claire Stanbrick. Go now and claim your identity." Right.

I lean back against the frigid metal of the dryer and close my eyes. I think of Astrid, picture her in a freshly pressed yellow dress with starchy white polka dots. She wears a party hat and opens birthday presents, each grander than the last. "Make a wish, Astrid," I whisper into the darkness.

I picture her on a pink bicycle with a wicker basket, riding down neatly paved sidewalks, training wheels guiding her way, keeping her safe. "I will keep you safe, Astrid. We will be okay." The image of Astrid is replaced unexpectedly with that of a gun, the steel barrel pointed at my chest. I try to look beyond the chamber to see who is holding the gun. The person looms, big, tall, but the face is hidden by a shadow. The sound of a shot rings through the air. The room whizzes by me as I collapse to the ground. My head throbs from the memory.

"No." I force my eyes open, wiping away the scene. Was that a real memory? My shoulder beats with pain. I place my palm over it. Who was holding the gun? An image of Roger shouting at me when he caught me cleaning his office juts through my mind. Is Roger the person who did this to me?

I press on. I need as many answers as I can get for myself, for Astrid, for our future.

Once I've made it through the entire notebook, I tiptoe past a napping Astrid into the kitchen, the cracked tile scratchy against the bottom of my feet.

I find the phone book and dial the number of the first agency beginning with the letter "B." Blood beats hard in my ears as I count the rings. After the third one, a woman's voice answers. "Bambi Temp Agency. How can I help you?"

"I have a question." I blurt it out.

"Okay?" she says.

She taps her fingernails against the handset, a busy lady. I speak as professionally as possible. "I am calling to inquire as to whether your agency has ever employed a temp by the name of Wanda Dellas."

"Nope," she says.

"Wait, how do you know that?" My toes curl against the kitchen tile, icy against my feet.

"Gotcha." She laughs, her voice a shrill crescendo piercing my eardrums.

I want to reach through the phone and smack her. But instead, I push out a fake laugh, in the hopes there is still a chance she can help me.

"Just kidding. Let me look," she says. "What was that name again?"

"Wanda. Wanda Dellas."

She continues to chuckle as she pecks away at her keyboard, and I can only hope she is really looking it up this time. Not playing another trick on me.

"Sorry. I don't see that name anywhere in our records."

"How far back do your records go? Ms. Dellas would have worked there a little over five years ago."

"I see nothing. I found a Wendy Dempster. Does that help?"

"No." I hang up to her saying "Let me know if I can help you in any other way."

Absolutely, if I want to feel like an asshole, she'll be my first call.

Frustrated but not deterred, I forge ahead and dial the next number in the notebook. I call it and two more agencies, each with the same outcome. Wanda Dellas worked for none of them.

Defeated, I bury my head on top of my forearms. The sound of shuffling pajama pants fills the room. The pads of Astrid's fingers tap my shoulder.

"What's the matter?" Her eyes are wide and thoughtful.

I rub my temples and force a smile. "Nothing. Mama's just sleepy."

"Nap time for Mama." She places her hands on her hips. "I don't like nap time, but you do. 'Let Mama sleep,' you always say."

A wave of guilt surges through me. I did used to say that.

She shrugs her shoulders. "But not anymore."

I think of the pills, and am glad to be done with them, even though sometimes I miss them, miss the ability to get away, to escape.

"I'm thirsty," she says.

"Then let's get you something to drink." I pull open the refrigerator. "What would you like?"

She squeezes herself in front of me, and peers into the refrigerator. "Apple juice."

She scoots onto her booster seat as I place the cup of juice on the table in front of her. But she doesn't drink.

"What's wrong?" I ask.

"Too cold." She rubs her hands together. "I want a straw."

I open and close cabinets, looking for the elusive straws.

After a few minutes, Astrid hops off her booster and walks over to the pantry. She pulls open the doors and points to a drawer inside. I tug it open. It is filled to the rim with junk: papers, takeout menus, plastic utensils. All jammed inside. I move the stuff around until I find a clear plastic bag containing a few stray straws. Beneath the bag is a packet of papers. I push broken pencils and erasers to the back of the drawer to get a better look.

It's a contract. But not just any contract, a temp agency contract. Between Wanda Dellas and Brighton Temps.

"Yes." I plunk a straw into Astrid's apple juice. She pumps her fists into the air, thinking my excitement is from finding the straw. I pull up a stool next to where she sits at the kitchen table and flip through the contract.

Most of it looks like boring legal-speak: the temp will get paid this much per hour, the agency is entitled to this percentage of the temp's earnings. Seems standard to me. I get to the signature page where Wanda's signature is jagged and erratic. I write the name Wanda on a napkin. Mine is swirly, nothing like hers. At first, I am excited by this, until I realize it most likely doesn't prove a thing. My handwriting could have changed since the accident, or I could have been in a hurry when signing or—I cringe at the thought of it—I could've been high.

Still, this is good news. I've found the name of the agency and an employment contract. I pick up the phone and am about to call them, when I notice a sheet of paper stuck behind the last page of the contract. A letter to Wanda.

> Dear Ms. Dellas,
>
> Thank you for your interest in working at Stanbrick Marketing Group. We have no positions, full-time or temporary, that match your qualifications at this time. We will hold onto your resume and will be in contact with you if a position opens in the future.
>
> Best of luck with your endeavors,
>
> Claire Stanbrick

The paper shakes in my hand. It doesn't make sense. A letter saying there is no job available, and yet I have a pay stub for work performed at Stanbrick Marketing Group and an employment contract from an agency that places people there. On the letter, Claire's name is crossed out in angry hash marks. Disturbing. I turn the page over. There are notes written on the back. A timeline. Marking Jack's movements and someone else's. Someone with the initials, "RL." Roger Lindsey? If there were no positions available, even temporary, how did I get hired?

Eager to get to the bottom of this, I dial the number listed at the top of the contract for Brighton Temps.

A receptionist with a smoker's voice answers the telephone. "Brighton Temps, here to serve your every staffing need. How can I help you?"

She barely finishes speaking when I cut her off. “What were the circumstances surrounding the employment of Wanda Dellas?”

“What?” she asks and coughs into the receiver. “Who is this?”

“I need to ask you a few questions about someone who used to work for you.”

“We have hundreds of temps coming through our agency. I am not going to remember each and every one of them.”

“Please, I need to know if you have information about this one person. Is there any way you could help me?”

“I can’t go around giving out information about former temps to anyone who asks. Ever heard of a thing called privacy?”

“I know, and you’re right,” I say. “It’s just I haven’t heard from my sister in years and I’m desperate to get in touch with her.” I lie.

There is a long pause and I think she might have hung up on me when she says, “I haven’t spoken to my sister in years either. Family feud?”

“Yes, but—”

“But you miss her and want to reconcile, huh?”

“Yes.” *I want to reconcile . . . reconcile who the heck I am.*

“You’re a better person than me.” She wheezes into the handset. “If that sister of mine ever wants to mend fences, she’s going to have to come chasing after me and even then, I’d probably tell her to go bounce.”

I pace around the kitchen, hopping over a line of splintered tile. Astrid claps. I press my finger to my lips, hoping she’ll quiet down.

“Bet your sister didn’t steal your boyfriend,” she says.

“No, she didn’t,” I say and sigh, growing impatient with this conversation. I’m looking for information from this woman, not to be her therapist. “Can you help me?”

She puts down the receiver, hacks for a few seconds, and clears her throat before returning to the line. "I'll try. But keep this between us. Got it?"

"Got it." I strum my fingers against the countertop, eagerness dancing through them.

"What's your sister's name?"

"Wanda Dellas."

"How many years ago was it that she temped for us?"

"A little over five."

A file cabinet opening fills the background. "Be patient with me. Our computers are down."

I press the receiver hard against my ear, straining to hear, as if I could somehow gather the information from the electric buzz of air traveling through the telephone wires.

"Oh my . . ."

"Did you find something?"

"So, your sister . . ."

"Who?"

"Your sister? Wanda Dellas?"

"Right."

"She did temp for us a little over five years ago, but only for a couple months."

"A couple months? Is that all?" I tug a strand of hair out of my head.

"Let me see if there's any other information in her file."

I twist the hair around my finger.

She coughs some more. "There's a note here that says she abandoned her position without notice."

"Abandoned her position?"

"Just up and left, stopped coming into work."

"What exactly does the note say?"

"It says, 'To Whom it may concern: I am writing this email to inform you that Wanda Dellas has not been showing up to work. She has neither reported to the office nor called in to tell us she will be absent. As such, we are permanently terminating her employment with our firm and we will no longer be paying a commission fee to your agency for her work. Sincerely, Roger Lindsey, Esquire."

Roger Lindsey.

"What is the date on the letter?" I ask.

"November fifth."

"Does it say what happened to her?"

She rifles through papers. "That's strange."

"What's strange?" I strain to better hear her.

"There's a note from your sister."

"A letter from Wanda? What does it say?" I can barely control my impatience.

"That she won't be needing to work for us anymore because she is moving out of state. It is also dated November fifth."

"Hold on one minute."

I scramble over to the other side of the kitchen, the curly telephone cord wrapping around my waist, and grab the magazine with Claire's picture on the cover off the counter.

"You still there?" A voice calls to me through the receiver as I shuffle through the pages.

"What was that date again?" I ask.

"November fifth," she says.

I press my pointer finger against the words in the magazine so hard they smudge. November fifth. The day Claire disappeared.

Chapter Twenty-One

Claire Before

Jack is waiting for me when I arrive back at the apartment, the table set, candles lit, their flames flickering in shadows against the dining room wall. I've barely stepped into the room and Jack can see I'm upset.

"What's wrong?"

I turn the bag so he can read the writing on the back. I point to the words.

He examines the bag, a trail of tomato sauce leaking from a corner. He presses his fingers against the words. "Is this what you're upset about?"

"It's clearly a threat," I say.

"Oh, I don't think so." He strokes my arm, still riddled with goose bumps.

"Why not?"

"It's an old proverb. 'Curiosity killed the cat.' Maybe this restaurant writes catchy messages on their take-out bags."

"I've never seen that done before," I say.

"It could be a new, hip, trend. Some coffee shops write funny things on their paper cups."

My head aches. I suppose it could be a new trend, yet for some reason, worry still winds within me.

"Why does this bother you so much? Are you nervous about something?"

An image of Wanda dressed like me spins through my mind, but that's just imitation, right? Harmless. "Funny, though, I also thought someone was following me."

He snaps his head around and stares at me. “Was someone following you?”

His response surprises me. “No. I mean I didn’t see anyone there.”

The muscles in his arms relax. He chuckles. “Then I’m sure all is fine. You just need some rest.”

Now that he mentions it, I am feeling tired. This pregnancy is taking a lot out of me.

He uncorks a bottle of Chardonnay. “Want some?” He offers me the chilled glass.

“Jack, that’s wine.”

“I read a pregnant woman can have a glass or two during pregnancy and it won’t affect the baby.”

“Well, I’m not going to do that. After everything we’ve been through, why would I take a chance like that?”

Hurt, he marches, wine glass in hand, into the kitchen where he tosses it into the sink.

I jump from the sound of the glass shattering. “What’s going on with you?” I say to his back as he stomps down the hallway toward our spare bedroom. “Jack?” I follow, but he closes the door behind him, leaving me standing alone, a stream of moonlight bouncing off the top of my feet.

***

The next morning, I peek into the spare bedroom. Is Jack gone? Already left for work? I rush into the dining room half-expecting to see the bag of last night’s dinner still sitting on the table where we left it. I brace myself for its pungent odor. But to my surprise, instead of the smelly bag, I see a folded notecard sitting beside a chocolate croissant and a glass of orange juice. I read the note aloud. "I'm sorry about last night. I over-reacted."

As I read the words, Jack's voice emanates from around the corner, "Can you forgive me?"

I nod my head. He meant well with the wine, and I didn't mean to hurt his feelings, to make him feel as if I think he doesn't care. For as long as I have known Jack, he's been sensitive. His feelings are fragile. My skin is thicker than his. Sometimes I forget that.

I pull him into a hug and run my finger through the stubble on his chin. He didn't sleep. Me neither. "It's okay," I say.

"It's the idea of you being in danger. It's more than I can handle."

I feel the same way about him.

"I think we should install more security at the office," he says.

"You do?"

"The opening of Stanbrick Financial has made us even more visible than before. We're almost like celebrities."

"Financial celebrities, I guess."

"I worry we could be targets."

I think about the words written on the take-out bag and my shoulders tense. A little extra security couldn't hurt.

***

It takes over two months before Jack can get the office maintenance guy to install a deadbolt lock at the top of my office door. Jack had to jump through hoops to get approval from the building in order to do it. I rub my belly as the maintenance man reaches into his toolbox and affixes the lock to the doorframe. Wanda walks by, her eyes wide with curiosity. Jack insisted the locks be put on all the office doors, not just mine. For added security.

The maintenance man finishes the job while I thumb through a file cabinet. When I look up, Wanda is standing in front of me, staring. I scoot my chair back, startled.

She laughs. “Here are the corrections on the Teason tables.”

I take them from her. “In the future, please knock before you enter my office.”

Her face falls. Hurt. “I thought you wanted them as soon as possible.”

“I do. But you need to respect my space.”

She looks down. “I thought we were friends.”

“We are work colleagues.”

She stands there looking at me, waiting for more, for a “colleagues who are friends” or something. When I don’t give it to her, she walks out in a huff.

Truth is, I don’t care. That woman needs to learn some boundaries.

I glance at the figures Wanda left on my desk. I should review them, but instead, I choose procrastination over doing my work. The morning flies by as I search the Internet for websites about babies. During my search, I find one with a baby calculator. All I have to do is punch in my due date and it tells me how big my baby is right now, alongside a picture of a fruit of corresponding size. Our baby is the size of a grapefruit. I’m staring at the photo on the screen, trying to imagine how a whole person can fit into such a small diameter, when there’s a knock on my office door. It’s Jack, his black hair slicked to the side from the palm of gel he applied this morning.

I turn my screen toward him. “Look at our baby.”

Jack chuckles. “I’m the proud papa of a grapefruit.”

“Yes, you are.” I rest my hand on my belly and laugh.

“I see you’re working hard today.”

“I know. It’s bad. I can’t help myself.”

He pulls up a chair and scoots beside me.

I toggle across websites to one with the year's most popular baby names. "Which do you like best?"

A worried look crawls across his face. "Do you think that's a good idea?"

"What?"

"To name the baby before its born. In case . . ."

My heart drops like a stone in my chest. I shut my laptop.

Jack kisses my forehead. "I don't want us to be disappointed again."

I pick at a hangnail. He's right, of course. Even though I am twenty-three weeks pregnant, I don't want to tempt the fates. We should wait before picking a name.

I look up and see Roger peering around the corner of my office door. "You were looking for me?"

"Not me," I say and feel a pang of guilt for not doing any work so far this morning.

"I was." Jack raises his hand.

"At your service." Roger fakes a bow. "What can I do for you?"

Jack reaches into the jacket pocket of his suit and pulls out a set of keys. "The keys to the river house." They jangle in the air before he drops them into Roger's outstretched palm.

"You're giving him the keys?" My blood pressure jumps up a notch.

"So he can give viewings to potential buyers," Jack says.

"There's something I want removed from the house before all of that showing-the-house business starts up." An image of a woman cradling her baby pirouettes through my mind.

"The painting?" Jack reads my thoughts.

I nod.

"I'm heading up there tonight," Roger says. "Want me to pick it up for you?"

"That would be great—" Jack says.

"No." I cut Jack off. Both men turn toward me. "No one touches that painting but me. And no one views the house until I've had a chance to remove it."

"Claire, we have a potential buyer stopping by tomorrow morning, one who seems like a solid lead. You don't want to miss out on that opportunity, right?" Roger asks.

"Then it looks like I'm heading up to Vintage tonight. I want to be there to keep an eye on it," I say.

"But I can't go with you tonight, Claire. I have a meeting," Jack says.

"You can ride with me." Roger stuffs the keys into his pants pocket.

I pause for a minute to think. I would much rather go up there a different day with Jack than go with Roger. But the buyer is coming tomorrow.

"What's the problem?" Roger asks. "I don't bite."

I know that. I do. Still, there is something tugging at me, a snagged thread of thought in my mind telling me that going up to the house with Roger is a bad idea. But I can't put my finger on why. I know the buyers probably wouldn't touch the painting. They likely won't pay any attention to it at all, except for maybe to joke about whether the multi-million-dollar painting comes with the house. Still, I can't seem to silence the alarm bells pinging in my head. Which risk do I take?

Jack rubs the back of my neck with his palm. "How about if you guys go tonight, and I'll meet you up there tomorrow afternoon?" He runs his hand down the length of my sleeve. "We can spend one more weekend there before selling the place. What do you think?"

It seems like a reasonable compromise.

"Don't worry, I'll be out of there as soon as the potential buyers leave. Let you two have your privacy," Roger says.

I look into Jack's eyes and see reassurance. It does sound nice. This could be just what I need, a weekend with Jack, enjoying the fresh scent of the pine trees, taking a boat out on the Wisconsin River. One last time.

***

That afternoon, Roger's station wagon waits beside the curb in front of my apartment building. The doorman covers my head with a black umbrella, shielding me from the rain as he walks me to the car. Roger pops the trunk, and the doorman slides my luggage inside. I slip the doorman $10 and wave a hasty goodbye.

The tires splash through the puddles on the street as Roger turns onto the tollway. Ramp I-90, Rockford. We are on our way. His car is older than I remember, more rundown. I can see from the maintenance sticker, peeling off the upper left corner of the windshield, that it hasn't been brought into the shop in over a year. Financial trouble again?

The rain beats down harder as the car speeds up, the wipers swinging back and forth. But it's a futile effort. I squint and strain but can barely see through the river of water flowing down the glass. As we fly along the highway, the drops hit harder, little pellets banging against the roof of the car. Hail.

"Maybe we should pull over." I knead my fingers together.

"We'll be fine. It's supposed to clear up once we cross the border into Wisconsin."

I wrap my arms around my belly. Nervous. This was a bad idea.

"It's okay." He leans across the seat, his arm brushing against my knees.

"What are you doing?" I turn my legs toward the car door.

He opens the glove compartment. "Grabbing a CD?"

I blush. Embarrassed.

"I thought some music would make you less tense. The radio is busted, but I have a CD with an 80's mix somewhere in here."

Still anxious, I laugh as he roots around the open compartment.

"What, don't you like music from the 80's?"

"No, I do." I take a deep breath and sigh. I do need to relax. This pregnancy has made me way too jumpy.

I close my eyes as he pops the CD into the radio and nod off as I think about the baby and Jack. I wake with a start to the car spinning, hydroplaning along the side of the expressway, the smell of burnt rubber rippling through the vents. I feel dizzy and nauseous as my fingers grip the leather seats as the scenery flies by. I check my seatbelt strap as we turn, making sure it is in the correct spot. The correct spot to protect the baby.

The car skids to a stop on the shoulder of the road, the front fender butting up against the post of the interstate expressway sign.

"Are you all right?" Roger turns to me, his face flushed.

"I think so." I pat down my arms and legs. "What happened?"

"We hit a slick patch and the next thing I knew, we were spinning."

"I have to call Jack." I pull my cell phone out of my purse and see that there is no signal. I look out the window. The sky is dark with storm clouds. My hands begin to shake.

"It's okay. You should get a signal once we get closer to Milwaukee." He pulls the gearshift into reverse and angles the car back onto the highway.

"Take it slow." I glare at him.

"I was." He clenches his jaw.

After an hour of sliding along the highway, we take exit 108A-B and merge onto I-39 North toward Vintage. A few minutes later we pull off the expressway and onto a narrow one-lane path leading to the river house. Two more winding turns and we inch up the driveway. Wet gravel kicks up against my heels as I step out of the car. The air is moist with pollen. The smell of damp leaves scratches my throat. I climb the paved stairs and stand beneath the sloped overhang while I wait for Roger to carry my luggage to the door.

He props my suitcase up against the wooden railing, tugs a key out of his pant pocket, and unlocks the door. He pulls a thick black box out of his bag and loops it through the door handle. With a spin of the numbers on the front, a metal plate slides open, and he drops the key inside.

"What do you want the code to be?" he asks. "It's a combination lock box."

"Don't they make electronic ones now that are more secure?"

"Yes, but those are expensive. So this is what we've got to work with."

"Whatever." I shake my head, still rattled from the turn we took on the expressway and eager to get inside the house.

"Let's go with 9390." He rests the base of the box in his hand.

"The address? Isn't that a bit obvious?"

"I wouldn't worry. No one is going to try to break in here anyway."

"Fine." I'm too exhausted and nauseated to argue with him. I watch carefully as he sets the code, his thick, clumsy fingers stumbling as they turn the dials.

"Do you need help bringing in your bag?" He motions to my suitcase.

I should accept his help. Being pregnant, lifting luggage is probably not the best choice. But desperate to be alone and to call Jack, I don't.

"I got it from here." I am grateful when he doesn't press the issue.

"I'll be back here at 9:00 am sharp. I'm staying at the motel just down the road."

I ignore him and tug my bag over the lip of the doorway.

"Call me if you need anything."

I keep pulling my suitcase forward.

"You know, like if things go bump in the night."

"What?" I spin around to look at him.

He laughs. "I'm teasing you. It's just an expression."

"Right." I fake a smile. "Just an expression."

I'm out here in the woods by myself, and he's tossing around expressions. Thankfully, Jack will be here tomorrow. As far as I'm concerned, he can't get here soon enough.

I close the door behind me and flip the deadbolt. Feeling chilled, I grab a fluffy sweater out of my bag. The gray wool scratches against my skin, but I don't care. I just want to feel warm. I slump down on the leather sofa in the family room and leave a message for Jack to call me when he gets home from his meeting. After an hour, my eyelids heavy, I decide to climb the stairs to the bedroom.

But I can't stop thinking about the key in the lock box. I am halfway up the steps when I decide to turn around and go back down again. 9390 as the code? The address as the code? Ridiculous.

I flip the lock and open the door. A strong wind whips at me as a splatter of rain pelts my skin. I cradle the lock box in my palm and spin the dials, my fingers numbing quickly from the chill. I think back on how Roger set the code and then I change it, turning each of the four numbers up and around, pressing them down to lock them into place. When I am finished, I close the door once more as a sense of calm washes over me like a wave. I lock the door behind me. New code. My due date. No one is guessing that. I drape my sweater over the railing and head upstairs to bed.

***

I wake with a start to a scratching sound coming from the floor below. I pull the covers up underneath my chin, squeeze my eyes shut, and hope it isn't real, that I am only dreaming. I wait for a moment and hearing nothing, settle back down to sleep. But a few minutes later, it starts up again: a tugging sound, a scraping. I jump out of bed, the satin sheets clinging to my thighs. I throw my robe around me as I reach for the nightstand, searching for my phone. It's not there. Did I leave it downstairs? I scramble into the hallway but freeze when I hear a new sound. Something sawing. Sawing metal. Too scared to venture down, I head back into the bedroom and lock the door. I flip on the light. Maybe if they see someone is home, whoever it is will go away. I walk over to the window, pull back the shades, and look onto the driveway below. I can't make out much in the darkness. I rub my eyes and see a rustle of leaves between the bushes. Beside them, I think I see a figure cloaked in dark camouflage clothing pushing through the trees. But when I look again, no one is there.

Trembling, I open the bedroom door, and step once again into the hallway. From the top of the stairs, I hear a faint buzzing. What's that? I step lightly along the smooth wooden steps and notice the sweater I hung on the banister earlier that evening is vibrating. My phone. I pull it out of the side pocket and exhale as I realize it is just a bunch of emails coming through, emails and a text from Jack. *I will call you in the morning.* Too impatient to wait, I punch in his number, trying to reach him. But it goes straight to voicemail.

Still shaken, I dial 911. After what feels like an eternity, a squad car with red and blue lights flashing pulls into the driveway. Two officers with navy hats and holstered weapons knock on the door. The light from the foyer catches on their badges as the younger of the two speaks.

"We searched the premises and found no sign of anyone suspicious." A toothpick dangles from the corner of his mouth.

No sign of anyone suspicious. His words play on repeat in my ears.

"We can keep an eye on the house for you this evening if you'd like, ma'am," the other officer says. He lifts his cap and scratches the side of his head, where his buzz cut is growing back in uneven patches.

I feel silly, like a nervous little housewife, fretting about the slightest noise. Roger's joke echoes in my mind, "things that go bump in the night." This is his fault. He put this thought in my head, making me unnecessarily nervous.

"No thank you. That's not necessary." I roll my sleeves up and down my arm. "Sorry to have bothered you."

"It's no trouble, ma'am," the younger officer says as he climbs into the squad car.

I am chastising myself for overreacting when my wrist bumps into the lock box.

"Ouch." The handle nicks my skin. I twist it around and notice ridges in the metal, jagged striations, as if someone tried to take off the box, as if someone tried to file it open.

"Wait." I wave my arms to try and get their attention. But it is too late. I rest my elbow against the doorknob and watch as their taillights disappear behind the hedges and they drive away into the darkness.

"I'm done with this thing." I blow on my fingers to warm them up before punching in the code. I pull out the key and drop it into the pocket of my robe. Then close the now keyless box and shut the door. Locking it behind me.

Again, I try calling Jack and again it goes straight to voicemail. He must have powered down his phone for the night. My adrenaline still pumping, I'm too restless to sleep. I grab the imitation nineteenth-century lantern I picked up at a local antique shop last summer and decide maybe a walk would calm my nerves. There's no chance I'm going outside, so I decide to walk the halls inside the house instead.

Everything looks different in the dim glow of the lantern, the light casting shadows upon the shiny wooden floor. I turn left past the expansive kitchen, jumping at my own reflection in the window as I pass. But it is after I make a right into the living room that my breath catches in my chest and I have to lean against the sofa to keep my balance. The painting.

The four-foot-by-four-foot canvas, “A Portrait of a Mother and Her Child,” hangs above the mantle. A rendition my mother created from an actual photograph, a painting of my mother and me.

I stare at the picture, squint my eyes as I try to remember her looking like that, to recall the lavender scent of her perfume, and the gentle curve of her jaw. But mostly, I try to understand her feelings for me. I often felt like a burden, an obstacle to her success. But this painting tells a different story, one I see clearly for the first time, the story of a mother’s love.

I press my palm against the cool glass of the end table, and tilt my head to the side, a new perspective. My eyes glance away from the painting as something wet drips down my thigh. I brush my hand against my leg and feel a sticky tackiness across my fingers. I grab the lantern and hold it next to my hip. And that’s when I see it, trails of red rivers weaving a path along my calf, my white socks splattered with crimson dots. I feel faint. I am bleeding. The baby.

Chapter Twenty-Two

Wanda After

The windows of the 151-bus fog up from the humidity and recent rain as we ride home from the offices of Bengal Cleaning Services in the Chicago Loop, where we picked up my final paycheck. Jack's hearing is tomorrow. Tomorrow he will plead guilty to Claire's murder. To my murder. An idea percolates in my head, bubbling to the surface. What if I go to the hearing? I could show everyone that I am her. What if that could change everything? The thought dances through my mind, as I chew on the "what ifs" of the idea.

Astrid and I peer out as the fancy buildings of the Loop turn into the apartments and townhouses characteristic of our neighborhood. We step off the bus, but instead of turning right toward home, I steer Astrid to the left, toward the pharmacy on the street corner. The tall glass doors glide open as we approach.

Astrid eyes a pair of pink socks with satin polka-dot bows sewn onto the top. I shake my head. Nope. Not a necessary purchase. Plus, we came here for a reason. There's something very important I need to buy. We make our way through the aisles until we reach the one with a sign above it that says, "Hair care." I pull the photo of Claire at the casino auction out of my bra and try to match the color of her hair to the swatches of color on the boxes of dye. Is "Copper Merlot" or "Apricot Caramel" the best match? I don't know. Unsure if I have enough cash for even one container of hair dye, I grab the one that looks like it's the closest to Claire's color off the shelf and bring it up to the counter.

The man behind the register wears a plastic name tag with the word "pharmacist" etched into it. He leans in close as he reaches for the hair dye, his breath sour and rancid, like stale cigarettes. The red light from his scanner flashes in my eyes as he rings up the total dollar amount, $15.94.

Whoa. My face flushes as I thumb through the bills in my wallet. The pharmacist stares at me as I count. My chin falls to my chest. $11. Not enough.

My head down, Astrid and I wind our way along the sidewalk toward home. I run my fingers through my hair, frustration a neon-red stop sign. No one will believe I'm Claire if I show up looking like this.

When we approach the house, Penelope is outside rooting around in her tiny garden. As soon as Astrid sees Penelope, she bounds away from me over to her. She squats onto the wet ground beside her and pokes at the flowers. Penelope snaps off her green gardening gloves and rests her hands on Astrid's shoulders.

"This is a chrysanthemum." Penelope brushes her fingers along the purple petals. She peers into Astrid's wide eyes. "It means cheerful." She taps her finger on the tip of Astrid's nose.

Astrid flings her head back and laughs.

"That's right, and this one is a daisy." She points to one at the far end of her garden. "It stands for hope."

"What about these?" Astrid walks toward a patch of fluffy flowers nestled against the siding of Penelope's house.

"Those are carnations, dear. So that depends on which color someone gives to you."

My curiosity piqued, I join the conversation. "What does the yellow one mean?"

"Funny you should ask. It means disappointment, and from the look on your face when you walked up here, that's what you are. Disappointed."

I dig the toe of my sneaker into the soil.

"What's the matter?" she asks.

"If I tell you, do you promise you won't laugh?"

She shoots me a wide grin and I'm not sure I can trust her not to mock me, but I go for it anyway. What's a little more humiliation going to do to me? "I didn't have enough money to buy the hair dye I need."

She looks at me, her face stoic. "What do you need to dye your hair for?"

I try to think of an acceptable lie but settle on the truth. "I'm going to Jack's hearing tomorrow."

"Why would you do a thing like that?" She wipes a drop of sweat off her forehead, leaving a streak of dirt in its place.

"Because . . ." I pause, unsure if I want to reveal the whole truth.

"Because why?"

"Because I am Claire."

"Not that again. That's what got you into this mess in the first place."

"If the judge sees how much I resemble her, maybe he'll give Jack a break and he won't have to plead guilty."

"Give yourself a break and stop this nonsense. Stop trying to recreate some wild version of the past. You're missing out on the present. And running the risk of destroying your future."

I try to let her words sink in. But they just bounce off. How can I have a future if I don't know who I am?

"This is all because you have a crush on him, isn't it?" She places her hands on her hips.

"What?"

"Before your accident, you were always talking in weird fantasies about him, comparing him to Carl."

"I was?"

"But you've got to give this up. That man is a criminal. He's worse than Carl." She slaps her gloves against her knees.

I doubt that. "Did I know him?"

"I don't know. You had a lot of secrets before the accident. Became real buttoned up about where you were working, what you were doing, all your comings and goings. If I hadn't been so persistent, you would have shut me out completely." She digs her knuckles into the dirt.

"I'm sorry." I rest my hand on her shoulder.

She shoots me a blank stare before pushing herself to a standing position and chuckling. "I'm nothing if not persistent."

I force a small laugh as a headache forms behind my left eye. I crave my pills. I'd only take one, so I can zone out, forget all this madness, or at least descend into a different kind.

"Just be yourself." Penelope breaks the silence hanging in the air between us.

"I don't know who that is." Frustration threads my voice.

"This wild goose chase is going to get you into trouble."

I grab Astrid's hand. "Come on, let's go home. I don't have to explain myself to someone who spends her days talking to her flowers."

Astrid and I trudge across the soggy lawn up to our front door. We are inside less than a minute when there's a knock at the door and a voice calls to me from the other side.

"Wanda? It's Penny. Open the door."

I press my back up against the doorframe, still too irritated with her to respond.

"Listen. If this is what you want, I can help you."

Feeling desperate and without good options, I open the door a crack. "How?"

"I can do it."

"Do what?"

"Dye your hair."

"I'm not taking money from you, Penelope. I don't feel right about that."

"We don't need to buy any dye. Stan hated when I wore my hair gray. Back before he passed away, I used to dye my hair myself all the time."

I can only imagine what that looked like.

"Come on. I can do it from things I have in my house." She squeezes my shoulder. "Let a lonely lady help you out."

Penelope coloring my hair? With things she has in her house? I pause for a moment. She takes my silence as acquiescence and tugs me out the door. Astrid follows and before I can change my mind, the three of us file into Penelope's house.

***

Astrid and I stop in the entryway hall, assaulted by the pungent scent of chicken soup and menthol. I peel Astrid's palm away from her nose, even though I don't blame her for trying to escape the smell.

Furniture covered in plastic lines the walls of each room. My eyes catch the glint of a bowl filled with dusty colorful candy on top of the coffee table. Astrid sticks out her tongue. Even her ever-insatiable sweet tooth can't stomach that.

"What are you waiting for? No one's been murdered here in a long time."

My feet anchor into the floor. "What?"

"Don't be so serious." Penelope pinches my cheeks so hard it hurts. "I'm just kidding. My supplies are in the kitchen."

I don't move.

"Come on." She presses against my back.

Despite my reservations, I allow Penelope to lead me through the musty hallway toward her kitchen, which looks almost identical to mine, complete with the same discolored and bubbled linoleum countertops.

Penelope opens and closes a few rickety cabinets and lines some items up beside the kitchen faucet. She runs her fingers under a stream of water until it steams and then puts a plug in the drain. "First we need to wash your hair."

"In the sink?"

"Would you prefer to use my shower?"

"No, nope. The sink is perfect." I crinkle my nose at Astrid, who giggles as she pulls a wooden stool from beneath the kitchen island and shimmies herself onto it.

Penelope scoots the other stool up against the lip of the sink and tells me to sit and lean back. She runs her fingers through my hair, and with a loud squeak squirts a pile of dish soap into the center of her palm. She rubs it along my head. I close my eyes and try to relax.

I breathe in as a memory washes over me. I'm at a salon and a woman with long fingers massages coconut-scented shampoo into my scalp. The water is warm and soothing. The words, "*You look so much alike,*" creep into my thoughts.

Water rushes against my ears, the world drowning out, washing away from me. Someone stands in front of me, their features distorted like a Picasso painting, shaded from view. They aim a gun at my heart. The floorboards smack as they rise to meet my falling torso. My hips bruise on impact. Then there's the cold, the pull of the current around me. Help. Help. Stop. I pop my head up, off the edge of the sink, as a waterfall of soapsuds cascades onto the kitchen floor.

"Settle down. You're making a mess." Penelope's voice echoes through the slush in my ears.

"I was drowning."

"Your face was up the whole time. You were breathing just fine." She mops up the floor with a fistful of paper towels as a stream of liquid runs down my cheek.

"It's the water. It was like I was in the river again."

"That you remember?" She tosses the paper towels into the trashcan, droplets raining down across the floor on their way in.

"I remember being shot, then in the water, fighting for my life. But I don't remember anything else. How I got there? Who shot me? Who I am? Nothing."

"Well, you aren't in the river now. You're in Penelope's kitchen." She wipes a cluster of bubbles off my forehead. "At this point, we've got to at least get that dish soap out of your hair."

I lean back but decide to keep my eyes open this time. Once the soap is out, she combs my hair, wraps my head in a towel and places a teakettle on the stove.

"Are you making tea?" I wave at Astrid to back away from the flame and mouth the word "hot."

"You'll see." Penelope drops four tea bags into a steel bowl before pouring the boiling water on top of them.

The room fills with the smell of vanilla rooibos.

"Let me see that magazine over there." She snatches a magazine with Jack and Claire on the cover off the splintered table. "Her hair is quite a bit redder than yours, and lighter."

My face falls.

"Don't lose hope. We can still make you look like her. Hers looks dyed too, just an expensive dye job. But not everyone gets to go to Penny's Hair Salon." She pokes at Astrid's shoulder and they both laugh. She tugs open the refrigerator and pulls out a jug of beet juice.

"Please tell me you don't drink that stuff." I scrunch up my face. Astrid imitates me and covers her mouth.

"It's delicious." She takes a swig right out of the bottle. "But it's also good for making hair redder." She pours a few drops into the now cooled tea water and mixes it with her finger, the tip of which comes out a faint shade of crimson.

She unwraps the towel, motions for me to lean back over the sink once again and pours the concoction on top of my hair. I startle initially from the sensation of the warm liquid rushing over my head.

“Too hot?” she asks.

“It’s okay,” I say, although secretly I scold myself for letting her do this to me in the first place. There’s a good chance I’m going to show up at Jack’s hearing tomorrow looking like a circus clown.

Moisture rushes down the drain as she wrings out my hair. Then she snaps a plastic shower cap on my head and stuffs my hair inside.

“You need to sit with this on for one hour.” She presses her palms against my shoulders. “Then we’ll rinse it out.”

The three of us squeeze next to each other on the couch in Penelope’s living room while we wait, the warm plastic sticking to our thighs. When the time’s up we head back into the kitchen. Penelope rinses my hair and grabs a pair of scissors out of a drawer.

I hold up my hand. “Whoa. You are not cutting my hair.”

“What have you got to lose?” She rests the shears against her hip.

It’s a fair point. I lost my dignity along with my memory a long time ago. “All right. But don’t take off too much. Try to make it look like hers.” I point to the magazine photo of Claire.

The blended sound of scissors snipping, and Penny’s sighs fills the air. Loose hairs fall onto my forearms. This is a mistake. She plugs in a hair dryer. It hums to life as the heated air stings my scalp. She runs a brush through it and shouts, “Voila.”

My eyes are shut as she leads me into the powder room and flicks on the light. I peek through my fingers before fully opening my eyes. I glance back and forth from the magazine photo to the person staring back at me in the mirror. I cannot believe it. The cut’s a little shaggier and the color a shade darker, and of course Claire doesn't have the scar across her cheekbone. But other than that, it's pretty darn good. I could pass for Claire. I could *be* Claire.

"Thank you." I wrap my arms around Penelope.

She beams into the mirror beside me. "Wait." She holds up her stained crimson finger and runs out to her garden. When she comes back, she has a flower with blue petals and a yellow center in her hand. She tucks it behind my ear.

"What is it?" I run my fingers across the silky petals.

"A forget-me-not."

***

Penelope and Astrid wave at me as I board the bus into the city. The smell of diesel fuel wafts in the air as I blow kisses to them.

"Mama will be back this afternoon," I say.

My heart breaks as Astrid buries her face into the folds of Penelope's jacket. I don't want to leave her, not even for a day. But I have to see Jack. I need to get to the bottom of this. For her. For us.

The tires of the bus kick up dirt as we pull away from the curb and head north toward the US District Court. The bus turns onto Dearborn Street and slows to a stop at the corner. Crowds of people line the sidewalk in front of the courthouse. Many carry signs protesting Jack's potential release from prison. A woman with a sign stating "Wife Killers Don't Get Second Chances" in bold pink letters crashes into me. I stand on the curb, not sure what to do next. It's not too late to turn back. But if I go home now, nothing will have changed. Nothing will ever change. I'll never get to the bottom of who I am. And if I am Claire, Jack needs to know. We both need to know.

I wrestle my way through the crowd and am cowed by the size of the building. Tall columns line the outside of the courthouse, like swollen bars of a concrete prison. A moment later, Jack walks out from between the columns, flanked on each side by his legal team, led by attorney Chris Brunson. Journalists with microphones and cameras snap pictures and shout questions at Jack and Mr. Brunson. I can't hear what they are saying over the shouting of the crowd. I can only make out bits and pieces.

I wedge my way closer until I am near the front, blocked only by a petite journalist shoving a microphone in Jack's face as she teeters in her high heels.

She calls out a question to Jack. "Mr. Stanbrick, if you are an innocent man, as you assert you are, why would you plead guilty to the murder of your pregnant wife?"

Jack turns to where the question is coming from. Mr. Brunson calls out, "My client does not need to answer that."

The color drains from Jack's face as he looks over the journalist's shoulder. His eyes lock with mine. Flashbulbs light up the sky as a sea of cameras spins in my direction. Blinding me.

Chapter Twenty-Three

Claire Before

I wake to the sensation of someone hovering over me, shouting my name. Jack kneels beside me, my head propped up against a throw pillow. My forehead throbbing, I run my fingertips across the matted crust of blood along my hairline. Sticky clots peel away from my skin, crumbling between my fingers.

I roll onto my side, into a fetal position, and bury my face in Jack's lap. "The baby."

He strokes my hair, wiping a sweaty strand off my cheek.

"I think the bleeding has stopped." I try to sit up, but slump back down, the room spinning.

"Not so fast. You hit your head." Jack places more pillows behind me.

"I hit my head?"

"You passed out. Good thing the arm of the sofa broke your fall and not the glass table."

The glass end table, an inch away from where I am lying. I cringe.

"I'm calling an ambulance," he says.

"No. I don't need one. There's nothing they can do, anyway." The words are thick in my throat.

"We don't know that. You need to see a doctor." His voice is stern, but his eyes are worried.

"No ambulance."

"Okay, but I'm calling an obstetrician. There's got to be one in town." Jack pulls out his cell phone and before I can protest, he is speaking with a receptionist. He interlaces his fingers with mine. "An appointment this morning is perfect."

Jack's eyes ooze with fear. A pang of sadness echoes through my heart. Would the baby have had his eyes? I bet the baby's heart was just as kind.

Jack brings a change of clothes down from the bedroom and helps me into them.

"I thought you weren't going to be here until the afternoon," I say.

"I wasn't, but when you didn't answer the phone this morning, I got worried and drove up right away and I'm glad I did."

He checks the time on his watch, a gift I bought him for Christmas last year. "We should get going. Our appointment is in twenty minutes."

Jack drapes my arm across his shoulder. We begin the trepid journey down the hallway when there's a tapping against the glass of the front door. Roger's face looks through the window. Jack gets me settled into a chair and opens the door.

Roger's face is red with frustration as he enters the house.

"What happened to the lock box? It's all scratched up and the code is different." He paces in the entryway.

"I changed the code." Dizzy, I lean my head against the wall to steady myself.

"The box is damaged." Roger holds it up.

"I thought someone was trying to break in last night. I called the police, but they found no evidence of anyone on the property."

"What?" Fear flashes in Jack's eyes. "Was someone here? Did someone do this to you?"

I squint my eyes against the light streaming in through the open door. "No."

"It was probably just some neighborhood teens having a bit of fun." Roger shrugs his shoulders.

"I'm not sure about that." Worry lines Jack's features.

"You don't look so good, Claire." Roger's eyes cut through me.

"She fell. Hit her head. We're going to the doctor now," Jack says.

"Good. The potential buyers will be here in about forty-five minutes." Roger scans the face of his watch and points to the dried blood on the floor. "I'll get this place cleaned up."

Jack shakes his head. "We should cancel today's showing. Claire needs to rest." He grabs my coat and helps me up off the chair.

"I'd hate to do that. These buyers seem like the real deal. It would be awful to lose out on the possible sale." Roger stuffs his hands into his pockets.

Jack looks at me, and I wave my hand in approval, not having the energy for a discussion about this.

"Just make sure they are out of here when we get back," Jack says.

"We'll be long gone by then, but I need the key," Roger says.

Jack turns to me and says, "Where did you put the key? Is it in your purse?"

I close my eyes. Where did I put the key? Blood courses through my head in painful beats as I strain to remember. In my mind, I replay the events of the night before and as the fear comes back, so does the memory.

"It's in the pocket of my robe," I say. "Upstairs."

I take a step forward, attempting to muster the strength to go up to the bedroom, when Jack interrupts me. "Nope, you stay here. I'll get it." He rests his hands on top of my shoulders and guides me back into my seat. Then he bounds up the stairs.

Roger and I wait in silence. I am annoyed he is here, angry he is showing the river house, selling the river house, even though I know it is Jack's decision to do so.

"Don't let anyone touch the painting," I say.

"No one is going to touch the painting." He sighs.

"In case someone wants to, don't let them. As soon as possible, I'm moving it out of here." Irritation bubbles out of my pores.

"Not a problem," he says.

"Damn right it's not." A sharp pain slices through my abdomen. I double over and shout for Jack. "Please hurry."

A second later, Jack comes racing down the steps, taking them two at a time. "What's wrong?"

My breath returns and I can once again sit up straight. "I don't know. I just got a horrible cramp."

"We need to go now." Jack loops his arm through mine.

"Do you have the key?" Roger hooks his thumbs through the belt loops on his pants.

I glare at him. As if the damn key and the house showing are the most important things on the agenda at the moment.

Jack fishes the key out of his pocket and tosses it to Roger.

I call out to Roger as we head out the door. "Don't forget to lock up when you leave."

***

The smell of pine fills the air as we pull into the driveway of the river house after the appointment. Gratitude beats through my heart. The doctor found nothing wrong with either me or the baby. Apparently, bleeding and cramping can be normal during a pregnancy. We even got to see the baby's heartbeat, healthy and strong. Relieved, Jack and I decide to sit out on the dock and enjoy the autumn breeze.

Jack rests a hand upon my leg. "We should come up with a name for the baby."

"I thought you weren't ready to do that."

"I wasn't. But after seeing the heartbeat, I am. I just am."

"But we don't know yet if it's a boy or a girl." A wave of nervous superstition percolates within me. I'm already so attached.

"If it's a girl, we should name her after your mother."

I don't have to say a thing. He knows I agree. With all my heart, I agree.

The afternoon passes in a lazy rush as I lean back in one of the patio chairs. Jack covers my legs with a checkered wool blanket, and we sit in silence as clouds float across the sky. He hands me a cup of hot cocoa. I blow on the steam, watching it billow against the chilled air, and wonder if it's really necessary to sell the place. Jack stands beside the grill. He covers our trout dinner with a thin layer of tinfoil and wipes his fingers on an apron draped across the railing overlooking the water.

We eat outside on the deck and watch ripples form along the river's bank. When we are done, Jack asks if I want to go out on the boat. The early fall sky still has a hint of light, despite it being after 7:00 pm. The glow from the moon casts a faint ray upon the water. Inviting. I agree to a boat ride, as long as we stay close to the shoreline.

I place one foot onto the metal lip of the boat when Jack calls out to me. "Wait. You're not going out on the river without one of these." He motions toward two orange vests dangling on a rack near the edge of the pier.

I chuckle. "I'm staying on the boat. I'm not going in the water."

"But what if the boat tips?" Jack tosses a life jacket to me.

"That's not going to happen." In all these years, neither one of us has ever fallen into the river.

"There are lots of things you can control, but nature is not one of them." Jack snaps the buckles into place and fastens the belt around my waist, leaving space open toward the bottom where my belly swells from the pregnancy.

"Do you think orange is my color?" I do a little catwalk, modeling it for him.

"I'm serious. The Wisconsin River is beautiful, but it is also dangerous. People have been sucked in by the undercurrent, never to be found." His eyes far away, he runs a palm along his five o'clock shadow.

I glance at the water churning white foam against the shoreline. He's right. The river is deceptive, attractive with a mean streak. It looks calm but is always roiling underneath.

"How about you put a life vest on too?" I toss him the other one.

He catches it and stretches his arms through the holes. "Yes, ma'am."

I twist him from side to side, making sure the vest is on tight. "Now can we go for a ride?"

Jack holds my hand as I climb into the aluminum fishing boat. It wobbles along with the motion of the water running beneath it. I spread my arms out to the sides to keep my balance as I head to the front of the boat. Once I am seated, Jack steps in and sits beside the motor. He tugs the cord. It whirs to life, and we are off.

We are only a few miles from the dock when the wind picks up, carrying with it the smell of dead fish and debris. Jack circles over toward a patch of river birch trees and shuts down the motor. We sit in silence for a few minutes as we watch the moonlight glint off the currents in the water. The boat bobs in rhythm with the waves, and we bounce along with it. Jack scoots beside me and squeezes my knee.

"You're cold." He checks the time on his watch. "Do you want to head back?"

"I can last a little longer." Since this could be one of our last times, I don't want to let the peacefulness of the moment pass. I look to where the river bends behind a row of trees and try to capture the beauty of the water in my mind. Imprint it in my memory.

Jack tilts his face up toward the stars then slaps a mosquito that's landed on his elbow. Dead.

From across the river, the lights at the house flicker, turning on and then off. "What was that?" I ask.

"Probably a power surge. It happens sometimes."

"We should go back now." I rub my hands together to warm them.

Jack slides across the edge of the boat toward the motor. As he moves, the boat sways. In an instant, I lose my balance, falling toward the crashing currents of the river. For a moment Jack doesn't move, panicked he stares at me. But before my back hits the water, Jack's firm hands grab me and pull me forward.

"This is why you wear a life vest." Jack's voice shakes as he settles back down on the lip of the boat. He sounds angry, but I know it is really fear.

With a purr and a hum, he tugs the boat to life, and we glide across the darkened water in silence.

The boat scrapes against the edge of the pier as Jack fastens a braided rope around a dampened post. Water splashes up onto the wood and squishes into my sneakers as I step onto the bouncing dock. Jack wraps a blanket over my shoulders, and we trudge across the leaf-covered lawn up to the house.

Jack slides open the patio door and flips on the light switch. A warm glow fills the room. I slip off my soggy shoes and bury my toes into the toasty fringe of the area rug. Jack calls to me from the foyer, but I can't make out what he is saying.

"I'll be there in a second." I walk into the kitchen, fill a glass with water, and head toward the front of the house.

Jack meets me halfway. His face is pale. He is trembling.

"What's wrong?"

He doesn't answer. A cool breeze blows into the house from the front door. Open.

I run into the living room, my feet sliding on the slippery wood flooring. "Please still be there." The words spill from my lips in a mantra.

The drinking glass slips from my fingers. It falls to the ground and shatters beside my feet. I look up. In the spot where "A Portrait of a Mother and Her Child" once hung, only a dusty outline, a blank wall remains. The painting is gone.

Chapter Twenty-Four

Wanda After

His eyes remain fixed on mine.

"Jack." I speak his name, a puff of breath.

I move forward, toward him. Until I see a man step out from behind. Roger.

Run.

I push and shove my body through the crowd. I don't know if someone is following me. Did people see what transpired between us? I look behind me but don't see anyone. I turn left onto Monroe Street and head East toward Michigan Avenue. I duck into a coffee shop, slide onto a stool in the back and hide. No one bothers me. No one even looks at me, their faces buried in their lattes or their laptops. I stare at the wrought-iron clock on the wall. A half hour goes by. Then an hour. My shoulders relax. Was it all in my mind? Did Jack even notice me?

I am about to leave when a shadow stretches across the table in front of me. A stranger, wearing a black polo shirt with a security logo embroidered in white stitches on the sleeve, leans across the table.

"Come with me." He grabs my arm.

"Leave me alone." I try to wriggle free.

He tightens his grip.

"I didn't do anything. Let me go or I'll scream." I take a deep breath, preparing for it.

"Mr. Stanbrick would like to speak with you."

I exhale. "He does?"

"Yes." He releases my arm and motions for me to walk in front of him.

My stomach, a ball of yarn, twists into a knot as we head north up Michigan Avenue to Washington Street. I follow the security guard down a flight of concrete steps to the Lower Wacker entrance of an unfamiliar building. He pushes open a glass door and the smell of garlic bread swirls through the air.

"She's here to meet with Mr. Stanbrick." The security guard points to a man in the back booth of the restaurant.

Only the back of his head is visible from where we stand, but it is enough. Enough for me to know it is Jack. The hostess, a tiny wisp of a woman in a tight leather skirt and red high heels, leads me to his table. "Your guest is here, Mr. Stanbrick."

Hesitant, I peer around the side of the booth. My hair falls in front of my face.

"Have a seat." He motions to the other side of the booth.

I don't even bother to move my hair from my face. I just slide onto the seat across from him.

His voice comes out as a shout, angry and insulted by my presence. "First I get an email from someone pretending to be Claire and now you show up at my hearing. Is this some kind of scheme to get money out of me? Well, I'm not going to be threatened into handing out money. You can forget that."

I squeeze my fingers together to stop them from trembling. He doesn't recognize me. He feels threatened by me.

"You're not the first person to try and insert themselves into this situation. Although most people are just looking to get their hands on the reward money, not pretending to actually be Claire." He gets up from the table.

"Wait." I scramble out of the booth, my hair falling away from my face.

He freezes. Like a deer blinded by headlights. He doesn't budge. He just stands there blinking until the hostess comes up behind him and asks if everything is all right. Jack's lips do not move. He stares at me. Like he's seen a ghost.

His eyes fixed on me he slides back into the booth. I follow suit. He leans toward me, takes my hand, and says one word. "Claire?"

Anxiety courses through me. Is this really happening? It's in his eyes, the urgency, the desire to be close to me. Jack recognizes me. Jack sees me. This is real. It has to be.

A wave of hesitancy washes across his features, as if he is questioning something, as if suddenly he is unsure of how to proceed. "I'm sorry about the last time I saw you."

I don't know what he is talking about.

"The argument we had." He pulls his hands from mine.

I shrug my shoulders. Confused.

"After your call with Nate?"

I purse my lips. "Who?"

"It was the last time I saw you. Do you remember the last time I saw you?"

Embarrassed. I shake my head. "No."

He doesn't speak.

"It's okay," I say. "Whatever we argued about, it's not important now." I run my fingers along cracks in the distressed wood of the table.

Relief washes over his features. "You're right, it's not important anymore. Do you know what this means?"

"What?"

"The fact that you are here sitting across from me now, talking to me?" His features glow in the light of the candle in the center of the table.

"That we can be together again?" I ask.

"It proves I am innocent. I took an Alford plea. Did you know that?"

"Yes."

"I had to plead guilty." His hands clutch the edges of the table. "Guilty of hurting you."

His eyes are filled with such sadness. I have to look away for a moment.

"Sure, I got to assert my innocence. But no one believes that. Everyone just hears the word guilty. Meaning, I did it. But I didn't. I would never hurt you."

"I know." The words come out with pure confidence. This is what I've been trying to tell people the whole time.

"Ever since news of the plea deal got out, investors have been pulling accounts from Stanbrick Financial. They don't want to invest if a convict is back in charge."

The reply email from Roger pulses in my mind. "Isn't Roger Lindsey the CEO now?"

Jack nudges a lone breadcrumb along the tabletop. "Yes, and he's been resisting giving up the title, even now that I'm out. But you being here proves I am innocent. There's no reason for me not to run the ship."

My face falls. "I see. This is all about business." I grab my purse and get up.

"No. You didn't let me finish. The best part, the very best part is we can finally be together again."

My fist balled up against my thigh, I let his words sink in.

"It has been awful living with the burden of people thinking I killed you, thinking I killed the person I love the most."

The person he *loves* the most. Present tense.

A waitress comes over, takes our order, and places a basket of warm garlic bread on the table. My heart feels as warm and buttery as the rolls.

Jack offers the basket to me first. I reach in, the bread hot against my fingertips.

"It'll be like when we first started. Just you and me, fancy meals out, long evening walks." He lists the names of a bunch of places.

I have never heard of any of them.

He gazes dreamily over my shoulder as he rattles them off in smooth succession.

All I can do is stare at him. I have nothing to contribute to these memories of his. They are all just generic words and places.

"Remember?" He raises his eyebrows.

I shake my head. "No."

"What do you remember?"

"Not much." I strain to think of something, anything, I can tell him about us before the accident.

"Do you remember what happened the day you disappeared?"

An image of the person with a gun assaults my vision. I shake the thought away. "No."

"How you got that scar?" His voice sympathetic as he points to the left side of my face.

I cover it with my palm.

He peels my fingers away. "You don't need to hide. You are stunning. You're my beautiful Claire."

I inhale his words. They fill me and expand my heart like warm air pumped into a balloon. I feel light and happy, as if I could sail, as if I could fly. I squeeze my eyes shut and repeat the words over and over in my head. Jack thinks I'm beautiful, so it must be true. Jack believes I'm Claire, so that must be true too.

"I like the way you're wearing your hair now. It's a little darker than it used to be, more raspberry colored."

I tug at the ends, smoothing the strands down past my chin. I blush.

"I've missed you. More than you can imagine." His voice cracks, overcome with emotion.

"I've missed you too."

He stares at me, his eyes wide and hopeful. And I feel as if I remember that look. As if I remember the crinkle of crow's feet stretching out at the corners of his eyes when he laughs, and the love dancing along his irises.

"Once I get settled back at work and can take a break, you and I are going to go on a long vacation. Maybe back to Europe. We can relive our visit to the Louvre." He looks toward the ceiling, dreaming.

Jack's words, "you and I," snag in my ear. I think of Astrid. I should blurt it out, shout it from the rooftops, "Jack, you're a father." But I'm worried if I mention her, he'll think I'm in it for the money, someone trying to scam him into paying for some alleged child of his.

"What's wrong? You didn't like our trip to the Louvre?"

"It's not that. I don't remember any of it. Memory problems." I point to my temple.

"Right. Sorry." His smile is so bright I think his face might crack. "I can't believe I'm laughing. It's been so long. You do this to me. You're the only one who makes me happy."

I blink away some of the caked-on mascara coating my lashes, as my eyes water with joy. "Or we could go to the river house."

His expression turns serious. "You want to go to the river house?"

"I guess."

"Why would you want to go there?" His tone is uncertain, concerned.

Caught off balance, I stumble to regain my composure. "I don't know."

"Do you remember something about the river house?" He asks.

I scan my memories, searching for some detail to share that would further prove I am Claire. But there is nothing. "No, I've seen pictures of it in magazines and on the news. I thought it was a place we liked to go."

"It was. Once. But speaking of memories, I have bad ones of that place. That's where they found the blood and the bullet casings. That's where this nightmare of losing you, of being without you, of being accused of hurting you, began for me."

I hadn't thought of it that way.

"You always did love that place. Maybe one day we can go there again. We did have good times at the river house before all of this. There are good memories there, too."

I exhale. "And we can make new ones."

"Yes. We can start fresh and make new memories." He wipes his forehead.

The waitress places two steaming plates of pasta with pink vodka sauce on the table. A panic comes over me.

"What's wrong?"

I thumb through the menu looking for the price of the dish. $30. I can't believe I didn't think about it. "I need to send mine back."

"Why? You love rigatoni with vodka sauce." He spoons some onto my fork. The smell of the tart dish increases my nervousness.

"I can't afford it."

"Of course you can. You are my wife. What's mine is yours and what's yours is mine, remember?"

"I guess I forgot that too." A flutter of guilt spirals through me. I need to tell him about Astrid. He deserves to know. "Jack?"

He balances his fork on the edge of his plate. "Really, it's my treat. Please, enjoy your meal. I want you to."

"It's not the food." I struggle to find the right words.

He reaches for my hand. "What is it?"

"I have a daughter." As soon as the words slip off my tongue, I want to suck them back in.

Jack stares at me, his features frozen as he processes what he's heard. "You mean the baby survived too?" His words come out in a whisper.

"Yes. She did." My heart warms as I think of Astrid. Her bright eyes and the way her dimples appear when she smiles.

"Tell me everything about her. I want to know everything. How old is she?"

"She's five."

He nods. "The timeline matches up."

"I know. I was pregnant at the time of my accident."

"Yes. Do you have a picture?"

I show him the background photo on my cell phone, a picture of Astrid standing beside Penelope's garden, her hair in pigtails.

"She's so beautiful." He traces the outline of her face. "What's her name?"

"Astrid." Just saying it makes me miss her, even though it's only been a few hours since I last saw her.

Jack's eyes shine with a knowing look. "And what made you decide to name her Astrid?"

"I don't know. It just felt right. Like that was what her name was always meant to be."

"So you don't know?"

I shake my head.

"Astrid was your mother's name."

My breath catches in my chest.

"But it's really not a secret. She signed it on every painting, her full name."

I think back to the photo of the painting, "A Portrait of a Mother and Her Child," from the magazine article. It's probably right there in the picture.

"It's funny," Jack lifts a forkful of pasta into his mouth. "She preferred to go by her middle name, Florence."

"Florence." I roll the name over my tongue and strain for a memory to surface, for any of this to ring a bell.

"Florence said she liked it better because it was the name of a town in Italy. A classy name, she used to say."

"I'm partial to Astrid." I wipe a streak of condensation from the side of my water glass.

"You always were. And you always let her and everyone else know it." He chuckles.

A song comes on the jukebox. Jack extends his hand to me. "Want to dance?"

Before I know it, I am in his embrace, our feet moving in time to the rhythm of the ballad. Our fingers interlaced, Jack places our hands over his heart. And it's as if it beats in time with mine, a unique rhythm. A song for Jack and me. I rest my head against his chest and close my eyes. As I do, I imagine myself as a bride, dressed in white, a big puffy veil on my head. Cream-colored roses and lavender lilac centerpieces fill a ballroom. I don't know if the memory is real. But in this moment, this moment that I never want to end, I'm not sure I care.

The sound of flashbulbs snapping fills the air, their brightness lighting up the darkened restaurant. Jack and I turn toward the cameras, and I'm certain my life is about to change.

Chapter Twenty-Five

Claire Before

I'm on hold with the Columbia County police department, listening to a recitation of County fun facts play on repeat. After what feels like an eternity, there's a click and a male voice says, "Officer Wyatt here."

"Officer, this is Claire Stanbrick. A very important, treasured painting was stolen from our home last weekend and I was wondering if you have any leads."

"From the Stanbrick residence, right?"

"Yes, 9390 Riverside Drive. Do you have any information?"

"Not yet. We have no witnesses. Plus, there were no signs of breaking and entering."

"But you're investigating, right?"

"Yes, ma'am. But honestly, I wouldn't get your hopes up. Often in cases of property theft, we never find the perpetrator or the missing object."

I sigh into the phone.

"We're going to keep looking. But remember, it's only property, ma'am. People have lost bigger things."

I wrap my arms around my abdomen, remembering the miscarriage. My voice squeaks out in a whisper. "I know."

"We'll call you if we hear anything."

Jack stands in the doorway to my office. He walks over and kisses me. His lips soft, he tastes like toothpaste and doughnuts and home.

"Everything is going to be all right."

I shake my head. Doubtful.

"They're going to find the painting. It's gigantic. Whoever took it is going to have one hell of a time hiding it."

That's true.

"And they can't sell it, because they'll most likely get caught."

Also true.

Roger walks into my office. He doesn't bother to knock. "I heard about the painting. I'm so sorry."

I can't even look at him. I can't shake the idea that if he hadn't scheduled a showing, called attention to the river house, none of this would have happened.

Roger leans against the doorframe. "While you guys wait for the police to catch the person who did this, you need to claim it on your insurance policy."

I wince. "No."

"You're not thinking clearly. There's no reason not to file a claim," Roger says.

"Isn't it too soon for that?" Jack asks. "Plus, they're going to find it. So then what? We'd have to return all the money."

"Or risk committing insurance fraud," I chime in.

Roger faces Jack. "You're entitled to that money."

"It would actually be Claire's money, not mine." Jack corrects him. "If she's not ready to file, then we aren't going to do it."

"I have no stake in it. I'm just suggesting what the best course of action is for you guys. But I'll do what you want." Roger rubs his temple.

"Perfect. Case closed." I look at Jack. "Let's get some lunch. The baby's hungry and kicking."

"We've got a meeting in thirty. Unless you want me to handle it myself," Roger says.

"No, no." Jack turns toward me. "Rain check?"

"Always."

***

The wind stings my face as I step out of the revolving door. I pull my maternity coat shut, wrap my paisley scarf around my neck, and turn left on Washington Street toward the sandwich shop. A cacophony of bells chime as I tug open the door. The restaurant smells of freshly baked bread. I inhale and peruse the menu. I decide to go for the tuna fish and rationalize that, even though the fish contains some mercury, it's not enough to harm the baby. Cold cuts, on the other hand, can harbor listeria. This pregnancy business is trickier than I thought it would be.

I sit on a stool beside the counter. The waxy paper of the sandwich crinkles as I unwrap it. I am about to take a bite when someone comes up behind me.

"Anyone sitting here?"

A smile washes from my face. Wanda.

"No, but I was about to leave."

She looks at my freshly made sandwich. "You haven't taken a single bite yet." Her eyes twitch and I notice she is wearing a paisley scarf, the same as mine.

"I know, but I just remembered I have a call in ten minutes." I rewrap the sandwich. "I'll eat at my desk. It's fine."

An elderly woman in line looks at us and grins. I give her a half-smile, which she takes as an invitation.

"You girls are so lucky." The woman dots her eyes with an embroidered handkerchief. "I always wanted a sister."

"We're not sisters," I say.

"Really? I thought you were twins or at least cousins."

I scowl. Wanda beams.

"It's like looking in the mirror, Claire." Wanda giggles.

I turn toward the door.

"Before you go, I need you to sign something." Wanda thrusts a manila folder on top of my re-wrapped sandwich. Only the bottom line of the document is visible, the signature line.

"What's this?" I tug at the folder, trying to flip through the pages. But she holds it shut with her thumb and forefinger.

"It's the form to re-order office supplies. Roger asked me to have you sign it."

I nudge her hand off the folder, flip it open, and scan the document. It appears to be what she says it is, an office-supply order form. What I don't understand is why Roger would need me to sign it. He has the authority to place orders of this kind.

Wanda drops a pen on the counter in front of me. "Are you sure you don't want to stay for lunch?"

"I can't." Selling that I am in a rush, I scribble my name on the bottom line, grab my lunch, and leave. The bells on the glass ring as the door closes behind me.

***

I finish eating at my desk while poring over a deck of bar charts for a client report when I feel the baby kick. One kick. Two kicks. Then another, and another. I sip my iced tea and rub my hand across my belly. A little bulge swims across my abdomen, doing the backstroke or the butterfly. I squirm from the force of another kick and my tea spills over the top of my shirt, dripping down the sides. Shoot. Now there's a smudge of brown tea splattered across the front of my shirt.

I head to the women's bathroom, hoping if I squeeze some soap on it fast enough, I can remove the stain. I open the door and catch a glimpse of Wanda posing in front of the mirror, admiring her pregnant belly, while talking to herself.

"Mrs. Jack Stanbrick," she says and extends her hand toward her reflection.

Confused, I scurry over to the sink and scrub at the stain. When I look up, her reflection in the mirror stares back at me. Twisted and smiling.

I don't bother to dry my shirt. I just leave and keep going, down the hall, stopping only briefly in my office for my purse. I march through the reception area, and desperate for some fresh air, out the door. A chilly wind slices through me, the wetness of my shirt multiplying the sting of the cold. A large, folded sign highlights a 20% off sale on some already marked-down items. I've been to this store before. Located in the Ashton Hotel, it's fancy although most of the clothing is not my style. But with goose bumps prickling my skin and having no interest in wearing this shirt for the rest of the day, I decide to give it a try.

A store clerk with a birthmark on her chin greets me. "We don't sell maternity items here."

I rub my arms to warm them. "Do you have an extra-large top that might fit?"

"Let me see." She rifles through a cluster of hangers and hands me an apple-green and gray cashmere sweater. She says it will compliment my eye color. In the changing room, I slip off my wet shirt and shimmy into the top. The fabric stretches across my belly, the price tag dangling at my side. $800. For one sweater? But I am cold, and I need to get back to work.

With my soggy old shirt draped over my arm, I head to the cashier to purchase the new sweater. I'm going to wear it out of the store.

I pull off the price tag and place my credit card on the counter. The store clerk swipes it.

"Denied." She shoots me a questioning glancc.

"That can't be right." I lean across to get a better look.

"I'll try again." Her manicured fingers push the plastic through the machine. "Sorry."

Figuring there must be something wrong with that card, I slide a different card across the counter.

"This one is also being denied."

"What?" I pull a third card out, one I rarely use, and hand it to her. "This one will work."

She tries again, her face sour. "It says you've exceeded your credit limit. It won't go through."

I open my wallet to see how much cash I have inside. Damn it. I've got some, but not $800.

"Would you like me to put the sweater on hold for you? You can come back and pick it up once you've resolved your credit card situation."

"No. Do you take checks?" I flip open my checkbook, scribble out a check, and paste it on the counter.

The salesclerk peers over the rims of her glasses. Skeptical. "This isn't going to bounce, is it?'

And for the first time in my life, I'm not sure.

***

My emotions ping-pong from one extreme to another as I walk back to my office. At one moment I am furious, eager to call the bank and scold them over the embarrassment they caused me. At another, I am concerned. Has someone hacked into my account? I've heard the stories, watched the late-night infomercials about identity theft. Has someone hijacked my identity? Maxed out my credit cards? Drained my accounts? I pick up the pace. I need to talk to Jack.

When I arrive at Jack's office, the door is closed, but the window blinds are open. Inside, Jack paces back and forth talking to Roger. Although he is not shouting, he is angry. I can tell. I am angry too. He sees me, and waves for me to enter.

"Aren't you a sight for sore eyes?" He wraps his arms around me, and I allow myself to sink into his embrace. Maybe everything will be okay.

"What's going on?" I ask.

It is Roger who answers. "A client pulled their account."

"Why?" I ask.

"They didn't trust their returns," Jack says.

"But you've been sending out detailed statements, right?" I stuff my hands into my pockets.

"We have. That's why I don't understand it," Jack says, his features clouded and concerned.

"Don't panic," Roger says. "It's just one client. Clients often bounce around."

"Yes, but the Feds are predicting a downturn in the market and that could lead more clients to pull out," Jack says.

"Let's cross that bridge if we have to. For now, it's the one client and it had nothing to do with market trends."

This seems to satisfy Jack. So I jump in. "I have some more wonderful news."

Jack covers his face. "No. What?"

"We have a problem with our credit cards. They're maxed out." I slap his desk.

Jack's shoulders relax. "That's no big deal. We can pay them off."

"But how did the balances get so high?"

"From all of the shopping for the baby we've been doing: dressers, changing tables, cribs?"

"No. Those charges were on the store cards, and I already paid them off."

"It's probably a mistake," Roger says.

I shoot him a 'mind your own business' look. "I'm going to call the credit card company."

"Good. They'll get to the bottom of it." Jack kisses my forehead and I feel reassured but unsatisfied.

Roger interrupts. "I'm glad you came in because I wanted to discuss something with you."

"What?" I place my hands on my hips, impatient and eager to get going.

"You might receive a call from the insurance company."

"Why?" Anger snakes through my veins.

"I raised the topic with Jack about a possible statute of limitations for filing the theft of the painting. I called the company to get information."

I scowl. "I said I wasn't ready to do that. Jack, did you know about this?"

"No. You should have checked with me first." Jack scolds Roger. It's embarrassing to watch.

"Now that you've called, what information did you get?" I ask.

"You have thirty days to file. And that's from the day of the incident."

"That's not very long." I glance at the calendar on Jack's desk.

"You need to decide soon if you don't want to miss the allowed time period."

"I need to think about it a little longer." I run my palm across my forehead.

"Take all the time you'd like." Jack rests his hand on my shoulder.

"I'm not trying to pressure you. But I want to make sure you don't miss out on something you're entitled to," Roger says.

Jack pats Roger on the back.

But as he walks out of Jack's office, I can't help but wonder why Roger cares so much. What's in it for him?

***

Back at my office, I can't stop questioning whether we should file an insurance claim for the painting, given the tight timeline. The best way to make any decision is with information, so I decide to give the company a call myself. To see what my options are.

I dial our insurance carrier's toll-free number. After following the instructions of an automated receptionist, I am finally connected with a human being. A young man with a fresh, enthusiastic voice picks up the line.

I give him my account number, and he asks, "How can I help you today, Ms. Stanbrick?"

"I'm inquiring about the statute of limitations for filing an insurance claim on a painting."

He clicks on the keyboard.

"A stolen painting," I say. "But you have to understand, that painting is precious to me. Priceless. I don't know why I don't want to file the claim. Maybe I can't accept it's really gone."

"I get it. I talk to people all the time who have lost irreplaceable items." The calm in his voice comforts me and I think I might have a chance to get what I want. And what I want is more time.

"So, can I get an extension on the time limit for filing the claim?" I pace around my desk.

"That's not a problem, ma'am. You can have all the time you want."

I want to jump through the phone line and hug him. "Thank you. How did I get so lucky?"

"It's not luck. There is no statute of limitations for filing a property claim of this nature with our insurance company. Never was."

My blood bubbles. "I don't understand. I was told by a colleague I only had thirty days."

"He must have been mistaken, ma'am." After a few moments of silence on my end of the phone, he says, "Can I help you with anything else?"

I am about to hang up when I think of something. "You still there?"

"Yes."

I pause, not sure if I want the answer to the question pecking at me. "Aside from this call, when was the last time someone called regarding the theft of my painting?"

His words spin through the phone line and confirm my doubts. "There was no last time. You're the first."

I hang up the phone. Did Roger lie to us, or did the agent have incorrect information? If he did lie, why would he do that?

I pull my credit card out of my wallet. On the back of the card is a number to call in case of problems with the card. Before calling, I log into our online account. I want to see exactly what the charges were that jacked up our credit card bill. A colorful circle spins on my screen retrieving my information. I squint at the data that fills in across the monitor. The debt is huge. The max credit limit exceeded. But when I scroll down, there are very few actual charges, just the occasional charge to a restaurant or grocery store. I click on a tab at the top of the screen where it says, "cash advances." And that is where I see it, withdrawal after withdrawal against the card. Thousands and thousands of dollars borrowed as credit against the account.

Clearly whoever hacked into our account is in serious need of cash. Alarm bells blare in my mind. Have our bank accounts been compromised as well? My fingers shaking, I dial the number on the back of the card and ask to be connected to the manager at our local branch.

A man with a hoarse voice picks up. “How can I help you?”

“There has been some unauthorized activity on my credit card and I’m concerned about the other accounts I have at your bank.”

“I’m sorry to hear that. Let me get some information from you and pull up your account.”

I answer every security question, all while feeling as if these questions didn’t do much to protect me if someone was able to hack into my account.

“There’s nothing to worry about here,” he says. “It can take a few days for the computer to fully update. The debt on this account is back to zero.”

“It is?”

“That’s good news, Mrs. Stanbrick.”

“I don’t get it. It looks like someone has been borrowing money against my credit card without my authorization.”

“The amount of withdrawals against the card did raise some red flags at the bank, but those have now been resolved.”

“And exactly how were they resolved?” I strum my fingernails along the wood of my desk.

He chuckles and I’m not sure what’s so funny. “You don’t remember coming into the bank about an hour ago?”

“I wasn’t at the bank today.” My knuckles turn white as I squeeze the handset.

“I’m sorry? You were here earlier. You took money out of your trust to pay off the credit card debt.”

“No. There must be some mistake. I didn’t take any money out of my trust. I never touch the inheritance from my mother.”

“You’ve been doing so quite frequently recently.”

"Did you actually see me?"

"Of course. I'm the manager here. I handle all the large transactions. We had a lovely conversation about when your baby is due. Don't you remember?"

It's not that I don't remember. It never happened. My pulse races, my face hot. "How much money did I take out?"

"Today, $500,000."

My chest tightens around my rib cage.

"Hello? Are you all right?"

"No." My heartbeat accelerates within my chest.

"You seemed fine an hour ago. I have the signed paperwork right here."

"Does the bank have any footage of me coming in today?"

"We have security footage filming at all times, but we can't release it to you unless there's a current investigation or if you have a warrant."

I hang up with more questions than before. Things are even less clear. But one thing is certain: I have got to get some answers.

Chapter Twenty-Six

Wanda After

That evening, I lie in bed and run my finger along the circular scar etched into my chest, just beneath my collarbone. Not far from my heart. I think about Jack. The feel of his breath against my neck as we danced in the restaurant, the press of his palm upon the small of my back as we swayed, the kindness in his voice as he hummed along to the music. Not to mention the gentle way he shielded my face from the onslaught of photographers as he guided me out the restaurant's back door and into a waiting car. A limo that brought me back here. I feel found.

Car headlights from the street below toss shadows across the ceiling. I want to share everything with Jack. Maybe he can help me figure out what really happened to me. My eyelids heavy, I strain to remember something, anything, about the day of the accident. But all I can conjure is the icy sting of the Wisconsin River, my throat choking on blood and water, fear flashing before my eyes. No matter how hard I try, I can't retrieve any memory of my life before that moment.

The sound of tires rolling to a stop along the pavement in front of my house jolts me to attention. Someone's outside.

A car door shuts. I don't dare turn on the light, but instead creep across the carpet toward the window and peek through the opening. A man exits the car, his legs thick, his torso rotund. A silver chain dangles from his belt. He weaves the chain between his fingers. There is a key on the end. He is headed toward the door.

I race past Astrid's room, hear the gentle pulse of her breath, and reassure myself she is okay. For now. I will kill that man if he goes near her.

I sneak down the stairs, ducking to avoid the window, and grab a ceramic vase off an end table. My back pressed against the wall I wait. But there's nothing. No scratching of the key in the lock. Just silence. I peer out the window, trying to see his face. But it is too dark out. The man rifles through my mailbox, tossing fliers and envelopes onto the lawn. What is he looking for? He tears open an envelope and shakes his head. Angry.

"Mama?" Astrid calls from the top of the stairs, barefooted in her strawberry-colored nightgown.

"Everything's okay, sweetie. Go back to bed."

"I'm thirsty." She scratches at her ankle.

"I'll bring up some water in a minute. Go to your room and close the door."

She pads away, down the hall to her bedroom, complaining. I turn back toward the door to see where the man is, to see if he has left. No one is there. I rest the vase on the floor beside my feet, take a deep breath, and stand up. Only to see a face staring at me through the window.

I gasp and flip on the outside light. If this guy is going to attack me in the middle of the night, I'm going to get a good look at him first. I am about to dial 911 when I recognize the face, the sunken eyes, the ruddy cheeks. Fucking Carl.

He holds the key up to the window, taunting me. "You might as well open the door. I've got a key."

"Go away."

"No can do." He laughs, his teeth crooked and yellow from smoking tobacco. He sticks the key in the lock.

I pick up the vase. "Take one more step and I swear, I'll smash you."

He chuckles as the doorknob turns. He pushes the door open and steps into the entryway.

"Don't come any further." I hold the vase over my head, fear coursing through my veins.

"Just give me the money, Wanda, and I'll be on my way." He inches toward me.

"What money?"

"The money you get from your cleaning lady job." He moves his arms around swaying, as if he were dusting the doorframe.

"I got fired."

"What the hell did you do now?" He slurs his words. Drunk or high, I can't tell.

"I don't have any money."

He pushes me aside and marches into the living room. "It's got to be here somewhere." He tugs open the drawers of the armoire and starts pulling out items. Old napkins and tablecloths scatter onto the floor.

"Stop it. There's nothing there." I grab onto his arms, and he shoves me onto the couch. At the top of the stairs, Astrid cowers, clutching her dolly. I motion for her to go back to her room. *Now*. She clambers to her feet and does as she is told.

I turn back toward Carl. His patience dissipated, he has resorted to tugging entire drawers out of the armoire and dumping out the contents. He heaves an empty drawer against the wall, where it splinters and cracks.

He charges at me and leans in close, pressing his nose against mine. "Where are the fucking statements?"

"I don't know what you're talking about."

"From the account at that convict's company. Where you invested all my workers' compensation benefits." Drunken spittle sprays my face.

"I did?"

"Don't play dumb with me. You can't be blamed for anything, right? Because you can't remember anything from before the accident."

"I wish I could forget you."

"I can't get my money out. When I call, they give me the runaround. But I'm going to get it or you're going to pay."

"I have nothing to give you."

He directs his attention toward the stairs. "Hey, where's that precious little girl of mine?"

"Leave her out of this." *She's not his. She can't be his.*

"I want to see her."

"No. She's sleeping."

He cranes his neck and looks upward toward Astrid's room. "Nah, she's awake. Her lights are on."

"She sleeps with her lights on these days. To keep crazy people away."

He tilts his head back and laughs. "So you've noticed too."

"Noticed what?"

"I'm not the only one who's been watching you, sweetheart."

"What the hell are you talking about? Who's been watching me?"

"Give me my money." He squeezes my wrist so tight I think it might snap.

"I don't have any money." I struggle to break free.

"Come on, baby. Why're you so worked up? We can chit-chat for a while." He tips his head from side to side as he says the words, *chit chat.* "I'll tell you all about what I've heard."

"No." I kick him in the shin, and he releases his grip. I lunge toward the coffee table and grab my cell phone.

"Who do you think you're going to call? The police?"

My finger hovers over the keypad. Threatening.

He chuckles. "From what I hear, the police have already been talking to you. Seems like you've been parading around saying you're someone you're not, someone who already got themselves murdered. You better be careful or you'll be 'swimming with the fishes.'"

His reference to water makes me shudder.

"You sure don't seem like the Wanda I used to know. You used to be wild, a real good time." He runs his fingers through his hair and gyrates his hips before stumbling and steadying himself against the chair.

I twist up my face. Disgusting.

He reaches for his back pocket and I duck, expecting a gun. Instead, he pulls out a cell phone and dials a number. I try to make out the digits, but he does it too fast.

"Yeah, I'm here," he says into the phone. "Bitch says there's no money. No statements in the mailbox either."

Silencc.

"All right. I'll meet you in twenty."

Silence.

"Oh, don't you worry. We'll find a way." He stares right at me as he hangs up the phone. "You're going to pay." He pulls open the door and points at me. "I'll be watching you, and I'm not the only one."

I shout at his back as he steps outside. "Who else is watching me?"

He walks toward his car, shaking his head, kicking up patches of lawn as he goes, and sings, "No money, no answers."

A gust of wind presses through the door's opening and all I can think is I better find out who I am and fast. Before someone tries to kill me. A chill curls up my spine. Again.

Carl's taillights turn the corner away from the house. As soon as he is out of sight, I slump down against the front door, my bare feet naked against the cold wood. I place my head between my knees and turn Carl's words over in my mind. He's been watching me. But not just him, others have been watching me too. I think about the flashbulbs at the restaurant, the photographs that are going to be splattered all over the papers by morning. What if someone followed the limo that drove me home? I stand up, flip the lock on the front door, and fasten the chain.

"Is he gone?"

I jump. It's Astrid. I pull her toward me and squeeze her tight. She smells like watermelon shampoo and sleep.

"Let me get you that water."

Astrid takes a few small sips before I tuck her back into bed.

Exhausted, but too shaken to sleep, I pace across the living room. The floor is covered in napkins, clothing, and old papers and I am pissed that Carl always makes a mess for me to clean up. I speed-walk across the piles when my foot catches on something sharp. Ouch.

A name tag sticks out of the bottom of my foot, the metal pin pressed into my skin. I tug it out and hold the badge between my palms.

The tag is yellowed at the edges, the plastic faded. The words, "Wanda Dellas Cocktail Waitress'" are written big in the center. The words, "Ashton Hotel" are printed in the upper right corner just above the cursive slogan, "Chicago's finest hotel and spa since 1929."

I don't think much of it. So what if I worked as a cocktail waitress? It's probably another dead end. My foot throbs. Stupid pin. I toss it across the room. But worried Astrid might step on it, I go look for it. I find it resting on top of a wad of thick folded paper, a brochure of some kind. I peel open the card stock, the layers cemented together from humidity and time. Although some pages are torn, I can still make out the weathered imprint of a pair of colorful rolling die and a set of fanning blackjack cards. The words, "Claire Stanbrick Presents: A Casino Night Auction" swirl beneath them. An image of the photograph I found in the laundry room flashes before me. The Ashton Hotel. It feels important. And I need to find out why.

***

Still clutching the name tag, I know exactly what's on the agenda for the day. The Ashton Hotel. I need to find out if I was working there the night of the auction. From the date on the photo I found in the laundry room, it took place before I started working as a temp at Stanbrick Marketing Group. If that's true, how did I go from working at the Ashton Hotel to working at Stanbrick Marketing Group? Did something happen at that event? Maybe someone from the hotel knows something. Maybe what they know will point to who's been watching me. I shiver.

The air is crisp, a cool ripe spring morning. Dew glistens on the thin strip of grass lining the sidewalk beside the bus stop. I help Astrid climb the steps onto the bus and offer her the only available seat. I hold onto the slippery metal post as the bus careens along the city streets. We arrive at LaSalle Street, three blocks north of the Ashton Hotel. Tired from the events of the night before, Astrid lopes beside me for the final block, repeatedly asking how much further.

But her eyes widen as we spin through the automated revolving door and step into the lobby of the Ashton Hotel. The Carrara marble tile shines with fresh polish. Astrid squeezes my hand, her Mary Janes slipping a bit as we walk. I survey the crystal chandeliers suspended from the high ceilings, but none of it triggers my memory. We take our place in line behind a family checking in for a visit, a vacation of sight-seeing, architectural tours, and pizza eating.

When it is finally my turn to approach the desk, I hesitate, suddenly flustered and embarrassed. Unsure.

"Can we stay here, Mama?" Astrid asks, her eyes hopeful.

"Do you have a reservation?" A woman with long curls hair sprayed into place stands behind the counter. The floral scent of her perfume makes me nauseated.

I don't answer.

She straightens her striped silk scarf and asks again, "What name is the reservation under?"

"I didn't book a room. I have a question."

She runs her tongue across her front teeth. "Okay?"

"I might have worked here once." I roll my sleeves up and down. Nervous.

"Is that your question? Whether you worked here?"

I fumble through my purse. "See, I have this." I hold up the name tag.

She leans across the desk. "I don't know anything about that. I've only been working here a few weeks."

"Do you think there might be some information on your computer about that night?" I point to the words, *Charity Auction*. "Any details at all would be helpful."

She glances over my shoulder at the line of guests forming behind me, getting longer by the minute. "I'm sorry. I don't have the authority to do that. If you aren't interested in booking a room, you'll have to step aside."

"But—"

Her face turns stern. "If you don't move, I'm going to have to call security."

I do *not* want her to do that. "Is there someone else I can talk to?"

She frowns and slides through a doorway behind the counter. When she returns a woman with a tidy gray bob is standing beside her. She whispers something in her ear. I scan her lapel for a badge, worried she might be a security officer, but none is there. The women laugh as the woman with the bob waves me over to the side of the counter.

"I'm the manager. You had some questions?"

"Is there a way to see if I once worked at this hotel?" I place the name tag and brochure on the lacquered counter.

She strums her manicured nails against the surface for a moment and picks up the name badge. "I don't recognize the name, 'Wanda Dellas.'" She thumbs through the brochure. "But I have seen this before. I wasn't the manager on call that evening, but it was a big event. Actually, I think we used an outside staffing agency to fill the gap on our wait staff."

"Do you know which agency you used?"

"No. Sorry."

I purse my lips. Another dead end.

"We stopped using temp agencies after that night."

Astrid taps her shoe against the base of the desk, making a scuff mark. I bend down and wipe it with my sleeve as I mouth the words, "Stop it," to her.

I look back up at the manager. "Why did you stop using temp agencies?"

"Like I said, I wasn't there that night, but I did hear there was an incident."

"An incident? What kind of incident?"

"If you were there, you'd probably remember." She starts to walk away.

"Wait, please tell me." I grab her sleeve.

She looks at my fingers grasping her blouse.

"Sorry." I let go and smooth out the wrinkles. "Please."

"I guess it's no secret. One of the wait staff was found—" She covers Astrid's ears with her hands. "—Fooling around with one of the event's guests."

"Really?" I peel her fingers off of Astrid, who now gives the desk a firm kick. "Do you know who it was?"

"No."

My shoulders slouch.

“But there were rumors the gentleman was the husband of the sponsor of the event.” She lifts the brochure and points. “Stanbrick. The guy who’s in the news these days.”

“Jack Stanbrick?”

She sees the distress in my eyes and places a hand on my arm. “But when the waitress was being reprimanded, a different man came forward, claiming he was the one carrying on with the staff member. He apologized for ‘taking it too far’ with the waitress. I heard Claire Stanbrick was furious at that man.”

“Do you know who he was?”

She shakes her head. “Gosh, I haven’t thought about this in years. Plus, we really tried to tamp down any discussion of it. We have a reputation to protect. We’re not that type of establishment, you know.”

“Of course not.” I try to hide my disappointment.

I grab Astrid’s hand and am about to leave when the manager calls out. “A woman’s name.”

I stop. “What?”

“The man who confessed had a last name that’s often a female first name.”

Roger Lindsey?

Chapter Twenty-Seven

Claire Before

The telephone rings as soon as I hang up with the bank manager. Assuming I must not have hung the phone up properly, I simply lift and replace. A moment later, it rings again. This time I answer.

"Did you hang up on me?"

I recognize the voice instantly. "Nate? I'm so sorry. I'm having trouble with my phone today."

"Well, there is some other trouble I need to discuss with you."

My stomach cinches into a knot. "It's not the third quarter report, is it? I triple-checked the numbers before they went out."

"It's not regarding the report."

I press the receiver hard against my ear. "What is it?"

"It's about my account with Stanbrick Financial."

I exhale. "That's Jack's area. I try to keep my nose out of his business as much as possible. Do you want me to connect you to him?"

"No. I'm forwarding an email to you now. Let me know when you receive it."

I pull up my email and see one from Nate. It is a chain of emails from Nate to Roger, including Roger's responses. I start at the beginning. The first email is polite and professional, just Nate asking for his most recent statements from Stanbrick Financial.

> Dear Mr. Lindsey,
>
> I was wondering if I could receive a copy of my most recent investment statement from Stanbrick Financial.
>
> Thank you,
>
> Nate

Roger's response was as follows:

Dear Mr. Teason,

Your statements were mailed to Teason Dairy's corporate address last week. Have you contacted the mailroom? Perhaps they are there. If not, I would be happy to resend a new copy to you.

Please let me know,

Roger

Roger's response is followed by a request from Nate to send the statements to his home address in Whitefish Bay, Wisconsin. Nate notes that since they recently moved their offices, some things have been lost in the mail.

Of course, I can send the statements to your home address. I will get them out to you today.

Roger

A week later, there is another email from Nate to Roger stating he still has not received the statements and is becoming concerned. Roger's response is:

Dear Nate,

I am sorry for the continued delay. We have had to make some staffing adjustments which has slowed our time in distributing the statements. You should receive them by the end of the week.

Roger

Another week goes by before Nate reaches out to Roger again:

> Mr. Lindsey,
>
> I believe I have been more than patient with regards to the receipt of my statements. At this point, I need to request a payout of 50% of my investment. Please mail a check for $421,000 to my home address in Whitefish Bay, Wisconsin, immediately.
>
> Nate

My breath catches in my chest. Nate wanted to pull some of his money out of Jack's business. The next email is even more disturbing. Instead of complying with Nate's request, as I would have advised Roger to do, Roger tries to persuade Nate to roll over his investments into an even more complicated-sounding fund package.

> It is a great opportunity. One we are only offering to our premier and most valued clients.

What the hell is Roger doing? Nate must have been wondering the same thing. His final response to Roger is as follows:

> Mr. Lindsey,
>
> I am not interested in rolling over my funds into any other accounts at Stanbrick Financial. I would like to receive my statements. If I do not receive them along with the money I've already requested, I will be forced to remove all of my funds from Stanbrick Financial and file a complaint with the SEC.
>
> Nate

I gasp. Jack's business is just starting out. A complaint filed with the SEC is not what he needs.

"It took threatening to pull all of my investments from Stanbrick Financial in order to get a damn statement," Nate says, his voice gruff.

I breathe a small sigh of relief. "So you did finally get a statement."

"Yes. But I still haven't gotten back the money I requested."

"On behalf of the company, I sincerely apologize for the delays in receiving your statements and the money you requested. I will speak to Jack. He will make sure this doesn't happen in the future."

"The statement shows significant growth." His displeasure carries through the phone line.

"I'm confused. Aren't you pleased with the growth in your investments?"

"I would be. If I believed it were true. I'm sending you another email with photos of my statement attached."

I open the attachment and immediately see why he has doubts about the veracity of the numbers. The returns are huge, too huge.

"Perhaps one could think I'm being pessimistic. I may just be a cheese guy, but I've invested in many companies over the years and I've never seen growth like this before. Nor have I ever had this kind of difficulty understanding the investments in general, receiving statements, or getting my money out upon request."

My instincts to defend Jack and his business kick in. There must be some mistake. If these numbers are true, big investors would be flocking to dump money into Stanbrick Financial, which is exactly what Jack tells me is happening. A large number of investors have signed up lately. My thoughts stall in my mind. But most of these new investors are from Roger's contacts.

"Have you spoken to Jack about this?" I ask.

"No. All of my dealings have been with Roger."

"I see. I think you should talk to Jack."

"No need."

Through the phone line, Nate pecks away at his keyboard. A moment later, another email pops up in my inbox, marked "urgent" with the subject line, "re: Teason account." It is not sent directly to me. Nate blind copied me on it.

> Dear Mr. Lindsey:
>
> This will be my last request from you to receive my funds from Stanbrick Financial after which point I will be terminating all transactions with Stanbrick Financial going forward. If I do not receive my money within 48 hours, I will be forced to file a claim with the SEC detailing my suspicions that Stanbrick Financial is running a Ponzi scheme.
>
> Sincerely,
>
> Nathan Teason

A Ponzi scheme? "There must be some mistake," I say, my palms sweating against the handset.

"Whether it is or is not a mistake doesn't concern me at this point. I want my money now or I will file a report."

Thoughts of my maxed-out credit cards, withdrawals against them, and the banker's words—that I was at the bank earlier today when I know I wasn't—spin through my mind. An image of Wanda, dressed like me, pregnant like me, trying to get me to sign something for Roger smacks my consciousness. A sucker punch. Roger and Wanda are in it together. They have to be, and they're scamming Jack and me out of everything we've worked so hard to build. I'm not going to let them succeed. I won't let them win. But first, I need to do damage control.

Make sure Jack and my interests are secure. Then we'll deal with Roger and Wanda.

I do a quick Internet search on Ponzi-scheme red flags. High returns with very little risk, unlicensed agents. Nate's earlier discussion with me about Roger failing to be registered on the SEC website jags in my mind. Complicated investment practices and investors having difficulty getting their money out. Damn it.

I clear my throat. "Again, I am so sorry for what has transpired and your lack of trust in Stanbrick Financial. You and I have known each other for a long time. Before you report anything, please give me a chance to make it right."

"I'm listening."

"Let me talk to Jack. We will find a way to get your money back. I just need a little time."

"You have until this afternoon. I'll be expecting your call."

"Yes, of course. Thank you for your patience. I will make this right. I promise."

I hang up the phone and race down the hall to Jack's office. I charge through the door. Jack's head pops up from the stack of papers he is poring over. I can barely catch my breath as I fill him in on my conversation with Nate.

"That can't be correct." He pulls up Nate's portfolio. "Everything looks fine. His investments are doing well."

"Check your other clients." I point to his computer monitor.

He toggles the mouse across the screen and opens a few more accounts. His eyes grow wide as he notices a number of accounts have less money than before, significantly less money. As if money were being taken from one account and being dumped into another as needed to create the appearance of growth. I don't need to say it—he knows. A Ponzi scheme.

"I think Roger has been stealing from investors." I look into Jack's eyes.

His face falls.

"I know this is difficult for you to hear because you have been friends with Roger for so long. But we both know he has gotten into trouble in the past for shady business ventures."

Jack covers his forehead with his hands. "I never thought he would do it to me."

"He's been running a Ponzi scheme. Taking money from one investor to pay off another. But those schemes can't last forever. One dip in the market, one big investor pulling out, and it all falls apart. He's probably already in too deep."

Jack shakes his head. Incredulous. "With the recent fluctuation in interest rates, some of our investors have been asking for draws on their investments, wanting their money out of the market until things stabilize."

I complete Jack's thoughts. "And pursuant to the mechanics of a Ponzi scheme, there is not actually enough money to pay these investors the promised profits."

Jack clenches his hands into fists.

"We need to stop the hemorrhaging," I say. "Nate says he is going to blow the lid on the entire thing if he doesn't get his money back in the next 48 hours. Report Stanbrick Financial to the SEC."

"If he does that, the business will collapse. No one will trust us with their investments."

"We're not going to let that happen." I place my hands on my hips. "I told Nate I would get him his money back."

"How?"

"I will take money from my SMG profits and pay him. That money is legit. I'm not taking it from clients. I will take from profits only."

"But you need that money to keep SMG up and running."

"If I need to file the insurance claim for the painting to reimburse myself, I will."

Sadness blankets Jack's features. "You didn't want to do that."

"I know. But keeping this from exploding is more important right now. I will call Nate and tell him I have his money."

"Do you think that's why Roger wanted us to file a claim for the painting?"

His question confuses me. "What good would that do him? He's not entitled to any of it." As the words escape my lips, Jack's meaning dawns on me. I picture Roger escorting Wanda into the bank, pretending to be me, forging my signature. "You think Roger was planning to steal it from us?"

"It pains me to say so, but at this point, anything is possible."

Anger pulses within me. "And he was enlisting Wanda's help to get to the money. So he could reinvest it in Stanbrick Financial."

"To keep the Ponzi scheme going." Jack slams his fist against the desk. "I'm so sorry."

"It's not your fault. Right now we need to focus on securing our future and the future of our companies."

"Yes. That has to be our top priority right now."

"You need to fire Roger," I say.

Jack kneads his fingers together.

I place my hand on top of his. "We also need to report him to the SEC. He should take the blame for what he did. I'll talk to Nate and see if he's willing to talk to an attorney with us, sign an affidavit about what's been going on, what Roger has done."

"Is it really necessary to get the law involved? I thought the purpose of paying off Nate was to keep things quiet."

"We don't want Nate to report anything unless we are doing damage control alongside him. We need to be working with him, all of us reporting together. Not him reporting against the company."

"This will ruin Roger's career forever." Jack's face looks pale.

"I know this is difficult for you because you trusted him. The only other choice is we bear the burden for what he's done, which will destroy our careers. That hardly seems fair."

"It's like my father all over again. Squandering the family's money. Putting us all at risk."

I run my hand across his shoulders. "When we care about someone, we often don't see these transgressions. We make excuses to protect them. To protect ourselves from the truth."

"Not anymore." He clenches his jaw.

I echo his sentiment. "No, not anymore."

"I think he's at the river house, preparing for a possible showing. I'm going to go talk to him now."

"You're going up there?"

"Yes. After I gather some documents as proof in case he tries to wriggle out of this."

I hesitate. "Do you think it's safe to confront him like that?"

"After all we've been through, I need to do this in person." He looks down at the floor.

"But you don't think he's dangerous, do you?"

"No. He's a white-collar criminal. He's not violent."

Fear and doubt scratch against my nerves, like nails.

"Everything is going to be okay." Jack pulls me into his arms.

I nestle my head against his chest, inhale the scent of his cologne, and pray he's right.

***

The call to Nate goes straight to his voicemail. His message states he is out of the office for the rest of the day. Working from home. If anyone needs to reach him, he can be reached on his cell phone. My fingers fly across my mobile phone as I dial his number. He answers on the first ring.

"It's being taken care of. You have nothing to worry about. I'm going to cover any losses you may have suffered."

"That's fine, but you still have an illegal situation going on at your husband's firm."

"I know. I spoke with Jack and we are going to terminate Roger. He will not be working at Stanbrick Financial or Stanbrick Marketing Group after today."

There is silence on the other end of the line.

"Forgive me if I don't trust the solvency of either of your firms. I will need the money today. You owe me $842,000."

"No problem. I can put a check in the mail to you as soon as we hang up." I pull my checkbook out of my briefcase, my pen poised over it.

"No. That will take too long. Transfer the funds to me electronically."

"Of course." In my panic, I hadn't thought of it. I slip my checkbook back into the briefcase beside my feet. Nate gives me the account and bank routing number for where he would like the money deposited. I toggle across my screen to check that the funds have been removed from my account.

"Got it," he says, confirming receipt.

I sigh, relieved. "So now that we are all squared away, there's no reason to go to the SEC, right?"

"I'm sorry. I still need to report this. I feel I have a duty to do so."

My heart deflates in my chest as I imagine everything Jack and I have worked hard for disappearing. "Wait, please. I need a little more time, so I can prove Roger was behind it, to preserve Jack's and my innocence in this situation."

"I don't know if I can do that."

The baby kicks and my heart breaks. What kind of future will the baby have if the company is embroiled in a financial and criminal mess when it is born? Maybe if I can explain this to Nate face to face. Maybe if he sees me, sees I am sincere and only have my baby's future in mind, he will work with me instead of reporting it himself. Maybe it will buy me some time.

"Is there any way I can meet with you? I can explain what happened and how Jack and I plan to make things right to you in person. We can report Roger to the SEC together."

I hold my breath as I wait for his response.

"Okay."

I exhale.

"But I am not waiting long. I expect you to come see me today so we can take care of this right away."

"Absolutely. If I leave now, I can get to your office by 5:30. If I hurry."

"Meet me at my home."

Right. He's working from home. "Of course."

My hands shake as I hang up. Still anxious Nate will file a claim before I can get to him, I lean over my keyboard and peck out a quick email.

> Dear Nate:
>
> I wanted to thank you again for giving me a chance to make things right. I promise we will make sure the person responsible for this situation will be held accountable with the SEC. It will never happen again.
>
> Claire

Outside the window, rush-hour traffic is building up on Wacker Drive. Storm clouds darken the sky, about to open up at any moment. I squeeze my eyes shut. Stanbrick Financial is Jack's dream, and for Roger to mess it up for him, for us, makes me furious. My eyes pop open at the sound of someone entering my office. Wanda. It's time to fire her, long overdue. She is done here.

She cradles her jacket and purse in her arms. Leaving work for the day early again, no doubt. She makes herself comfortable, knocking my jacket and purse off my guest chair as she sits down.

"Not now." I refuse to even look at her. I will deal with her on my way out.

She exits my office. I slam the door shut behind her and finish gathering up some documents to bring with me to Nate's. I stuff his file into my briefcase, grab my purse, and head to the reception area. Looking for Wanda. Time's up for her at this office. At this point, I don't care if she tries to sue us for wrongful termination. I'll press charges right back at her, for impersonating me and forging my signature, for stealing from me. I'll get that warrant and force the bank to produce the videotape of her taking money from my account. I know it was her, her and Roger. She messed with the wrong person.

My frustration builds as I round the corner. When I do, I notice that not unexpectedly, Wanda is nowhere in sight. But what is surprising is her desk is neat and tidy, completely cleaned out, all her stuff gone. Did she just quit? That's okay. After I get everything squared away with Nate, I'll find her. The temp agency will have her information. She can't hide for long. I catch a glimpse of the clock on the wall. It's already 3:30. I've got to leave. Wanda is soon to be part of Jack's and my past. It's the future I need to focus on right now.

Chapter Twenty-Eight

Wanda After

It's dark when Astrid and I arrive back at the house. We slide off our wet shoes and leave them on the mat beside the door. Astrid bounds up the stairs to play in her bedroom. I head into the living room and jump as a pair of eyes stare back at me. My heartbeat stalls in my chest. I flip on the light. It takes me a minute to process, to recalibrate. I exhale. Penelope.

"What are you doing here?" I ask.

She straightens out a newspaper folded in her lap. "I've been worried about you."

"Why?"

"I knew you were out on your wild goose chase. But you were gone so long, I thought maybe something happened to you and Astrid."

"We're fine. But what are you doing in my house?"

"Waiting for you."

"In the dark?"

"It wasn't dark out when I got here. It's been hours."

"And how did you get in here?"

"The door was unlocked, and I always say, 'an unlocked door is an invitation.'"

Did I really forget to lock the door? An image of Carl's key dangling from his pocket chain flashes before me. "Was anyone in the house when you got here?"

"Nope. But a man stopped by."

"Was it Carl?" I swear that man refuses to leave me alone.

"It wasn't Carl."

My nerves fire, hot beneath my skin. "Who was it?"

"He didn't give me his name. But he gave me this." She unfolds the newspaper so the front page is clearly displayed. A full-page photo of Jack and me at the restaurant dancing, our arms wrapped around each other.

The heading on the article asks, "Who's That Girl?" It goes on to question whether I am an imposter Jack hired to make himself look innocent. After all, only a guilty man would accept a guilty plea, right? Wrong.

Penelope places her hand on top of mine. "All of this attention is going to get you into trouble. You need to give this up."

I squeeze my eyes shut and recall the feel of Jack's body pressed against mine as we danced in the restaurant, and the promises he made about our future together. "I'm not giving up on proving who I am, and that Jack is innocent."

She looks down at her sneakers, grass-stained from her time spent in her garden.

"I'll be okay. I know what I'm doing."

"Do you? How do you know you aren't putting yourself and Astrid in danger?"

A thread of worry snags on that last part. The idea of Astrid being in danger is more than I can bear. And yet, her words strike anger in me. "I take great care of Astrid. I'm a terrific mother."

"That may be, but you're playing a dangerous game."

"It's not a game. Astrid deserves to know Jack is her father. Jack is not dangerous." I place my hands on my hips. "What did the man who stopped by want, was he some newspaper delivery guy or something?"

"He said he needs to talk to you. Said he'll be back."

"Is that all?"

"He seemed nervous, ill at ease. Seemed like he wanted you to go away." She steadies herself against the end table.

"Can you describe him in more detail?"

"Bald head and when he walked away, I noticed a limp."

Roger Lindsey? My defensive attitude toward Penelope falls away. A chill slices through me as Carl's words ping-pong in my mind. *Someone is watching.*

"Have you found the gun I lent you yet?" Penelope asks.

Although Penelope has asked me many times since my accident whether I've found her gun, this time her question registers differently with me. "Why did I want a gun?"

"I don't know. Before your accident, you asked me for it. Said you might need to take care of something."

Thoughts whir through my mind as I try to recall the memory. Did I think I was in danger?

"That fellow who stopped by made me uneasy, his eyes darting around, as if he was up to no good. You need to drop all of this."

"I can't." I plead with her, as if she is the decision maker here. She's not.

"How can you trust Jack? He pled guilty to killing his wife."

Anger bubbles up within me. "He did not kill his wife. I am his wife. Jack would never hurt anyone."

Doubt shades Penelope's features. "I read an article that said Claire's will left everything to her offspring if something were to happen to her. Skips right over Jack. That's motive right there. She was pregnant at the time she disappeared. Don't you think he might have tried to get away with killing her and the baby, so he could get to her money?"

"Nope. You're wrong there." I take a deep breath and do my best to piece together the little bit of information about Illinois probate law I learned from an article I read. "Jack pled guilty. That means he can't inherit any money from Claire's estate. Illinois law doesn't allow people to profit from crimes where there is a guilty verdict against them."

Not following, Penelope squints her eyes at me.

"If he were after the money, he would have held out for a new trial and a verdict of not guilty. Then he would have gotten all the money. Instead, he forfeited any claim to it by taking the Alford plea. Ha."

"Even if that were true, you've still gone and made yourself a target. How do you know the person who hurt Claire isn't going to come after you?"

A shudder slithers up my spine. I can't bear to listen to any more of this. I am so close to having everything I've ever wanted. She has to stop. "If you're my friend, you'll support me. You're jealous because you lost your husband and I've found mine. I finally have a purpose to my life."

She looks at Astrid. "You've had a purpose this whole time."

"You don't want me to be happy." As soon as I speak the words, there is a knock at the door. I instruct Penelope to go into the living room, to stand out of sight, in case Roger came back.

Outside, a delivery guy holds a huge bouquet of flowers. My shoulders relax.

"Delivery for Claire."

"That's me." I smile at Penelope who is peeking around the corner.

A floral scent fills the hallway, lifting the tension and creating warmth to the room.

"Is there a card?" I check the outside wrapping but can't find one. "Maybe it fell off." My eyes scan the ground. Nothing.

Penelope helps me search, but there is no card.

"Do you think they're from Jack?" I inhale the sweet scent coming from the bouquet.

Penelope peels back the neon crepe paper and glances at the flowers. "I hope not."

"Why would you say that? Someone sends me flowers. Of course, we hope it's Jack." Anger beats at my temples. I gaze into the bouquet. "Plus, these are roses. Roses mean love." I brush the soft petals against my cheek.

"Not these roses." Penelope purses her lips.

"All roses symbolize good things."

"Not all." She opens the tissue paper to give me a better look. "These are black roses." She knocks the bouquet out of my hands, the flowers scattering across the floor. "Black roses mean death."

"Stop it. You're just trying to scare me." I scoop up the flowers.

"I'm trying to protect you."

"No one asked you to do that, and if you can't be supportive of what's important to me, you can leave." I point to the door.

She turns away from me. "I will leave. Wanda or Claire or whoever you think you are. But don't say I didn't warn you."

I shut the door behind her.

***

Later that evening, I can't sleep, unable to push my argument with Penelope out of my head. I check the door. Again. Deadbolt turned, chain on. The flowers sit in a chipped vase on the entryway table. I grab them, walk straight into the kitchen and toss them into the garbage can. *Now I'm afraid of them. Thanks, Penelope*. If those flowers mean what she says, if they were meant to frighten me, I bet they were from Carl. That seems right up his alley. I wipe my hands on my nightshirt and climb up the stairs. I'm sitting on the edge of my bed, not sure if I should call Penelope and debate the whole flower issue again, when my cell phone rings.

I know the voice as if it were my own. Jack.

"Am I calling too late?"

"Never," I say.

"It seems like the press has really run with our story."

"I know. It was on the cover of the newspaper."

"Everyone loves a fairy-tale ending."

"And you think our story is a fairy tale?" The doubt Penelope planted in me, needles its way to the surface.

"It is now. Now that I have you back."

"Thank you for the flowers. They're beautiful." I throw it out there. To see where it lands.

"What flowers?"

"You didn't send me any flowers today?"

"No. I'm sorry. Did you want me to?" Embarrassment laces through his voice. "Do you want me to send you flowers? Because I will."

So it was Carl. Or Roger. My skin turns cold at the thought. "It's not that."

"What's wrong?"

"I'm not sure I'm safe." The words scrape the back of my throat.

"Why would you say that?" His voice shakes with worry.

"I'm sure it's nothing. Someone sent me creepy flowers. It's silly, really."

"If it's silly, why are you worried about it?" He sounds concerned.

"Because a man stopped by today. I think it was Roger."

"Roger? Why? What did he want?" He stutters into the telephone. Nervous.

"I don't know. I didn't talk to him. He spoke with my neighbor. Said he needed to talk to me. Kind of indicated I should back off."

"That proves to me even more what we need to do now."

I smooth out a few wrinkles on my comforter. "And what is that?"

"We need to make all of this public. That you are Claire."

My heart warms at the sound of it.

"I missed you so much and now that I have you back, I want to be with you all the time. I want to get to know our daughter."

An image of Jack, Astrid, and I walking hand in hand, pirouettes across my mind.

"It's time for you to be back where you belong. At the company and by my side."

"How do we do that?"

"You and Astrid should meet me tomorrow at 10:00 in the morning at Stanbrick Financial. We'll get you all set up at the company."

"But I don't remember how to do any of the work."

Jack chuckles. "It'll come right back to you. I'm sure of it. No worries, though. We'll take baby steps. First, we'll get you settled in, then gradually find an account or two for you to work on."

I close my eyes and try to picture it and it feels right, like I belong there.

"The work will be a little different from before, because you'll be working on Stanbrick Financial accounts until we can get your old company, Stanbrick Marketing Group, up and running again."

That's right. SMG dissolved after the disappearance.

"But I assure you, we will get SMG operating again and you will transition back to the marketing work you love so much."

That sounds like me. I can picture it. Coming into work in a tailored suit, classy high heels, giving presentations, running things.

Jack interrupts my fantasizing. "I want things to be how they used to be before."

Before someone tried to kill me. The thought comes out of nowhere. Penelope's worries triggering a fear within me. I push it out of my mind.

"Don't be surprised if there are some reporters when you arrive. They've been outside the building every day since I took the Alford plea. I'm sure they'll be there tomorrow, too."

My stomach tenses at the thought of it. Especially given Roger's visit and the anonymous flower delivery.

"It'll be all right. Remember, it's their job to report the story. There's no harm for us in letting them do so. We have nothing to hide."

My muscles relax.

"Sometimes it's best to get things out in the open. Once the truth is out, things will settle down. Roger won't be able to tell you to back off because everyone will already know everything. No one will think I'm a killer because people will see you are alive and doing well. Then you, me, and Astrid can be the family we were meant to be."

It's everything I've hoped for. We'll show the world Jack is innocent and that I was right about my past. Even Penelope will have to believe it. Then Jack, Astrid, and I will finally be able to have a future together.

***

The next morning, Astrid and I approach the corner of Madison and LaSalle Street. A cluster of reporters gather outside the Creighton Building. We stop and wait for a walk sign to light up when Astrid's grip on my sleeve tightens. A hand taps my shoulder. A man's face glares back at me. Carl.

"I like this little scheme you've got going, Wanda." He snuffs out a cigarette butt beneath his shoe.

"I'm not Wanda. I'm Claire."

"You don't have to put on your act with me. I know what you're up to." He leans toward me, and I gag from the stench of alcohol on his breath.

I step back. "I'm not up to anything."

He chuckles. "I know you, and you are always up to something. Always got some angle you're playing." He reaches for Astrid. "How are you doing?"

Astrid buries her face behind my legs.

"Leave us alone," I say.

"I'll leave you both alone if you cut me in on your game."

"I told you. There's no game."

Carl squeezes my arm. "You're pretending to be that dead woman so you can get at her money."

"No, I'm not." I wince in pain as he tightens his grip.

"I bet that convict is in on it too. There's nothing like a rich dead wife." His eyes glaze over, wistful.

"Unlike you, Jack isn't interested in the money. And anyway, he didn't kill her. I mean, kill me."

Carl bends over and laughs. "I'm telling you, he's using you so he can get to her money."

"You don't know what you're talking about."

"Oh yes I do, and I want my share. I want the money you invested in that stinking company of theirs. You better cut me in on whatever you're going to get out of this."

"Or what?"

"I'll blow your cover. Tell everyone who you really are."

"Tell everyone I'm Claire Stanbrick?"

"That's right, stay in character until you get the money. And once you do, I better get a piece of it or you will be like that Claire woman. Dead."

"Are you threatening me?" I shudder as I picture a bouquet of black roses resting on top of a coffin. My coffin.

"This is your warning, Wanda. Now go be a good girl and get us some of that dead lady's money."

Carl stumbles away pointing a finger at me.

Astrid peeks out from behind my legs. "He's a bad man," she says.

"Yes." I kiss her forehead. Carl is wrong about me. He's wrong about everything.

Flashbulbs snap and crackle in our direction as Astrid and I turn onto LaSalle Street and approach the Creighton Building. I shield Astrid's face from the eager cameras.

Before we even get to the building's entrance, Jack spins through the revolving door to greet us. He pulls me into his arms and kisses me.

He extends a hand toward Astrid. "It's nice to finally meet you."

Astrid returns his handshake.

Reporters line the sidewalk outside the building, pushing and shoving for position. They thrust video cameras and microphones in my face. Being part of a high-profile murder case makes me suddenly somewhat of a celebrity. I'm overwhelmed by all the attention.

The camera lenses pan to the left as Jack's lawyer, Mr. Bronson, steps out of the building. He stands beside Jack as the reporters begin calling out questions.

A woman with a high-pitched voice and long dangly earrings sticks a tape recorder beneath my nose. "If you are Claire Stanbrick, where have you been the past five years?"

I answer her question as best as I can. "Suffering from amnesia and struggling to find my way back to who I really am."

"When did you first realize you were Claire Stanbrick?" the reporter asks.

Before I can answer, Mr. Bronson cuts in. "No comment." He motions for Jack to come forward. "Mr. Stanbrick is thrilled to be reunited with the love of his life, his beloved Claire."

Jack loops an arm across my waist. And it feels right, like he should always be there beside me. He kisses my cheek. I close my eyes. I can't believe this is real.

A slew of questions come at me all at once. Camera flashes snap from every direction. My head dizzy. My eyes dart from one reporter to the other, trying to focus through the flashbulb afterglow shading my vision. I strain to see but can't follow who is asking what. One reporter calls out to me, "I have a question for you, Claire. If that's who you really are."

Jack leans toward the microphone. Then in a calm, controlled tone says, "That's exactly who she is. Trust me."

"And why should we trust you?" A journalist with frizzy hair and coke-bottle glasses asks.

"A man knows his wife. I knew from the moment I saw her my Claire had returned to me." Jack presses his nose against my cheek and smiles.

"But how can you be so sure?" The journalist persists.

Mr. Bronson places a hand upon Jack's shoulder and answers for him. "Anyone can tell by looking at this woman that she is Claire Stanbrick."

A young journalist with long raven hair sticks a microphone in Jack's direction. "This is all fine and good. But how do you account for the evidence presented against you in court? The evidence that led to your conviction in the first place?"

Jack's jaw tightens. He furrows his brow but remains silent.

The reporter pulls her hair over her left shoulder and continues. "For example, luminol showed the existence of cleaned-up blood on the floor of your river house. Your footprints were scattered throughout the residence. Do you have an explanation for this?"

A wave of panic gushes through me. What *is* his explanation for this? Mr. Bronson rushes to step in. "Mr. Stanbrick was the first on the scene. When he arrived, he saw no sign of Claire. You all will remember no body was found. Plus, during the course of Claire's pregnancy, she had a tendency to bleed. Since the blood had been washed up, the prosecution was never able to prove the blood was not from one of those incidents."

The journalist refuses to let it go. "And how do you explain the bullet casings and the fact they are the same caliber as the gun Mr. Stanbrick owns, a .45 caliber semi-automatic pistol?"

"Mr. Stanbrick did indeed have a semi-automatic pistol of that caliber licensed to him, but that gun was never found. And Mr. Stanbrick reported it missing long before the day of the incident." Mr. Bronson massages his chin. "In fact, the case against Mr. Stanbrick was based almost entirely on circumstantial evidence. I'm surprised the prosecution was able to secure a conviction on such a weak case. I suggest you look to the court transcript for any other questions you have regarding evidence presented at the murder trial."

A reporter in a pinstripe business suit chimes in. "If Mr. Stanbrick is innocent, why would he accept an Alford plea, a guilty plea?"

"First of all, Mr. Stanbrick has continued to assert his innocence which is an inherent component of the Alford plea. As previously reported, Mr. Stanbrick was granted an appeal for a retrial. His choices were to sit in prison and await the retrial, which could take months, possibly even years, without knowing if the same shoddy treatment of evidence would result in the same baseless conviction. Or he could accept the plea now, assert his innocence, and be released from prison immediately."

Jack states, "I chose to get out of jail. If you were wrongly convicted, you would do the same, I guarantee."

Murmurs circle through the crowd as a wiry reporter with a goatee stands up and asks, “Who is Wanda Dellas?”

My heartbeat freezes in my chest. I take a deep breath and think of Jack’s words, that we need to make all of this public, that we have nothing to hide. “That is who I thought I was. As you can see from the scar on my face, I was in an accident. The result of which was a loss of all memory. My memory of the accident itself and who I was prior to the accident.”

“Given that you can’t remember anything, how do we know you really are Claire Stanbrick and not Wanda Dellas pretending to be Claire Stanbrick?”

My palms sweat as I look at the pack of reporters. It’s a fair question. One I’ve been struggling to find the answer to myself. Telling them I am trusting my gut isn’t going to cut it. My eyes dart from one journalist to another, and then I notice Carl in the crowd. He runs a finger under his neck and mouths the words, “You’re done.”

He’s right. I am done. I’m done being threatened. I’m not going to allow him or anyone else to intimidate me anymore. I know the truth and I’m going to prove it. I straighten my back and tilt my head up. “We will be able to know for certain that I am, in fact, Claire Stanbrick because I am going to take a DNA test.”

Jack smiles and drapes his arm across my shoulders as I continue. “That test will show that not only am I Claire Stanbrick, but that this child is Jack’s biological daughter.”

Jack dips me and kisses me in front of everyone. Flashbulbs go off like fireworks. Astrid jumps up and down and claps her hands beside us.

Once upright, I glare at Carl as he grumbles and slinks out of the crowd.

Mr. Bronson places his hands on our backs and announces. "Results of the DNA tests will be made available upon receipt. No more questions."

Mr. Bronson leads us through the revolving doors of the Creighton Building. And all I can think is, we're back. Jack and Claire Stanbrick working together once again. Just like it was always meant to be.

Chapter Twenty-Nine

Claire Before

On my way out, I stop by Jack's office to tell him about my conversation with Nate, and that I am going to go see him now. But when I round the corner, his office is dark. Lights off. He must have already left to confront Roger. A nervous chill spirals through me. How dangerous is Roger? What lengths would a man like that go to in order to protect himself?

I slide onto the smooth leather of my sedan and type Nate's home address into the navigation system. Before shifting the gear into drive, I pull my cell phone out of my jacket pocket and peck out a quick text to Jack.

`On my way to meet Nate. I'll text you as soon as I'm done.`

My stomach churns. I drop my cell phone into the car's cup holder and drive toward the Ohio Street onramp. I veer left and merge onto I-94 West toward Wisconsin. The Western Avenue exit is barely in my rearview mirror when I hit traffic, bumper to bumper. Shoot. I don't have time for this. The illuminated numbers on the dashboard clock flash. 4:00. Damn it. Cars honk as I move across the crowded lanes that merge with I-90. I pass the O'Hare exit, the clock taunting me. A half hour goes by before traffic lightens up.

Trees dot the hills along the side of the expressway. They fly by in my peripheral vision as I try to convince myself everything is going to work out. Once Nate sees me, sees how sincere I am about correcting the situation, how honest I am, he'll be satisfied and won't file any charges with the SEC until after Jack and I report Roger. That way, Jack and I will have covered our asses and be able to handle the situation ourselves and with some lawyers. We can even hire a public relations firm to rebrand both Stanbrick Financial and SMG, to present us as victims here. Which we are. And to undo the damage Roger has caused. I can only hope we get the chance to do so. If Nate reports us first, I don't know what we'll do.

A thought stings the back of my mind. What about the other investors? Nate can't be the only client affected by Roger's Ponzi scheme. A bug crashes into my windshield, dead on impact. I turn on my wipers. Smudged guts smear across the glass. It will take more than a quick fix to clean up Roger's mess this time. We're going to have to find a way to pay them all back.

My phone buzzes in the cup holder beside me.

> Drive carefully. We are going to be all right. We have each other and the baby. We'll get through this.

He's right. I just need to take it one step at a time. First make sure Nate is happy. Then figure out how to provide restitution to any other clients with losses. We will get through this. Somehow. I take Exit 78 toward Silver Spring Drive and my navigation system instructs me to turn left onto North Port Washington Road. My heart beats wildly in my chest as my anxiety over meeting with Nate kicks in. What if he's changed his mind? What if he got impatient and decided to report Stanbrick Financial?

I take the turn onto Nate's street quicker than I intend to, my tires screeching against the road. The spectacular view of Lake Michigan lies ahead of me, peaceful and calm. A stark contrast to the way I feel. I am almost there. I remember Nate telling me how much he loves living on the water, treasures the soothing nature of the waves he sees from his balcony. I could use some of that reassurance now. I've always been fond of Nate. We have a lot in common, Nate and I: our dedication to our businesses, our work ethic, our love of the water. Maybe when things settle down, Jack and I can buy a place on Lake Michigan. Put this craziness behind us. Jack, the baby, and I, can start fresh.

My tires slow, hot against the road. I hear the sirens first. They echo through the air as my navigation system directs me closer to Nate's residence. Then I see the lights, red and blue, bouncing off the pavement. Police cars. And an ambulance. Blocking Nate's driveway. Passersby gather on the sidewalk in the cul-de-sac in front of his house. An officer wearing a navy-blue police hat taps on my window as my wheels crawl to a stop.

"You can't come any closer, ma'am."

"What's going on here?"

Another officer sets up police barricades, stringing yellow tape between them.

"This is a crime scene."

"At the Teason residence?"

"Yes, ma'am."

"Is everyone okay?"

"I can't give you any more information. This is an active crime scene. You need to turn your car around."

The officer means business. But what about Nate? I need to speak to him. Is he even all right? I don't know what to do. The officer waves me along. I shift my car into reverse, make a three-point turn, and head back in the direction from where I came. On a side street a block away from Nate's cul-de-sac, I parallel-park my car beside the curb. I fling my seatbelt off, hop out of the car, and race down the street toward Nate's house. I need to get some answers.

Crowds have formed along the perimeter of Nate's house. People are huddled in groups, pressing against each other, trying to get a better look at what is going on. I sidle up beside a woman wearing a sea-foam green fleece and tap her on the shoulder. She turns toward me, her features harried, her eyes wet.

"What's going on?" I ask.

She looks away from me. I follow the direction of her stare and notice a stretcher being pulled from Nate's house. A person lies on top in a sealed gray body bag. My hand covers my mouth. Nate? I stand on my tiptoes to try to get a better look.

"It's so sad." The woman wipes her eyes.

"Do you know who's on the stretcher?" My voice shakes.

"Nathan Teason."

No. "What happened?" I feel frantic. A headache forms at my temples.

"I don't know. His wife came home from shopping and found him lying in a pool of his own blood. Shot to death. Poor thing."

I gasp. No.

"Investigators think it might have been a burglary gone awry. Valuables and priceless heirlooms are missing from the home."

A burglary? "Do they know who did this?"

"There are no suspects. I am terrified, a killer on the loose in our neighborhood. My husband and I moved to this area twenty years ago and we've never seen anything like this. It seems no one is safe anywhere anymore."

An image of Roger screeches across my mind.

"Did you know him?" The woman asks.

"Who?" I look at her.

"Nathan," she says.

I think of Jack on his way to the river house. "I've got to go."

My heels click against the pavement as I hustle down the sidewalk toward my car. I am almost there when I notice a beat-up blue station wagon perched at the end of the block. Roger? Was Roger here? Did he kill Nate? Roger knew Nate was going to report the Ponzi scheme to the SEC. Maybe he took matters into his own hands, made it look like a burglary, to avoid suspicion, to get away with everything. I squint my eyes to make out the features of the person sitting behind the wheel. The headlights blink on, blinding me. I turn away from the brightness. As I do, the car's engine revs to life. It's moving toward me. My heart thumps in my chest. I run down the street to where my car is parked. My keys fumble between my fingers as I search for the unlock button. Open, open, open. Somehow at the last second I find it and manage to wrangle the door open. I hop in just as the car speeds past me. Gone in an instant, too fast to catch a glimpse of the driver or the license plate.

With no time to waste, I peel down Shore Drive toward the expressway. I need to get to Jack before Roger does. If Roger did this, if he is capable of murder, who knows what he might do if he learns Jack is on to him. Jack's life could be in danger. There is no way I'm going to let him hurt Jack. I need to get to him. Now.

I speed toward the interstate when the orange gas icon lights up on my dashboard. Shoot. In my hurry to get to Nate, I didn't bother to check the tank. I don't have time to stop for gas. But then again, I don't have time to get stranded on the expressway either. A yellow hexagon sign appears out my window to the left. A gas station. I angle my car beside the pump and type a quick text to Jack. To warn him.

`Don't talk to Roger.`

No time to go into the details. I reach for my purse, nestled against the leather of the passenger seat, unzip it, and fish inside for my wallet. I push the items around. A pre-chewed wad of gum balled up in a receipt, a cracked leaky pen, and a melted fire-red tube of lipstick. None of this stuff is familiar to me. The leather of a wallet brushes against my hand. I flip it open and look at the driver's license. And it dawns on me. This is not my purse at all. It's Wanda's.

Chapter Thirty

Wanda After

We've barely reached the elevator banks of the Creighton Building when Astrid's feet screech to a halt. She refuses to budge. Her eyes say it all, and I get it, get why she doesn't want to go any further. I scoop her up into my arms and kiss the side of her head. The last time we were here, her last memory of this place, is of being locked inside. And of me being escorted out in handcuffs.

The elevator dings and Jack holds the door open. We don't move.

"We had a little mishap here," I say, unsure of how much information he has about my alleged break-in. Nervousness shakes through me.

"I know. I've been working to get the charges dropped."

I exhale, but nonetheless feel the need to defend myself. "I never intended for it to play out that way. I was just trying to make ends meet and to find a way back to you. Then it all went wrong." I clench my fists. "I had no choice but to go in and get her." A hint of the old anger seeps out with my words.

Jack places a hand on my sleeve and motions for me to get onto the elevator. "No need to explain. Like you, I would do anything to save someone I love."

The elevator doors open and my heart beats double time as we step into the lobby of Stanbrick Financial. I smooth a few wrinkles from my skirt, feeling both out of place and at home simultaneously. The secretaries rise to their feet as I walk by, nodding and calling out polite "welcome backs."

Jack interlaces his fingers through my own as Astrid skips along beside us. "I want to show you something."

He leads me down the hallway toward Claire's old office, toward my old office. He pushes open the door and I am amazed by what I see. The once-dingy office-turned-storage-room is now bright and airy. The blinds on the windows are pulled all the way open, allowing the late morning sunlight to snake its way onto the freshly polished mahogany desk.

Jack turns me so I face him. "This is all for you."

Freshly cut flowers line the windowsill, the sun casting a glow along the petals.

"I wanted you to have some beautiful flowers, not like those creepy ones you told me about."

"What kind are these?"

Jack looks at me, somewhat embarrassed. "I don't know much about types of flowers. Roger is usually the one who coordinates with the office staff regarding any greenery at the company. This time, I decided to ask them to fill the office with flowers. But I didn't know to specify a certain type. Still, I hope you like them."

"I do. Very much." I twist the stem of a lavender one toward me as a shock of sadness curls around my heart. I miss Penelope. She'd be able to identify each and every flower. I feel horrible about our last conversation. But at this point, I need people around me who believe me, who will support my new life as Claire Stanbrick. Penelope made it clear that is not her.

A knock at the door shakes me from my thoughts. Mr. Bronson stands in the doorway with a woman dressed in nursing scrubs, a medical kit resting in the crook of her arm.

"Ready for your DNA test?" She snaps on some gloves and pulls four tubes off the tray. She opens the first tube and hands me the swab. "Now rub it around the inside of both sides of your cheeks for about one minute."

Astrid watches me wide-eyed.

"It doesn't hurt, honey." I hand the nurse the first swab.

"We always do two." She gives me a second one.

I repeat the scraping around the inside of my cheeks and place it into the tube. Then it's Astrid's turn. At first she is nervous, but by the time she gets to the second tube, she is a pro.

"All done," the nurse says.

"When can we expect to get the results?" I kiss Astrid's head.

"Mr. Bronson has asked to expedite things, so you should have them within the next one to three business days."

"Excellent." I'm not worried about what the results are going to say. I already know the answer. I am Claire Stanbrick. The sooner the tests confirm that, the sooner Jack and I can prove it to the world and move on with our lives together.

Mr. Bronson turns toward the door. Before he goes, he hands me his business card and tells me he'll be in touch. But if I have any questions in the meantime, I should reach out to him. I slide the card into my pocket.

After Mr. Bronson and the nurse leave, I look around the office. Everything seems so fresh. A new beginning. I run my fingers along the surface of the desk and across the keyboard.

"You seem at home here." Pride laces Jack's words.

I sit down in the leather desk chair and rub my palms together. "So where do I begin?"

Jack chuckles. "You always were ready to work." He comes up behind me and wraps his arms across my shoulders. "Today is Thursday. I think we should cut out of here early and take a long weekend together."

I look over at Astrid. I'm not prepared to go anywhere without her. Not yet.

Jack senses my anxiety and turns his attention to Astrid. He squats down to her level and looks into her eyes. “You are definitely my kid. You are just like we imagined you would be.” He taps her nose with his pointer finger. She giggles.

Jack continues, “Why don’t you pack up some things. You, Astrid, and I can spend a long weekend together while we wait for the DNA test results. Plus, that will give a little time for the press craziness to settle down, too.” He kisses me on my chin, my cheeks, and finally my forehead.

“Where would we go?”

“I would suggest our old condo, but Roger sold it to cover some of my legal expenses. So we can’t go there.” There’s solemnness to his voice.

The mention of Roger’s name chafes my skin and I suddenly want to get as far away from the city as possible.

Jack stares out the window. “The weather is warming up. We could spend the weekend at the river house?”

It seems like a reasonable suggestion, close enough to Chicago if Mr. Bronson gets the DNA results and wants us to return to the city, but far enough away for us to have some privacy.

Jack stuffs his hands into his pockets. “It’ll be like old times. The good ones.”

I shrug my shoulders, not knowing what our old times at the river house were like.

“The river house used to be a special place for us,” he says. “It’s time to make it a happy place again.”

I run that idea through my mind. “I like that. A lot.”

Astrid plays with a cluster of paper clips bunched up on the corner of my desk. She is getting restless.

“I think she’s had enough for today.” I stand up.

"I'll have a car drive you home and send another to pick you up around eleven o'clock tomorrow morning to bring you both to the river house."

"Will you be riding with us?"

"I'll meet you there. I may head up early to get the place organized." Jack loops his arms around my waist and kisses me. He rests his forehead against mine. "I'm so grateful to have you back, Claire."

"Until tomorrow then," I whisper. Astrid follows me to the door and then turns around and runs to Jack.

A smile spreads across his face. He picks her up and twirls her through the air. "My baby."

My heart swells with joy. I can't believe it. I did it. Astrid is getting the father she deserves. I am back where I belong, back to being who I was always supposed to be, who I always was. Jack, Astrid, and I can finally be the family we were meant to be. Everything is going to work out. Everything is going to be perfect.

***

I awake early the next morning and peek out the window to see if the limo has arrived. The clock flashes, 7:00 am, way too early. I close my eyes and picture the river house. Even though I have no memory of the actual place, it's as if I can see it in its entirety: the deep woodsy siding, the wall-to-ceiling windows overlooking the river, and the smell, that wonderful smell of pine trees, and fresh dew-covered grass. A ribbon of excitement dances through me. I bet it's exactly like that.

With Astrid still sleeping upstairs, I start packing. I can get a lot done before she needs my attention. I flip on the morning news. A weatherman comes on first, grinning a hokey grin, an oversized yellow umbrella slung over his shoulder. "Looks like there's going to be rain this morning, but it'll be all dried out by afternoon."

Good. Hopefully, it will stop before Astrid and I arrive at the river house. I grab a basket of clean clothing from the laundry room and start folding them on top of the dining room table. I run my fingers along the gouged-out scratches etched across the surface. Bye, bye junky table. As soon as Jack and I move in together, I'm going to purchase the nicest table I can find.

I toss a few pairs of Astrid's too-small socks onto the floor to discard, as a newscaster references yesterday's press conference outside Stanbrick Financial. My pulse quickens as video of Jack and I fill the screen. The image of Jack dipping and kissing me blankets the television and I wish I could freeze time, live in that moment forever.

But the moment doesn't last and in the blink of an eye, the newscaster points his pen in the direction of the station's sports reporter. The sportscaster scrolls through a list of stats for a couple professional baseball teams. About that, I don't care. It all seems the same to me. Interchangeable.

I take the stairs to the unfinished basement to see if we have any suitcases tucked away. I flip the switch and a light bulb dangling from a copper wire buzzes to life. The glow barely illuminates the room, and I jump at a shadow moving along the wall. My own shadow. Relax. Not too much longer and you'll be out of here for good.

The back wall of the basement is lined with rows of wooden shelves, warped and sagging. I push aside a veil of cobwebs and find two suitcases covered in dust. One is clearly larger, a full-size suitcase, the zipper partially undone. The other is much smaller, about the size of a carry-on, perfect for Astrid.

I pull them across the puckered basement floor and up the cement stairs. Once back on the main level, I pause to catch my breath before dragging them into the living room. I am about to head into the dining room for a stack of clothing when a red banner with bright white letters fills the television screen. "Breaking News."

The newscaster stares into the camera. "We have a new development to share with you." He furrows his brow.

I take a deep breath and reassure myself it's probably just some new scientific discovery. Any moment and he'll report Pluto is once again a planet. The grandfather clock ticks away reliably. If I want to finish packing before the limo arrives, I don't have time for this.

I march into the dining room and scoop up a pile of shirts. I balance them on my forearm, using my chin to keep them in place. My feet skid to a halt when I read the words now emblazoned in bold yellow letters across my television screen: "Claire Stanbrick's Body Found."

The shirts tumble from my arms and scatter across the floor. I race to the TV and clutch the sides. No. That can't be true. That can't be right.

A woman with long blonde hair and manicured fingernails holds a microphone. The damp wind whips through her hair as she stands on the bank of a body of water, its currents toiling in the background.

I am kneeling in front of the television trying to make sense of the reporter's words when Astrid calls out to me. "Are we going to go see Daddy soon?"

"Hang on, honey."

"Are you okay?"

"Mama's fine. I just need to hear this."

She shuffles into the kitchen as she rubs the sleep out of her eyes.

The newscaster continues, "A body was discovered early this morning in Prairie du Chien, near the mouth of the Mississippi River." The newscaster holds the microphone in front of a middle-aged man with gray hair poking out from under a fisherman's hat. He stares straight into the camera, a stunned look blanketing his face.

The newscaster leans toward him and says, "We have here Cappy Johnson, the owner operator of Missy Cruise Lines. Mr. Johnson, when did you first notice the body?"

"Early this morning. I was cleaning and preparing my boat for the day's tours when I spotted what looked like a discarded duffel bag pressed up against the rocks." He clears his throat.

"But it wasn't a discarded duffel bag, was it?"

"No, ma'am. Once the waves started hitting it, I knew it was a body, a dead body. I called the authorities right away."

"It has been reported that the body is significantly decomposed from being in the water for such a long period of time, to the point that the feet are missing, severed above the ankles. Given all of the disfigurement, what made you believe this was missing woman, Claire Stanbrick?"

"I found some identification on the body."

"What kind of identification?"

"There was a wallet."

"And whose wallet was it?"

"Most of the papers inside were destroyed due to being in the water for so long, but the plastic driver's license held up."

"So you could read the name on the license?"

"When the police officers arrived on the scene, they read the name."

"And what name was that?"

"Claire Stanbrick, ma'am."

"Thank you for your help, Mr. Johnson," the reporter says. The camera follows Cappy as he walks away mumbling. He wipes at his forehead, still shell-shocked by the discovery.

The newscaster flicks her hair away from her face and looks into the camera once again, flashing polished, white teeth before directing her attention to a police detective now standing beside her. "Officer, can you tell me how this body could possibly wind up at the mouth of the Mississippi?"

The detective clears his throat. "Since the Wisconsin River is a tributary of the Mississippi River, it is likely that the body of what is believed to be Claire Stanbrick flowed downstream from somewhere in the northern part of Wisconsin. From the looks of the body, it appears it was initially weighed down at the ankles, then became wedged beneath some kind of obstruction for a long time until it just recently broke free due to heavy flooding in the area."

No, no, no.

The newscaster speaks into the microphone next. "It is interesting to note that Mr. Stanbrick, husband of Claire Stanbrick, owns a home on the Wisconsin River, in the northern part of the state, the same home that was designated a crime scene at the time of her disappearance."

No. I rise to my feet and begin pacing. I pick up my cell phone and dial Jack's number. It goes straight to voicemail. Crap. What do I do now? Think. Think. Think. I shake out my hands. I can call Jack's lawyer. Mr. Bronson gave me his business card yesterday. I run up the stairs, taking them two steps at a time, and grab the skirt I wore to Stanbrick Financial yesterday off the corner of my mattress. I rifle around in the pockets until I feel the card. I clutch it between my palms like I am holding on for dear life and dial the number.

A harried sounding receptionist answers the phone. Through the line, I can hear the other telephones ringing off the hook.

"I need to speak with Mr. Bronson, the attorney for Jack Stanbrick."

"I'm sorry. Mr. Bronson is in the middle of some important business and is not accepting phone calls."

"Please. I need to speak to him now."

"Who's calling and what is this in regards to?" Her voice is stern and intimidating. Still, I press forward.

"It's Claire Stanbrick." The words now sounding funny and false, like cotton, as they roll off my tongue. I'm not sure who I am anymore.

There is a pause on the other end of the line and I worry she might have hung up. Until I hear, "Connecting you to Mr. Bronson now."

"This is Chris Bronson."

"Have you seen the news? They're reporting they found the body."

"Slow down. To whom am I speaking?"

"It's Claire. Claire Stanbrick. At least, I thought I was Claire. Now I don't know what to think. Is it true?"

"It is true a body believed to be that of Claire Stanbrick has been discovered."

I hang onto his words, "believed to be" and lasso them against my heart. "So they're not sure it's her body, right?" I ask.

"Not yet anyway." His words spill out in a slow drawl, and I can tell he thinks the body is hers. He's just waiting for confirmation.

"So, there's a chance it's someone else?"

"I suppose there's a chance."

"I can't reach Jack. I need to talk to him." My words sputter out in a panic.

"We all need to talk to Jack. The problem is no one knows where the hell he is."

"Jack's missing?"

"We're not ready to commit to phrasing like that just yet. We haven't made it public. If it gets to that point, what we'll say is we're still in the process of trying to get a hold of him. You understand, of course."

The press will be all over it if they catch word Jack is on the run.

"He's been staying at a hotel in Milwaukee until he could find a more permanent residence, but when we tried to reach him this morning he was gone." Mr. Bronson clicks his pen in the background. "I'll be honest with you. While he can't be charged with the same exact crime twice, I know the prosecutor will find a way to put him in jail with a related charge. Things are not going to look good for him if he doesn't turn up soon."

"What do I do now?" My palms sweat.

"Stay put. Don't talk to anyone and don't call any attention to yourself."

"How will I know when you've heard from him?"

"I have your phone number. But to tell you the truth, if that body does turn out to be Claire Stanbrick's, even you aren't going to be able to help him."

He hangs up. Stay put. I peek out the window. The street below is quiet, not a reporter or news van in sight. I guess I'm not where the action is. Yet. For now, the action is at the mouth of the Mississippi River. Where the body was found.

But where is Jack? If he is hiding, it may not be because he's guilty. He could be afraid, unsure of what to do. Everyone is assuming the body is Claire's, but it might not be. I place my hands on my hips. Indignant. But even as I think the words, a cloud of doubt blows in. Have I been deluding myself this entire time? I cringe at the next thought. Have I been Wanda all along?

I think back to my visits to the library, to my research into Claire, to see if any of it might shed some light on the situation. I strum my fingers against the top of my desk when I remember the emails I printed out from Claire's old account. I pull them out of the drawer. The top one is Roger's defensive response to my initial email to Jack. My stomach turns just looking at his name on the letterhead. I flip through the rest of the pages. Most are advertisements I printed because I didn't want anyone to see what I was up to. But as I thumb through them, my eyes catch on one in particular. I recognize it immediately. It's the email I came across when I was cleaning Roger's office the day Astrid became trapped inside. I hadn't been able to read it at the time because Roger interrupted me.

It's marked "urgent" with the subject line, "re: Teason account" and is addressed to Roger Lindsey. But Claire is blind copied on it. My eyes fly across the page, my heartbeat knocking in my chest. In the email Nathan Teason, a man who appears to be a client of Stanbrick Financial, is requesting to have Roger return his money to him. Nathan states if he does not receive his funds within 48 hours, he will file a complaint with the SEC. My eyes grow wide with disbelief as I read the next line. He will alert them to the Ponzi scheme taking place at the company.

Stanbrick Financial was operating a Ponzi scheme? My blood bubbles in my veins as I flip to the next email, this one from Claire to Nathan Teason. In it, Claire thanks Nate for giving her a chance to correct the situation. She also promises she will report the person responsible to the SEC.

I clutch my chest. Suddenly it is difficult to breathe. Claire knew Roger was using Stanbrick Financial as a front for a Ponzi scheme and she was about to implicate him when she went missing. I scowl. I knew he was a rat. Did Roger know about this email from Claire? Did he know she was on to him? What about Nathan Teason? The name sounds so familiar. Maybe he has some information.

I grab my cell phone and type his name into the search engine. My hand flies to my mouth as I read the words, "Nathan Teason, Owner of Teason Dairy, murdered in a home burglary."

How can that be? I scroll up to look at the date of the murder. A little over five years ago. November 5th. The same exact day Claire went missing. What are the chances of both crimes happening on that day? At the same time Claire and Nate were on the verge of reporting Roger? Is that what put both their lives in danger? The coincidence is too great to ignore.

I am about to call Mr. Bronson back to tell him this when a thud emanates from the floor below and Astrid says, "Uh oh."

"Are you okay, honey?" I call out to her.

No answer.

I race down the stairs and into the family room, where I find the suitcases toppled over and Astrid sitting crisscross inside the larger one. She has something in her lap.

"Uh oh," she says again and holds it up.

The blood rushes out of my face. I stifle a scream. It's a gun. My baby is holding a gun.

My breath pushes out in rapid staccato beats as I speak. "Astrid. Honey. Put. Down. The. Gun."

She raises it above her head, struggling with the weight of it. I have no idea if it's loaded.

"Give Mama the gun." I hold my palm out flat.

She sees the panic in my eyes, and I know she is feeding off of it. My fear is making her more afraid. Her face turns red. She is about to have a meltdown.

"No, no, it's okay. Everything's all right. You can just put it down next to you. You're not in any trouble."

She lowers the gun and turns it toward her face. She peers into the steel barrel.

My heart stalls in my chest. I want to shriek at her, plead with her to stop, but I moderate my voice. To stay calm. So she stays calm. "Please. Astrid. Give Mama the gun."

She nods her head, the gun shaking along with the movements of her body. I steady my breath as she drops it onto the wooden floor. I lunge for it as it falls, as if I could stop it. As if I have the power to stop a flying bullet. My ears sting from the sound of the gun vibrating as it lands. I squeeze my eyes shut. It doesn't fire.

Astrid climbs out of the suitcase toward me. She tackles me as the gun rattles to a halt beside us. I turn Astrid from side to side, making sure she is okay. I exhale. Not a scratch on her.

She presses her face against my shoulder. I rest my cheek against the top of her head. “You’re okay.” I rock her back and forth.

A body found, and there’s a gun in *my house*.

Penelope’s words, that I borrowed her husband’s gun, spiral through my mind. Did I feel in danger from someone? I think back to the picture of Claire from the casino night, the one with her face scratched out and the email from Roger to the temp agency intentionally hiring Wanda. Was I in cahoots with Roger? Maybe I didn’t feel threatened by anyone at all. Maybe I was a threat to someone.

I cringe. If the body they found is Claire’s, if I am Wanda . . . I stop and try to push the possibility away from me, make it implausible and untrue. But it blows into my consciousness like a hurricane. Am I Claire’s murderer?

The sound of Astrid’s crying shakes me from my thoughts. No. It can’t be. I grab the gun off the floor and stick it into my purse. The gun feels smooth and slick in my palm. Comforting. I am not a killer. Or am I?

Astrid sits, hugging her knees, still rattled. I must get to the bottom of this. It’s the only way to know once and for all who I am and what I was involved in.

Stay put, Jack’s lawyer said. Not a chance.

Chapter Thirty-One

Wanda After

I rush Astrid along, slip her Mary Janes onto her feet as she pushes her arms through the sleeves of her purple windbreaker. We race out the door.

"Where are we going?" she asks.

"Penelope's house. I need her to watch you for a little while." I hustle her down the front steps.

"Why?"

We cross the soggy grass that separates our house from Penelope's. "Mama has an important errand to run."

"Can we get ice cream after?"

"What?"

"Ice cream. Can we?"

"Sure." After I solve a murder. If I'm not in prison for committing it.

I pull open the screen door leading to Penelope's house and knock, hard and fast. No answer. Where the heck can she be? With Astrid in tow, I hop off the front stoop and run around to the side of the house, fully expecting to see Penelope hunched over her beloved flower garden.

But there is no sign of her.

Shoot. When I didn't care, she was around all the time. But now that I need her, she's nowhere in sight. A pang of remorse spirals through me as I regret our last conversation. I shouldn't have treated her the way I did. I hope I get the chance to tell her.

"Looks like you're coming with me." I reach for Astrid's hand.

She stares at me confused.

"We need to go to the river house."

"Are we going to take the fancy car again?" Astrid points over my shoulder.

I follow her gaze. The limo Jack ordered for us is waiting in front of our house. I shuffle Astrid to where the car is parked and pray Jack is inside.

"Jack?" I tap on the tinted glass.

The driver lowers the passenger side window. "No, ma'am."

"Do you know where he is?"

"Sorry. I just go where I'm assigned to go." He lifts a tablet off the seat beside him. "This ride was arranged and paid for yesterday afternoon. No one called to cancel, so I showed up."

Shoot. Even he hasn't heard from Jack.

"Do you want me to leave? You'll still have to pay for the ride. You won't get a refund."

"Don't leave. We're coming." Astrid and I climb onto the smooth leather back seat.

The ride takes over two hours, which feels like an eternity. My feet tap the floor as horrible scenarios flood my thoughts. What if the body they found really is Claire? I can't go back to my life as Wanda. I can't. Goosebumps bristle my skin. What if I'm Wanda and Claire's murderer?

The limo pulls into the driveway of a large wooden house, resembling a modern log cabin. Astrid and I hop out of the car and thank the driver. I am about to ask him to wait for us, give us a chance to make sure everything is okay, but he pulls away. The car's taillights fade into the distance as a wave of panic crashes down on me.

There's an uneasiness in the air here, a discomfort I can't pinpoint. Something bad happened. I don't know exactly what it was, but the feeling intensifies within me as I climb the steps to the front door.

An image of a gun, a muzzle flash as it fires, and the subsequent pop, rattles my memory. I want to turn back, leave this place, but my need for answers propels me forward. I slide my fingers under the flap of my purse, cradle the handle of the gun in my palm, and keep going.

I am surprised when I turn the doorknob and the door opens. We step onto the marble tile foyer. I call out Jack's name over and over. Astrid spins through the streaks of early afternoon sunlight that dances along the walls.

"Jack? Are you here?"

No answer.

I walk down an open hallway, lit by the glow coming through a skylight in the vaulted ceiling. A light emanates from an upstairs bedroom. I run my fingers along the dusty wood of the banister and climb the stairs as if pulled, propelled by a force not my own. The door to the bedroom is ajar. I peek inside.

"Jack?"

No answer.

I step across the threshold and see the bed. A feeling of disappointment, of heartache, of fear assaults me. A throbbing pain shoots across the scar from my injury. But the room is empty. What is going on?

A voice calls out to me.

"Mama!"

My head whips toward the sound. "I'm coming. Stay there." This was a mistake. We need to leave. We're not safe here.

I skid as I scramble down the stairs and into the entryway, expecting to see Astrid waiting for me. She is not there. Frantic, my eyes scan the room, flitting from side to side. I notice a back door is flung open, leading out to the river. To water. No.

Without missing a beat, I move across the foyer and out of the house. My shoes slosh along the damp dock, toward the sound of Astrid's voice. And then I see her. And I see him.

Roger. Standing at the edge of the dock, his clothing a ruffled mess, his pants dirty and splotched with river water. My heartbeat drums in my chest. He is holding Astrid, dangling her over the river's edge.

"Stop," I call out, my voice a shrill cry.

"It's not what you think. She was about to go in the water. I was trying to stop her."

"Mama!" Astrid tries to wriggle loose from his grasp, the toes of her Mary Janes dipping in the water.

"Let her go. I'll do whatever you want."

"I need you to listen."

I lunge toward him but stop as Astrid's feet swing wildly over the churning currents of the river. "You killed Nate."

"No."

"You knew he was going to report you to the SEC, so you made sure to stop him. And you knew Claire was going to do the same, so you killed her too."

"You're wrong."

Astrid twists, trying to break free from his grasp. "Mama!"

My heart pounds, what if he drops her? What if she falls into the river? She can't swim. "Try to hold still. I'm going to help you." My attempt to comfort Astrid and control the panic bubbling within me is not working.

Astrid kicks him hard in the shin.

"Stop it, little girl."

I reach inside my purse, wrap my fingers around the smooth handle of the gun. But I hesitate. I don't even know if it's loaded. Plus, I've never shot a gun before, at least not that I can remember. What if I miss? What if I hit Astrid by mistake?

"You are a criminal, a murderer, and you let Jack take the fall for everything," I shout.

Roger's face is red and angry. "You've got it all wrong. The person responsible is—"

I am about to pull the gun out of my purse when a loud gunshot goes off behind me.

Astrid screams. I lunge toward her as she falls from Roger's grip. She lands on her knees on the dock. I grab her as Roger topples backwards into the river. A gush of crimson water splashes onto our legs. I kneel beside Astrid and pull her into my arms. She is trembling. I shield my eyes from the afternoon sun and try to make out the face of the person standing above me. Jack.

Chapter Thirty-Two

Claire Before

I smack my fist against the steering wheel. Why do I have her purse instead of mine? An image of Wanda knocking my belongings off my office chair pellets my memory. The gas light flashes in my peripheral vision. Damn it. How am I going to pay for gas? Wanda's wallet rests in my palm. Screw her privacy. I open the top flap and pull out what's inside. Two dollars. I stick my fingers into the wallet's folds, root around looking for scrunched-up bills. But there's nothing other than her driver's license. For a moment I feel sorry for her. I can't imagine what it must be like to live the way she does. Desperate. Constantly pretending to be someone she is not. I toss the wallet back into the purse.

The car engine makes a puttering sound. Running on fumes. I'm wasting precious time. I've got to figure out something. I scrounge around in Wanda's purse, scoop out a fistful of coins scattered and stuck to some kind of sticky residue at the bottom. I gag.

A tally of the coins tells me I only net six dollars. Nowhere near enough to make it all the way to Vintage. I survey my options and remember what brought me to Wisconsin in the first place, a visit to Nate. Per his request, I paid him online. But initially I was going to write him a check. I say a quick prayer that my checkbook is in my briefcase and not in my purse. I reach across the passenger seat, feel around in the zippered side pouch, and am relieved to find my checkbook nestled inside. That's how I'll pay for the gas.

The sun is lower in the sky, already hiding behind the trees as I head along the expressway. I've got a good hour's drive ahead of me. Less if I speed. Just a little. I step on the gas as the Wisconsin landscape flies by in my rearview mirror. My heart rate kicks up a notch as I pass the familiar Vintage welcome sign. I'm almost there.

As I steer onto the driveway of the river house, I notice a blue station wagon parked on the grass behind the garage, partially hidden from view. Roger. He's here. I don't see any sign of Jack's car. Did I beat him here? It's possible. Maybe he stopped at the bank after he left the office. He did mention he wanted to organize some documents in case Roger tried to lie his way out of things. Not this time, Roger.

I know I should either wait until Jack gets here to confront Roger or call the police. He could be the killer who murdered Nate. But what proof do I have? That he used our company as a Ponzi scheme and Nate was going to report us? If I tell the police that, it will blow the lid on things before I'm ready. Implicate us. I need to control how information about the Ponzi scheme gets revealed to ensure our interests are protected.

The minutes tick by on the dashboard clock. When I can't wait any longer, I decide to sneak into the house. It is not until I get to the top of the steps that I remember I don't have my purse. No key. I go around the back where we keep the spare key and enter through the door overlooking the dock. I freeze. Noise emanates from the upstairs bedroom. It sounds like a struggle. Panic hits me. I didn't check the garage. Maybe Jack is here. Maybe Roger is trying to hurt him like he hurt Nate. I race through the living room, but in the dim light, my foot catches on something. I bend down and recognize the tangerine leather, my purse, my actual purse. Is Wanda here too? What's she doing here? I climb the stairs and push open the bedroom door. As I do, I see the silhouettes of two figures beneath the covers, their faces hidden. A naked leg pokes out from beneath the sheets. What the hell? Are Roger and Wanda having sex in our home?

"Get out!" I shout.

The bodies beneath the covers freeze. Wait until Jack hears about this. I slam the door behind me and charge down the stairs toward the front of the house. My pace increases as footsteps follow behind me. I have almost reached the doorway when the weight of a barrel presses up against my back. A voice calls out to me, the words echoing in my ear. "You couldn't just let it be. Curiosity killed the cat, Claire."

A car weaves its way up the driveway. A red convertible. Jack. Jack's here. Can he see me? I can't see him through the glare of the setting sun reflecting off the car's windshield.

Still, just knowing Jack's car is here gives me a jolt of courage. "Help!" I scream.

I turn toward the sound of someone coming down the stairs.

As I do, a loud bang pierces my eardrums. The burn of a thousand firecrackers sears through my skin. I fall to the ground and clutch where the bullet tore into my chest. My vision blurry from pain, I look up at my shooter, but can't make out their face, the features a moving kaleidoscope.

A cramp sears through my abdomen and all I can think about is the baby. Please be okay. Panic courses through me, I can't lose you. This can't be the end. We deserve a future. I steady my breath and try to make out the argument taking place around me. Angry, frantic voices echo through the air. Lie still, I tell myself as gray dots cloud my vision. Play dead.

My muscles tense in agony as the sound of another gunshot spirals through the air. I wait for the pain, brace myself for where the bullet will hit me. But it doesn't come. A body falls to the floor beside me, mouth open, eyes blinking, wide and fearful. Wanda. Wanda's been shot too.

I choke on a mouthful of blood and pray for my baby. Pray for myself. The room begins to move, swaying in time with my labored breaths and the weakened rhythm of my heart. A boot kicks me in my back. I stifle a scream. And all goes black.

Chapter Thirty-Three

Wanda After

Jack brushes my hair away from my face, exposing my scar. He squats down beside us and tucks the gun into his back pocket. "I couldn't live through this. Not again."

My words come out in a panic. "They're looking for you."

"Not anymore. I just got off the phone with Bronson. Told him I was coming here to meet you."

"Jack, I think I might be Wanda. I think I might have had something to do with all of this awfulness. I might have been working with Roger before the accident."

Jack doesn't respond.

"They found a body. Claire's body." My voice shakes.

"No. Not Claire's body."

"You're not listening to me. A body was found. Claire's body was found," I insist.

Jack kisses my head. "Can't be."

"Why not?"

"The DNA results came in. They show with 98% certainty Astrid is my daughter." His smile is bright, and warm, and kind. "They also show you are Claire."

"They do?" Sunlight glints off ripples in the water.

He extends his palms toward me. Open and welcoming. "They do. It was Roger, the whole time. I should have listened to you. You tried to warn me. He was my oldest friend. I trusted him. I don't know if I'll ever be able to forgive myself for that."

"So, Roger was behind the Ponzi scheme all along?" I ask.

"Yes, he and Wanda were stealing from the company. They stole from your bank accounts and even took your mother's most prized painting to try and get the insurance money to fund their Ponzi scheme, to keep it going."

An image of a portrait of a woman cradling her child flashes before me. I can't believe Roger and Wanda would stoop so low as to take that too. I think of the painting and remember it now. Not just from the picture in the magazine article, an actual memory. I look at Astrid. A warm feeling floods through my veins. That must have been how my mother felt about me.

Jack puts his hand on my forearm. "He made promises to Wanda. Told her he loved her and that she would be a financial beneficiary of their scheme. Until . . ."

"Until we found out about it and were going to report them." Thoughts spin through my mind as I try to put the puzzle pieces together. What I do know for sure is Roger just threatened Astrid. And Jack is innocent. Thank goodness he showed up when he did. I shudder to think what could have happened if Roger tossed her into the water.

Jack kisses the back of my hand and pulls out his cell phone. "We need to report Roger to the police." He holds the phone against his thigh and his face saddens. "You're both soaked. Why don't you go dry off? There used to be some towels in the guest house." He points to a small log cabin wedged behind a cluster of trees.

Still cradling Astrid in my arms, I press myself off the ground. Jack tucks a loose strand of hair behind my ear. "Everything is going to be all right now. Roger is gone. We can finally be a family. I promise. And I don't break my promises."

Too weak for words, I nod, and carry Astrid to the guesthouse. I turn and see Jack talking into his cell phone. He looks at me, and smiles. I whisper to Astrid, the same words Jack just said to me. "Everything is going to be all right now." I promise.

***

The guesthouse smells of mildew and abandonment. My hands fumble along the rows of logs that make up the walls, until my fingers find a light switch. Green tufts of moss poke out from the edges of once expensive, now cracked floor tiles. Boxes threatening to topple over are stacked high in each corner of the main room. A linen closet is built into the far wall. Inside I find a pile of colorful yet musty towels. I drape one with red and blue stripes across Astrid's shoulders. She sits on the floor, cradling her knees in her arms. I wrap a second one around her legs, drying her feet and the bottom of her pants.

"Is he gone, Mama? Is the bad man gone?" Astrid shivers as she talks.

"Yes. Roger can't hurt us anymore." Relief flows through me.

When I am done drying her off, I drop the towels onto the top of a dresser. A plume of dust billows as they land. One of the towels slides behind the dresser. Shoot. I tilt the dresser toward me and try to reach it. As I feel around for the soft terrycloth, my hand brushes up against something, something firm but pliable. Curiosity getting the best of me, I pull the dresser all the way out. In the dim light of the ceiling fan, I see a shape, a huge square hidden beneath a satin sheet.

A cloud of soot wafts into the air as I tug it off. Astrid coughs. I cover my face with my sleeve and take a closer look. And then I see it, beneath the sheet. A painting.

A portrait of a woman with long flowing brunette locks, cradling a baby with auburn hair and bright green eyes. The missing painting. A memory wades through me, like a seashell washing onto the shore. My mother, her fingers speckled with paint, pulls me onto her lap. She points to the portrait hanging above the mantle. "You and me," she whispers. And I feel warm, and velvety, and safe. She rubs a dry paintbrush along the palm of my hand. It tickles and I giggle.

I am pulled out of the memory as Astrid rests her head on my shoulder. We crouch down together to get a better look. She can feel it too, the love in the painting. She knows it's how I feel about her.

I run my fingers along the splintered edges of the frame and feel a forgotten sense of completeness finally return to me. A missing piece now put into place. I can't wait to show Jack what I've found. He's going to be thrilled. Everything is coming back together. Everything is going to be as it should be. I want to surprise Jack, bring it to him.

The painting is large and bulky, but I don't dare slide it. I don't want to damage it. This painting is precious and must be treated with the utmost care. Instead, I lift it. Curl my fingers around its edges and hold it tight in front of me.

Astrid opens the door, and we walk out onto the wooden porch attached to the guesthouse. With great care, I lean the painting against the outside window.

Astrid spots Jack standing near the river. She waves at him. We call out to him as we move toward where he stands. A misty fog hovers over the water as Jack pulls me into his arms and kisses Astrid on the cheek.

"You're never going to believe what I found." I can barely control my excitement.

"What?" Jack's face is bright and interested.

I point to the guesthouse porch. "The missing painting. My mother's missing portrait."

Jack pulls away.

This confuses me. This is a wonderful thing. "I found it. Can you believe it?" I force myself to still sound upbeat.

“You found it.” His tone is nervous.

I don’t understand.

He motions toward his back pocket, but stops.

As I try to process what is happening, a white light shoots across my mind and a memory flashes before me. I picture myself pressed up against the window, the barrel of a gun pointed at my back. Jack’s car pulls into the driveway. But this time, as the car veers along the driveway’s curve, the glare from the sun is shaded, for only a moment. But in that moment, I can make out the face behind the wheel. Roger? Roger was in Jack’s car. Which means . . . no. The realization sends a jolt of terror through me. It means . . . Jack was in the river house. With me. And Wanda. Anger bubbles in my veins as the devastation of this discovery comes flooding back. For the first time, I can see who is holding the gun, his features no longer distorted in my memory, his face clear. The face of a man I used to love, a man who promised to love me. Jack.

My hands clench into fists. We need to get out of here. Now. Astrid stares at me innocently, and before I can say anything, before I can warn her, she moves toward Jack. I grab her shoulder and hold her back.

Jack’s eyes are fixed on the painting when his features relax and a smile spreads across his face. “I was right, Roger did steal the painting. I’ve been wondering where he hid it.” His voice suddenly calm, reassuring.

I keep a firm grip on Astrid and take a deep breath. “Except it wasn’t Roger, was it? You were orchestrating it the whole time. Roger was trying to warn me.”

“You’re not thinking clearly. That memory of yours is getting in the way.”

Is he right? Am I remembering it wrong? My thoughts jumble in my mind.

"I would never hurt you. Ever. I love you." He presses his hand against his heart.

And I want to believe him. Maybe I am just confused, so much has happened today and my memories, my messed-up memories, I can't count on them.

"It was Roger and Wanda. I didn't have anything to do with it. I'm a victim here too." He takes a step toward me.

I flinch.

"Please don't be afraid of me. You can trust me. Deep down, you know you can. You always have. It was your belief in me that helped you find your way back to me."

That is true, my love and trust for him is what brought us back together. Maybe I've got this all wrong. My shoulders relax.

"That's right. Now we can put this behind us and start over." He turns toward the painting and as he does, I get a good look at the gun sticking out of his back pocket.

Every fiber within me screams. It can't be. But I know from the photo in the magazine that it is. A semi-automatic pistol. .45 caliber.

Jack glances at me over his shoulder. He follows my gaze to where my eyes meet the gun. And he knows. Just then, Astrid breaks free from my grasp and runs to Jack. She throws her arms around his legs.

"Astrid, no." I reach for her.

A twisted smile blankets Jack's face. "Hello, my darling."

My stomach turns. How could I have been so stupid to ever trust this man? How could I have once loved him? Loved a man who was capable of stealing from me, capable of hurting me.

"You're so stubborn, Claire. Everything had to be your way. It was your business. I worked for you. Then I tried to start something for myself. So what if I cut a few corners? We could have used the insurance money from the painting to cover any losses or dipped into your inheritance. But you wouldn't allow it, would you? The money was yours, always yours. You had to be in control of it all."

"So you stole from me?"

"You gave me no choice." He is defiant. "And then that snitch Nate. He was going to report Stanbrick Financial to the SEC. Can you believe that?"

"So you killed him and you tried to kill me too."

He doesn't answer, just stares into space.

I motion for Astrid to come to me. She doesn't budge. She doesn't understand what's happening.

"Don't forget about Wanda." He laughs.

A chill crawls across my skin. Is that pride in his voice? Is he proud of what he's done? "If I'm Claire, where is Wanda?" I both desire and fear his answer.

"You know that body they found near the Mississippi River? Say hello to Wanda." He waves his hands at an invisible Wanda. Astrid thinks he's playing and waves her hands in time with his.

My thoughts spiral. "You killed her too."

"She didn't understand her place. She always wanted more from me. More promises." He chuckles, sending a wave of nausea through me. "She actually believed I wanted to start a life with her. Be a father figure to her baby. Yeah, right." Jack strokes Astrid's hair. "I was going to keep her around a little longer, though. But then she messed everything up that day at the river house. Threatened to spill everything to the cops if I didn't commit to her. She knew too much. I had to get rid of her. Stupid bitch."

These words Astrid does understand. The profanity. She's heard too much of it from Carl. She knows this is not a game. She runs away from Jack and buries her face against my hip.

"Everything was going to work out this time. But you had to go digging." His words are laced with anger.

"It's not my fault you murdered Wanda or that her body was found."

He doesn't respond, just pulls out his gun. "My name was about to be cleared. I was going to go back to running Stanbrick Financial. And you and I could go back to our charade of being a happy family."

So that's what it was, a charade. How did I allow myself to be so deceived? Not once, but twice.

Jack holds the gun at his side and paces across the dock.

I nudge Astrid behind me and block her with my body. My eyes fixate on the gun. I need to find a way out of this. He's not the only one who can lie.

"We can still be together," I say. "We can be a family. No one has to know the truth about the past. Remember, my memories are distorted. So you can tell the story however you like. No one would believe me, anyway." As I speak, I remember Jack calling the police as Astrid and I went to the guesthouse. I just need to stall until they show up. "The police are on their way. When they get here, we'll tell them Roger was behind everything. I'll back you up."

Jack laughs. "What do you think I am, stupid? I didn't call the police. I wasn't sure how this was going to play out or whose side you'd really be on."

"I'm on our side. Remember, everything is going to work out now that we're back together. We just need to present a united front."

"Maybe." He rubs his fingers across the stubble on his chin and I think I might have convinced him. "No. You see, I still won't have access to your money. It's got me thinking." He stares out across the water. "How can I get my hands on Claire's money? That's right, I can inherit it."

"But you can't inherit any money from me. You've already been convicted of killing me. It's the law."

"You disappoint me. I thought you were smarter than that. Think DNA."

My chest tightens as I realize what he is saying. The DNA tests prove Jack didn't kill me.

He nods as recognition scrolls across my face. "This time, I'll make it clear that Roger killed you. I'll be the grieving husband who tried to stop him. I'm not taking any chances. No more convictions for me."

I reach for my purse, but Astrid is clinging to it, tugging it behind me. I slink my arm along my back and fumble for the zipper as Jack talks.

He stares at Astrid. "Too bad you had to bring the kid into things."

I grasp behind me, trying to get my hand into my purse. "I didn't bring her into anything. She was born, and I am so grateful for that."

Irritation radiates from Jack's eyes. He smacks me across the cheekbone. "Don't talk back to me."

Astrid screams as I fall onto the wet wood of the dock. She pulls on my arm. "Get up, Mama. Please, get up."

Jack's black loafers approach me. He grabs my hair, presses his nose against my forehead, and inhales.

I wrench my head away from him and get a glimpse of Astrid cowering beside a patio chair.

Jack tugs my face toward him. Spittle flies from his mouth as he speaks. "Too bad you wouldn't change your will. Now if something happens to you, the money skips right over me." He slams my head against the ground.

My vision unsteady, his words spin through my mind. I think back to my last conversation with Penelope and her warnings about the will. That because I was pregnant, the will could've been Jack's motive for trying to kill me. We were going to have a child. If something happened to me after the baby was born, my entire inheritance would go to that child. Not Jack. A wave of adrenaline courses through me. And if Jack gets away with killing me now, my trusts, my mother's paintings, everything, would go to . . .

"Astrid! Run!" I lean on my elbow and point in the direction of the trees.

Astrid tries to race past Jack, but he is too fast for her. He grabs her and walks toward the edge of the dock.

"Please, don't hurt her. You can have it all." I forgo my pride and beg. "I'll give it to you. I'll sign it all over to you. Just please leave her alone."

"It's too late for that." A satisfied grin crawls across his face.

As he speaks, I slide my hand into my purse and wrap my fingers around the cool handle of the gun. I say a silent prayer it is loaded.

But before I get the chance to use it, he tosses Astrid into the river, into the water.

"No!" I scream.

I scramble toward the end of the dock where Astrid grips the edge, barely holding on. I reach for her, but he pulls me away, away from my baby. Terror rains through my muscles, my legs kicking and thrashing, as he slides me across the damp wood. I cry out as my spine crunches against the dock. He grabs me by the neck and lifts me to my knees. He wedges the barrel of his gun between my ribs. I tug at his fingers and try to loosen them from my throat. But they don't budge. Stars pepper my vision.

An eagle flies overhead, calling out in a high-pitched song. Jack turns toward the sound and momentarily loosens his grip. I muster all my strength and grab the soft tissue underneath Jack's arm. I pull down.

Hard. His voice reels with pain. He releases me and clutches at his skin. The gun falls from his hand and lands on the dock.

Without missing a beat, I pull my gun out of my purse and point it at him.

He laughs. “Look at that cute little girly pistol.”

“Stop talking.” My voice shakes.

“Oh, you want to play?” He bats the gun from my hands, like a cat with a ball of yarn. It lands beside him. He grabs it and points it at me.

Then pulls the trigger.

Click. I brace myself for the pain. But the gun is not loaded.

We look at each other, stunned, before he tosses it in the river. Then we both lunge for his gun lying dormant on the dock. He elbows me in the face. A bruising pain grows along my cheekbone as I fall to the ground. With my heel, I kick the gun across the dock, away from his grasp, and try to scramble toward it.

But he is too quick. He pulls me backwards by my ankle, his grip a steel clamp against my skin. He pins me down, his forearm wedged beneath my chin, and reaches the gun. I bite down on his arm as hard as I can, drawing blood. Red droplets splatter on my face as he cries out in pain. I knee him in the groin. The gun slips from his hand. I roll toward it and grab it.

My body aching, it takes all my might to climb to my feet. Writhing on the ground, Jack clutches his bleeding arm. I stand over him, my face swollen and pulsing with pain. I point the gun just above his abdomen, at his heart. The sound of river water churns in the background, echoing in my ears.

He reaches his hands toward me. “Come on now. Be a good girl and give me the gun. You’re going to hurt yourself.”

My finger trembles against the trigger as memories flood through me. So much coming back. When we met and the immediate connection

I felt to him, the love I thought we shared. Our wedding. The four-layer yellow cake, covered in white frosting and hope. This can't be happening to us. How can this be happening?

Jack interrupts my thoughts. "That's right." He props himself up and crawls toward me.

More memories flood my mind, pelting me with everything he has done, all the harm he has caused, still wants to cause. No more.

A scream slices through the air. And a splash. Astrid.

I squeeze the trigger. A bullet hits him in the chest. He falls back onto the dock, his mouth open, gasping for air, like a trout on a dry pier.

I bend down, my eyes fixed on his, and whisper into his ear. "I am Claire Stanbrick. And I am not disappearing twice."

I leave him there, choking on his own blood and race toward the river, screaming Astrid's name. My feet pound against the wood of the dock as I run to its edge. My eyes scan the water for Astrid. Where are you? Please show me a sign.

"Mama!"

Astrid floats down the river, carried away by the current, her arms flailing in the air. I stare into the depths of the water beneath me, dark and opaque, a jolt of panic courses through me. Water. Danger. I can't. I can't go in. I'm afraid.

Astrid's body flips and twists along the foamy river. Yes. I. Can. To save my baby, I can. I jump in after her, the cold water stinging my face. My fingers frozen, I paddle toward her. I need to catch up to her, but she is so far away. Muddy water splashes into my mouth as I gasp for breath and push myself forward along the river's current.

Another scream pulsates against the sound of churning water. I can't see her. I don't see her. I call out to her. I look from side to side, pulled along by the force of the river, desperate to find her.

And then I do. A flash of her purple windbreaker caught on a tree branch. Her arms and legs kick, but she is tangled, unable to get free. I paddle sideways against the tug of the current, grab onto a tree branch, and unwind her jacket from its grasp. Then, with all my might hoist her onto the riverbank.

She climbs onto her feet. I exhale. My baby is safe.

Just then, the splinter of wood beneath my arm snaps as the branch gives way. Astrid's face grows smaller as my body is tossed along the river. Numb, my arms and legs shiver, useless in the icy water. Then a crack as my head smacks into a rock. And there is pain, electric, fierce, searing pain pulsing behind my eyes.

In that moment, my past no longer matters. All I want is a chance, a chance for a tomorrow with Astrid. I say a prayer. And then there is nothing, nothing but silence. And darkness.

Until . . . I squint from the flash of sunlight stinging my eyes. And the weight of strong arms lifting my drenched body out of the river. Streams of dirty water drip from my clothing as two paramedics lay me on the river's edge. Panicked voices fill the air, my head throbbing from the sound. Lead palms press against my chest in an aching rhythm. Muscular hands turn me onto my side. My lungs burn as I cough, filthy river water spilling from my mouth. Astrid runs out from between the pine trees, a police officer guiding her toward me. Dirt kicks up from her feet as she races to my side. I suck in air and try to speak. My voice comes out in a scratch of a whisper. "Astrid."

She lays her head upon my shoulder, and I think about the day she was born. How the delivery nurse placed her tiny body upon my chest, this beautiful new life. My heart bubbles with joy. I stroke her wet hair, bury my face in her cheek, and inhale. A new beginning.

Chapter Thirty-Four

Eight Months Later

News cycles move quickly. The revelation of the Ponzi scheme, and Jack's renewed attempt to murder me, are splashed across the front page of every newspaper. Jack's guilt surprised no one, not even me any-more—making me question how I missed it, both before the accident and after. How did I allow myself to trust so completely, to put my heart and my life in Jack's hands? Twice.

What people are surprised about is that I am Claire. No one expected that, except me. It didn't take long for authorities to identify the body on the banks of the Mississippi River as Wanda's. DNA is a magical thing. The body also told the story of how Jack weighed her down at the ankles to keep her body submerged. Oddly, my ankles have no marks, no scarring. Nothing. Did Jack just toss me into the river after he shot me? That's what the investigators think, anyway. But I can't figure out why he would do that. Maybe on some level, he did love me, even just a little. I shake the thought from my mind. I suppose there is still a small part of me that wants to believe Jack had some good in him somewhere. But he didn't. I know he didn't.

Occasionally, when I look in the mirror, I think about Wanda, the real Wanda, and my emotions catch me off guard. Mostly, I feel anger toward her. For the role she played in dismantling my life. But some-times, in the quiet of the night, I remember what it was like to live as her, and a sort of sympathy creeps in. After all, Jack tricked her too.

The El train rattles above Astrid and me as we stand at the corner of Wacker and Washington Street. The sun peeks through the metal tracks. The traffic light changes, and we cross the intersection. A warm breeze ruffles against my pant legs. We pause beside a bakery, the smell of fresh croissants billowing out of the air-conditioner vents. I kneel in front of Astrid, straighten the front of her dress, yellow with multicolored butterflies.

She wraps her arms around my neck. "Today is a special day, right Mama?"

"It most certainly is." I kiss her petal soft cheeks.

"I'm wearing my new dress and fancy socks."

I laugh. I don't know why. It just bursts out of me. It feels funny, and foreign, and wonderful all at the same time, this thing called joy.

Astrid flings her head back and giggles, full-bellied, and my heart swells. This. This is what we need. Astrid and I are going to be all right.

The old Marshall Field's clock, green and tarnished, a remnant of the city's history, shows the time and I realize we are running late. Astrid skips beside me until we get to the bright blue awning of a storefront, its doors flung wide open. Welcoming.

A logo blankets the glass. I breathe a puff of air onto it and wipe a smudge off the bright, bold, letters. "Penny and Claire's Forget-Me-Not Flower Shop."

Astrid runs through the doors and into Penelope's arms.

Penelope grins, her face resting on Astrid's shoulder. "It's opening day."

A floral scent coats the air, the perfume of a hundred flowers, fills the shop. Red roses, lavender tulips, yellow and white daisies line the walls, a store of sunshine and promise.

"What do you think?" Penelope stuffs her hands into her pink striped apron.

"It's perfect."

"I heard on the news they are finally closing the investigation into what happened to you and Wanda, putting it all behind us," Penelope says.

I stare at the lacquered floor tiles and think about the way I treated Penelope while I was trying to figure out my past. I didn't treasure her like the friend she is. "Thank you for forgiving me."

"You were kind of a handful. So stubborn." She crinkles up her nose, and smiles.

Although I know she is teasing me, still, a pang of guilt peppers through me. "I should have listened to you. You were right."

Astrid runs her fingers across the petals of the flowers.

"What did I tell you about dwelling on the past?" Her gloved hands leave traces of soil on her apron.

"It's not the past that matters. It's the present and future."

"Ding, ding, ding. You got the correct answer. You win a prize." She plucks a deep purple flower off the shelf. Water droplets fall from its stem as she places it in my hand.

"Which flower is this?" I ask.

"An iris."

"What is its meaning?" She'll know. She always knows.

"Hope."

I press my face against the petals, and breathe it in, the softness of the scent filling my soul. It smells like the future. My eyes well with tears.

Penelope gives me a playful nudge. "Don't go getting all sentimental on me now." She wipes at my cheeks with a gloved finger. "After all you've overcome, this is what's going to make you cry?"

A customer enters the store, a woman looking for a bouquet for a friend. Penelope leads her to a colorful arrangement in a refrigerator. Astrid runs behind the cash register. I kiss her head and motion to Penelope that I'll be back in an hour.

I pause at the edge of the sidewalk. Through the window, I see Penelope helping Astrid wrap up the flowers. She guides Astrid's hands as she covers the bouquet with cellophane. Penelope stretches an orange ribbon around the plastic wrap, cinching it at the top. Lovely.

***

The revolving doors of the Creighton Building stick as I press through them, echoing my resistance to being there. Again. I ride the elevator to the 123rd floor to meet with the lawyers. Memories wash over me as we sit around the conference table. It's strange. Sitting here, I find myself thinking more of Nate, and his kind smile, than of Jack, or Wanda, or anything else.

The attorney for the investment firm buying Stanbrick Financial slides the papers across the table to me. I'm shocked any company wanted to take it over, given its history. I certainly don't want anything to do with it anymore. But then again, my offer to use a portion of my trust money to reimburse the losses incurred by Stanbrick Financial clientele couldn't have hurt. Stanbrick Financial clientele, including Carl. I reached out to him recently to tell him. Funny how much nicer he was once he learned he was going to be paid back. He's still a jerk, of course. But in some ways, he's a victim too.

With a quick slide of my pen, the last remnants of Stanbrick Worldwide are no more, vanished into thin air, like much of my memory.

Later that evening, I am packing up a pile of toys Astrid left scattered across the living room of our new condo in Streeterville. Our condo with a big open foyer, a spacious living room, and floor-to-ceiling windows overlooking Lake Michigan. Overlooking the water. I'm not afraid of it anymore. Not since Astrid and I began our weekly swim lessons at the local gym.

As I drop the last toy into the toy box, Astrid pads out into the living room. She runs her fingers through the colorful streamers cascading from the handlebars of her new, pink bicycle. I scoop her up in my arms and we twirl around the expansive room. I pause, out of breath. She clings to me like a baby koala bear as we face the painting hanging above the sofa. My mother's painting, A Portrait of a Mother and her Child.

And the thing is, Jack almost took it all. The painting. My inheritance. My identity. But none of those things are what really matter. I still don't remember all of my past, and honestly, there are some things I'm glad to forget. But I know now I don't need to reconcile my past in order to figure out who I am. I kiss Astrid's head. Together, we have our present and our future. And I can't think of anything else I'll ever need . . . to remember me.

About the Author

Lisa has always had a passion for stories and the fictional worlds created by her favorite authors. Her love of words led her to pursue a BA in English Literature as an undergraduate. Her interest in jurisprudence led her to law school, where she attained her Juris Doctor degree. Later, Lisa rounded out her love of writing by obtaining an MFA.

Lisa has always been fascinated with the "why" behind people's actions. As a writer of psychological thrillers and women's fiction, she hopes readers will enjoy getting a sneak peek into what makes her characters act the way they do, especially when faced with challenging or extraordinary situations.

Upcoming New Release

LISA SHERMAN'S

FORGET ME NOT

YOU BELONG TO ME

BOOK TWO

Possession is nine-tenths of the law…

Now that I know who I am, I thought it was okay to move on. It was supposed to be safe. And it was safe. Until…

I'll never let you forget…

Danger once again arrives at my doorstep, and I am forced to take another look at my past. A past where new details about dark secrets hide and things are not what they seem. A past that clouds my present. And a present where someone vows to never let me forget exactly where I belong.

You belong to me…

Upcoming New Release

BRIAN FELGOISE / DAVID TABATSKY

FILTHY RICH LAWYERS

THE EDUCATION OF RYAN COLEMAN

BOOK ONE

"The lightning paced humor provides a serious message about corruption in class action litigation. This is a hilarious satire about a very real problem." —Matt Flynn, author, *Milwaukee Jihad*

For more information
visit: www.SpeakingVolumes.us

On Sale!

MARK E. SCOTT
A DAY IN THE LIFE
DRUNK LOG
BOOK 1

For more information
visit: www.SpeakingVolumes.us

Made in the USA
Middletown, DE
23 August 2022

72010896R00184